LUMINOUS

Dawn Metcalf

LUMINOUS

DUTTON BOOKS

An imprint of Penguin Group (USA) Inc.

DUTTON BOOKS
A MEMBER OF PENGUIN GROUP (USA) INC.

Published by the Penguin Group | Penguin Group (USA) Inc., 375 Hudson Street, New York, New York 10014, U.S.A. | Penguin Group (Canada), 90 Eglinton Avenue East, Suite 700, Toronto, Ontario M4P 2Y3, Canada (a division of Pearson Penguin Canada Inc.) | Penguin Books Ltd, 80 Strand, London WC2R 0RL, England | Penguin Ireland, 25 St Stephen's Green, Dublin 2, Ireland (a division of Penguin Books Ltd) | Penguin Group (Australia), 250 Camberwell Road, Camberwell, Victoria 3124, Australia (a division of Pearson Australia Group Pty Ltd) | Penguin Books India Pvt Ltd, 11 Community Centre, Panchsheel Park, New Delhi - 110 017, India | Penguin Group (NZ), 67 Apollo Drive, Rosedale, Auckland 0632, New Zealand (a division of Pearson New Zealand Ltd) | Penguin Books (South Africa) (Pty) Ltd, 24 Sturdee Avenue, Rosebank, Johannesburg 2196, South Africa | Penguin Books Ltd, Registered Offices: 80 Strand, London WC2R 0RL, England

This book is a work of fiction. Names, characters, places, and incidents are either the product of the author's imagination or are used fictitiously, and any resemblance to actual persons, living or dead, business establishments, events, or locales is entirely coincidental.

The publisher does not have any control over and does not assume any responsibility for author or third-party websites or their content.

Octavio Paz. Excerpts from *The Labyrinth of Solitude*, copyright © 1961 by Grove Press, Inc. Used by permission of Grove/Atlantic, Inc.

Library of Congress Cataloging-in-Publication Data
Metcalf, Dawn. Luminous / Dawn Metcalf.
p. cm. Summary: Sixteen-year-old Consuela suddenly and inexplicably finds herself in the parallel universe of the Flow, where she and other teens with extraordinary abilities safeguard a world where they no longer belong.
ISBN 978-0-525-42247-1 (hardcover)
[1. Supernatural—Fiction. 2. Interpersonal relations—Fiction. 3. Hispanic Americans—Fiction.]
I. Title. PZ7.M5656Lum 2011
[Fic]—dc22   2010038063

Published in the United States by Dutton Books,
a member of Penguin Group (USA) Inc.
345 Hudson Street, New York, New York 10014
www.penguin.com/youngreaders

Designed by Irene Vandervoort
Printed in USA | First Edition | 10 9 8 7 6 5 4 3 2 1

For Mooma and Dad,
who always believed,
and for Jonathan,
who made it come true

LUMINOUS

chapter one

"I believe that myths, like every living thing, are born, degenerate and die. I also believe that myths come back to life."

—OCTAVIO PAZ

CONSUELA wrestled with an armload of jeans, trying to catch the hangers on insufficient hooks. Squeezing into the tiny dressing room, she tugged on the first pair. No good, she pulled them off. Tried another pair. And a third. Step-step on, step-step off. It was as if the room had been specifically designed to make her feel big. Consuela hated shopping for jeans. It made her want to eat a donut.

Eventually she found two pairs that weren't *too* bad; the question was whether they were worth buying or not. Consuela compared price tags. She didn't like them enough to buy both. It was tough to feel good when clothes were made for size-four white girls. She felt heavy, unsuccessful, and annoyed—the exact opposite purpose of her coveted shopping therapy break.

Screw it.

Consuela pulled her T-shirt over her head, unhooked her bra, and posed for herself a few times, half naked in the dressing room mirror. She flashed a smile over her shoulder. Perfect white teeth—no cavities—her smile was her best feature. She spanked her hip, feeling better than she had all morning.

Getting dressed, she decided to keep one pair of light denims and hand the rest back with the two plastic, yellow "6" cards. She hung the remaining eleven hooks neatly in her palm for easy counting. The baggy old attendant lady had glared at her earlier as if she suspected Consuela of shoplifting. Like she could hide a pair of True Religions in her cleavage. She could all but hear her best friend's voice in her head: *You know, you probably could!* Allison could always make her laugh.

Consuela held her head high as she stopped at the dressing room exit. The old woman lifted her hangdog eyes.

"Find anything?" the woman asked, only because she had to.

"Yes, thank you."

The gnarled, arthritic hands took the jeans as a sudden lurch of vertigo brought Consuela to her knees.

Hangers clattered against the floor. Head spinning, Consuela groaned; nausea kneaded her throat and her vision slipped sideways. The three-way mirror in the corner bent out of shape. Points of light winked and wobbled like candle flames. Consuela tried to focus on her reflection and saw surprised eyes looking back—but they weren't her own. Dark eyes, wide with urgency, had appeared just inside the glass.

// Know thyself. //

It was an electrified sound, like synthesized violins given voice.

Consuela blinked.

The bizarre image and dull pain shattered.

She slapped a hand to her forehead, squinting against the sudden needle-stab prickles in her eyes. She heard distant voices and felt soft hands touching her back and face. She shrugged them away and fought the wash of cold sweat crawling over her skin.

"I'm all right," she mumbled, embarrassed and shaken. "I'm fine."

Several strangers helped Consuela to sit.

"Are you sure?"

"Sit here."

"Did you faint?"

An employee hurried over. "Hang on, I'll get you some juice."

The old dressing room attendant remained on her stool behind the pressboard podium. She glanced down at Consuela and shook her head.

"Gotta watch them mirrors," she advised in a croaky voice. "They'll play tricks on you if you're not careful. I see it all the time." The old woman looked away. "Mm-hm. *All* the time."

Speechless, Consuela sat numbly on the floor. She drank the small bottle of orange juice, fumbled with her cell phone, and hung up when there was no answer at home. Someone shoved a clipboard at her. Flustered and self-conscious, she dutifully signed the accident report, scribbling her name and forgetting to give back the pen.

Consuela waved off any more offers of help and hurried to take her place in the checkout line, nervously brushing her hair from her face and folding the jeans over her arm. She wanted to pretend that everything was normal, that nothing weird had just happened, and go straight home.

She took out her credit card and adjusted her necklace over her collar. She felt the clasp catch.

"Ouch," she grumbled. Consuela tried untangling the snarl of gold and fine baby hairs.

She rubbed the back of her neck and felt something move.

teNDeR dropped to a crouch, rising slowly as the Flow ebbed and swirled around him like a cloak. He looked back to where the window had appeared between worlds. He wasn't used to looking over his shoulder. Others were usually watching their backs around *him*.

"Did you see that?" Wish whispered, eyes wonder-wide under his greasy mop of hair.

Tender was tempted to say no. Instead he admitted, "I saw the rift. But I didn't see who was on the other side." He felt obliged to state the obvious. "Someone's coming through soon."

"Never saw that before," Wish added, tugging his denim jacket covered in old novelty pins. "Shone like a mirror."

"Yes," Tender said. "I suspect V got a good look. He's always somewhere lurking about."

"You should talk." Wish grinned up at Tender. Tender glared through his too-long blond bangs and oppressively thick, black eyebrows. Wish tapped one of the buttons on his left pocket that said IF YOU CAN READ THIS . . . YOU MIGHT AS WELL INTRODUCE YOURSELF! and winked. Tender sighed and readjusted the heavy silver belt buckle riding low on his hips.

"Come on," Tender said, jerking his head into the void. "I've got things to do. Whoever it is will get here soon enough."

Tender strode away, the Flow twisting in impossible directions as the world bowed beneath his feet. The gray-and-opal mist parted. Wish wiggled his loose tooth and broke it off with a snap. Blowing a long, cool breath through his fingertips, he pushed a dusty white moth into flight. Both boys turned away as it flew jaggedly up into black nothingness, slipping like a satin ribbon between pages of night.

CONSUELA walked around her room, absently rubbing the back of her neck and trying to figure out what was wrong.

She ran a finger over the skin again: it gooshed under pressure.

Prodding experimentally around the base of her skull, she thought the lump was about the length of her little finger and the width of her thumb. It was soft and squishy, following the line of her spine. It didn't hurt, but touching it made her feel uneasy. Still, she couldn't stop. Like picking a scab.

Her mother handed her two small white pills and a tall glass of juice. Consuela stopped rubbing her neck as Mom watched her swallow. The citric acid tasted like vomit.

"I called Dr. Cooper," her mom said, stroking Consuela's hair. "He recommends heat, rest, and a double dose of ibuprofen. If the lump is still there in the morning, we can make an appointment."

"Great," Consuela mumbled.

"Does it hurt?" Mom asked.

"No," Consuela said with a flashback feeling to when she first got her period. Mom had wanted it to be a "moment," while Consuela hadn't. It just hadn't been one of those bonding mother-daughter things for her. She wanted it to go away and get on with her life. Like now. "It's gross."

"Let me see," her mom said.

Consuela turned around and ran her fingers down the back of her neck. Her mother pushed Consuela's glossy black hair aside and gently dabbed a fingertip over the lump's surface.

"It's not bruised," Mom said. "Did you bang it somehow?"

"I think I would've noticed getting smacked on the back of the head."

"I would think so," her mom admitted. "Still, if it doesn't hurt, we'll wait until morning. Try soaking in the bath and I'll go find the heating pad." Her mother hesitated by the door, as if debating whether to admit this was a big deal or not. The pause was scarier than the lump itself. "If it starts hurting, tell me right away and we'll go straight to the hospital. Okay?"

What else could she say? "Okay."

Both of them smiled uneasily, projecting *Everything is going to be fine,* while checking to see if the other one believed it.

"Don't worry," Mom said, squeezing her hand. She went downstairs, probably to call Dad. Consuela closed the door.

Okay, so it's a big deal.

She distracted herself by playing with the bathtub faucets, trying to get the water temperature just right. She paced her bedroom while she undressed, grabbing a hair tie and throwing her keys on the vanity, hitting the pile of blank Statement of Purpose sheets from her college applications. The truth was that she had no idea what she wanted to major in or where she should apply, let alone what she wanted to do with the rest of her life described in one thousand words or less. Every time she tried to start, she ended up doing laundry or going online shopping. Anything to avoid the fact that she obviously had no Purpose in life.

Lavender-scented bubbles perfumed the warm air as she unwound her robe and hung it on the back of the door. Dimming the lights, she tied her hair into a knot on top of her head.

Slipping one foot into the hot water, Consuela waited for the initial sting to soften. She climbed in, goose pimples rising all over her legs. She settled into her shell-shaped bath pillow, inching down so that the water lapped the back of her neck. Consuela closed her eyes and tried not to think about anything.

Unfortunately, the moment she tried thinking about nothing, everything else flooded in. She wondered what was wrong with her, whether she'd go to the doctor's tomorrow or end up in the ER tonight. She should've listened in on her parents' phone conversation—she hated not knowing what was going on! Should she dress for a hospital stay? Should she insist on staying home? Going to school? Would anyone notice the lump? She resolved to wear her hair down and her new pair of jeans.

She shifted in the water. Why did Allison have to be out camping this weekend, totally unplugged? Consuela itched to text her. Allison would have made a joke, told her not to worry, and known whether or not that second pair of jeans was worth buying. That made Consuela remember the changing room, the fall, and the creepy old attendant. Consuela squirmed. She couldn't *believe* she'd stuck around to buy a pair of jeans!

The whole experience had been uncomfortable. Buyer's remorse struck. Luckily, she'd kept the receipt.

Consuela wiped tiny beads of sweat and steam from her face and examined her pedicure. Ten little squares of Ruby Matte with gold decals floated beneath the surface of the bath like buried treasure. Pumping foam into her palm, she slid it thickly over her arms and legs. She soaped and rinsed her whole body, drained the tub, and sprayed herself with the handheld showerhead before daring to check the lump.

Sliding her fingers over her scalp, she slowly worked her way down—the skin changed from normal to mush. Consuela grimaced. *Nope, still there.*

She felt around the giant soft spot at the base of her skull. Bracing herself, she pushed a little harder. Her finger slipped—*pushing inside?*—and stopped suddenly. She shrieked and yanked her hand in front of her face.

Consuela stared at her fingertip: nothing. Not even blood. She checked the back of her neck and pulled her hand away—nothing. She ran her fingers over the lump again—not a hole, or even a scratch. It was smooth, unbroken skin.

She swallowed. *I imagined it.*

But she knew she hadn't.

Steadying herself, Consuela kept her right finger straight and pushed slowly, but firmly, into the lump. She *felt* her nail sink inside, all the way through, until she touched something hard—*my spine?*—and stopped.

Consuela sat in the empty bathtub with her finger stuck through the flesh of her neck and her heart hammering in her chest. *What the hell?!* Consuela kept her eyes closed, drinking in air. Her mind spun. *What now?* She thought desperately, *Call Mom? She'd freak. I'd freak,* she admitted to herself. *This is me, freaking!*

She took a few deep breaths that shuddered on the exhale. Her eyes stayed shut, spots of light winking behind the red. Using both hands, she traced her fingers along the edges of the gap, feeling along the edge of puffy skin and the bony nubs beneath, trying to determine whether this was or wasn't real. She couldn't quite decide yet. She had to be sure before she screamed.

Chin on her chest, Consuela slipped a second finger alongside the first, parting the skin at the back of her skull easily. It didn't hurt—*It doesn't hurt*—but it felt . . . strange. She tried a third, her pinky stuck into her hair as the rest of her hand cupped inside her neck.

She closed her eyes, trying to picture it . . .

Her fingers broke through, melting a line of cool heat

down her back. Her body opened like the seam of a sandwich bag.

She felt the cold kiss of air on her naked spine.

Almost without thinking, Consuela slipped her skin over her head like a sweater. She pulled her arms out of their long gloves and stepped gently out of the warm, wet suit left puddled at the bottom of the bathtub. Keeping her eyes on her feet, Consuela stared at the collection of thin, tiny bones suspended in a sort of liquid shadow holding them together, surreal against the peach bath mat. She looked up into the full-length mirror and saw herself.

Consuela was a skeleton.

Rich and shining, her bones gleamed—the steam giving her an aura, a halo. She was smooth and shiny, like pale mother-of-pearl, almost glowing in the muted half light. A thin translucence clung to her, outlining where her skin ought to have been. She traced the ghost of her curves, powdered with dew. Hard but soft, luminous as shell, she was firm, beautiful, strong, alive.

She moved lightly, as if the weight of her was measured in the tiny gaps of nothing between each of her bones. Flexing her hand, she watched the delicate cage of fingers floating in darkness. She opened and shut her mouth, watching her jawbones slide together, marveling at the motion. She breathed deeply the warm smell of the air, seeing her rib cage expand and lift—free of organs, but hardly empty. She exhaled, and saw her clavicle and shoulders settle straight.

She wanted to smile, but she was already smiling. She realized she'd always been smiling on the inside. Now she could see it—her perfect white teeth in two, perfect lines: her forever-smile. Admiring herself, she knew that this was *her.*

This is who I am, she thought. *The rest is just skin.*

She looked down at the empty suit of Consuela Chavez, feeling curiously detached. She picked it up and inspected her surface body, feeling the soggy weight of it in her hands. Consuela knew there should be muscles and organs and blood—*and pain?*—but there wasn't. There was only the skeleton and her skin.

She cradled it in her arms like a precious thing, a gown of tan silk with black satin fringe, and hung it gently on the door hook to dry.

She laughed.

Consuela felt suddenly, impossibly whole. *Shining. Pure. Powerful. Alive!* She knew that Consuela Chavez, high school good girl smiling shyly in the back of the room, *never* felt like this. But, like this—for the first time in her life—she felt like the real Consuela Louisa Aguilar Chavez. Completely.

As if imagined, she heard a whisper like music.

// *Know thyself.* //

Consuela turned in the hazy glow, tracking the sound. She didn't see anyone, but she had the feeling of being . . . not "watched," but "observed."

She stepped toward the mirror and gently wiped away the clouded moisture. Condensation dripped like tears where her bones scraped the glass. She tried peering into the silvery reflection.

A pair of lips surfaced. Smiled. Withdrew.

She stepped back.

The ghost of violin sound quieted and she was alone.

Consuela tapped the mirror. *Nothing but glass.* The steam slowly obscured it once more.

Know thyself.

The air slipped like a secret between her pieces. She suddenly needed to feel the world breathing. Consuela climbed onto the edge of the bathtub, unlocked the window, and let the night in.

Her nonexistent eyes slipped closed in their sockets as she arched her back, gripping the edges of the windowpane like a pirate ship's Jolly Roger in full sail. Consuela let the wind buffet her and blow in-through-around her body. Like an autumn gust through apple trees, it smelled crisp and wild and real. She wanted to feel it— wear it like a second skin.

The thought came out of nowhere, but it seemed so logical, effortless. *Why not?* Consuela stepped onto the window ledge, curling to sit on the sill, legs dangling out the second-story window high above the porch. The air swam like tadpoles around her toes. She slipped a foot in.

She watched her toes disappear into the wind, although she still felt them there, buoyant and cool. Consuela reached down, pulling the edge of air up her legs, under her knees. It felt more comfortable than any pair of jeans she'd ever owned.

She stood up before she'd realized what she'd done: slipping the skin of air over her butt, she was now suspended in nothing at all. Threading her arms into sleeves of breezes and cupping a mask of wind to her face, she inhaled the intoxicating scent of seasons and pulled it impossibly over her head. The seam up her back slipped closed and sealed.

The world snapped open.

The world snapped shut.

Consuela opened her eyes to the roar of the weather. She smelled the northerly wind and saw its currents run. Like a moving sidewalk, a river road, paths rushed and parted as they rode warm and cool hillocks of pressurized air.

Consuela stepped out onto one of them. Turning east, she rode it like a comet into the night.

chapter two

"Death as nostalgia, rather than as the fruition or end of life, is death as origin. The ancient, original source is a bone, not a womb."

—OCTAVIO PAZ *(ref. to Villaurrutia's* Nostalgia de la Muerte*)*

tHIS place called to her. Consuela had never seen it before, not really, although she'd passed the park many times, but this was the first time she was truly aware of it. The little park bench pulled at her. She could feel it in her bones.

She blew past the concrete sign reading SUNRISE PARK framed in potted marigolds and mulch-covered earth, down the gravel path, and toward the person hunched in a worn leather jacket. The young man stared at his hands, ignoring the cold, while absently flipping a butterfly knife.

Consuela watched the thin silver blade spin like a toy pinwheel. The man stared at it with an intense, child-like fascination; the scene carried with it an undertone of blood. She circled around him to look at his face.

Haunted, was the first word that rang in her mind. *Scared. Determined. Awful. Alone.* He stared at the knife wheel—past it, through it—something pressing upon his thoughts like a stone, slowly pushing him toward resolve. Consuela could feel his anxieties, his fears, like a ripple in her mind.

Suicide.

She realized that he was waiting for something; some sign to prove that this was right. But this wasn't right. It was wrong, she knew, although she was surprised to find that she wasn't afraid about witnessing a possible suicide. It was something out of balance, off course, and worth correcting.

She was calm, distant, slipping silently on feet of breeze. Although he didn't see her, she knew that he felt her there because he was so attuned to finding *something,* he couldn't help but hear her. She wanted him to hear, so she told him:

"Don't."

He jerked up—surprised, embarrassed, and angry. He glared around with staggered glances, like a startled moth, seeing nothing, erratic and unsure. His fear was almost comical. Consuela smiled her forever-smile.

"Don't," she said again, and let her fingertips of air lift the hairs from his brow, drying them instantly of sweat and *fear.* His breath came coughing in short gasps.

"Breathe," she advised. He did. She listened as his lungs filled with the smell of forest pine, his senses tickling him back to wakefulness and away from the ledge in his mind. He sighed, relieved. She ruffled his hair playfully and helped him to stand, the strength of the wind lifting him up like a child.

"Go home," she said gently. *"Go."*

The knife found its way into his back pocket, forgotten. He crossed himself reverently and kissed a gold cross hanging from its chain around his neck. Dropping his eyes, he left quickly. Consuela watched him go.

Peace trickled in.

She stood quietly by the park bench, watching the nettles tremble and the dead leaves turn; soft, rustling sounds after the lingering crackle of danger had passed. She'd stopped someone from hurting himself—maybe dying. Consuela smiled to herself as she turned the thought over in her mind. She hadn't felt nervous or afraid or embarrassed in the least; she'd just *done* it. Like she was meant to do it. Like she was meant to be here. To stop him.

She jumped when a phone rang.

Consuela knelt in the windblown garbage that had collected under a tree, following the insistent, electronic buzz. She found the cell phone buried beneath a crumpled newspaper, jammed inside the remains of an open Happy Meal box. She pressed the green button, answering it.

"Hello?" she said while realizing that the call couldn't possibly be for her.

"I see you," a gentle voice said with a hint of humor. "Care to see me?"

Consuela turned in place on the balls of her feet, searching. She wasn't afraid, but she was curious. "Yes."

"Good," said the girl's voice. "See a yellow-gray light?" Somehow, Consuela was not surprised that she could. It stretched like some dull reflective tape through space. "Follow it to me. Leave the cell phone on—it's your receiver. Oh, and bring the box." The connection cut.

Obediently, Consuela tucked the flimsy container under one arm. Something rattled inside it, but she didn't bother to check. She held the cell phone out like a divining rod—an invisible flashlight searching the dark corners of nothing—and followed the sulfurous trail into dawn.

CONSUELA entered a comfortable room of plush carpet and indirect lighting. A basement office, she figured, given the lack of windows and the large computer screen. A young woman about Consuela's age, maybe a little older, sat in an oversized leather chair, the kind pulled tight and bulleted with brass buttons.

Consuela thought that the girl was meant to be pretty, someone from a wealthy prep school or senior class president—suede skirt, expensive shoes, soft sweater, pearl earrings, and perfect waves of honey-colored hair framing a face that was half gone. It was odd how that didn't bother Consuela more.

Without a word, Consuela offered both the cell phone and the Happy Meal box to the girl's left hand—the right one was noticeably missing at the wrist.

"Thank you," the young woman said as she took the phone and shut it off, placing it to the right of the mouse pad on her desk. She set the box in her lap and delicately reached inside. "My name is Cecily Gardner. Call me 'Sissy,'" she said with an amused chirp. "Wait a minute, I want to get a good look at you . . ."

Sissy withdrew her hand from the container and dropped something into a tall glass of water. An eyeball bobbed gently to the surface, its blue iris spinning lazily like a planet. Sissy fished inside, plucking it up, and tapped her wrist against the edge of the glass, shaking the excess moisture free. Sweeping her hair aside, she rolled the eyeball expertly at the top of her cheek; thumbing it into the socket with a soft, wet pop. She blinked and wiped away a tear. Both blue eyes turned to look at Consuela.

"There you are." Sissy smiled with genuine welcome. "I watched you with Rodriguez. You did everything like a pro."

Consuela wasn't quite sure what to say. She was a mixture of things—shocked, curious, anxious, afraid—but it was blunted, folded in a soft, airy blanket in her chest. She felt oddly peaceful and serene.

"Thanks," she said.

"You're welcome." Sissy turned to type something single-handedly into the computer. She hit enter with a flick of finality and swiveled the chair to face Consuela. "Do you want to sit down? Something to drink?" Consuela didn't know. She hadn't thought about fleshy things in a while. Sissy seemed to understand. "How do you feel?" she asked.

"Strange," Consuela said truthfully, "but in a good way. Powerful, light . . ." She hesitated, laughing a bit. "It's tough to describe. Could be that it's the air I'm wearing."

Sissy nodded. "Do you want to take it off?"

Can I? Consuela wondered.

"There are some hangers in the closet," Sissy added, gesturing with her left hand at a tall, open door. Consuela wafted over, trying on the idea of hanging up her skin like a coat. She slipped her fingers into the lump at the base of her skull, unzipped the seam of her spine, and stepped out of the invisible covering as easily as she had her own skin. Choosing a heavy wooden hanger, she threaded it into the empty shoulders. Her suit of air hung in the closet, where it swayed gently in its breeze.

"Beautiful." Sissy had been watching and breathed her approval. Her left fingers curled demurely in her lap. "I've been looking forward to meeting you. You're the first person who's . . ." She shook her head, admonishing herself. "Sorry. First things first: do you have any questions?"

"Questions?" Consuela gaped.

"I'm obliged to ask," Sissy said.

Only about a million . . . "Where are we?" Consuela asked.

Sissy smirked. "Not an easy one for starters, but I'll try my best. We're in an image of my father's office in the basement of our home in the Valley. On the other hand, we're in a sort of reality running parallel to the real

world—we call it the Flow—and you are somewhere between Bristol, Wisconsin, and Aurora, Illinois, and I'm
slightly north of Los Angeles. Does that help?" Sissy said
with a grin.

Consuela shook her head, laughing despite herself.
"No." She could appreciate the humor of a ridiculous
situation.

"I wouldn't think so," Sissy said. "May I preempt the
next question?"

"Sure."

"'*Why* are we here?'" Sissy swiveled in her chair.
"That's a somewhat easier question. You and I exist in
both worlds, although this one only admits people like
us. Everyone here can *do* things, things that affect the
real world, usually for specific people and usually for specific reasons. Mainly, we keep certain people from dying
before their time."

Consuela's mind spun, thoughts and implications
whizzing around her head; she couldn't seem to settle on
just one. She wondered aloud, "Like who?"

"Like Tony Rodriguez. Like Sophia Crane. Like little
Killian O'Shea, not six weeks old in his bed in Roxbury."
Sissy recited the names with pride.

"I don't understand," Consuela said. "What's so important about them?"

Sissy shrugged. "I don't know. We don't know," she said. "Sorry. No one here really knows. There are theories, but nothing solid. New people arrive here all the time, replacing those who've recently left. It's a temporary position for who knows how long, but in the meantime, we just do what we came here to do—what we're meant to do. Save these select people from dying prematurely, however we can with whatever we've got. It's who we are. You understand."

Consuela recalled the pride at recognizing herself in the bathroom mirror. *Know thyself.*

"Yes," she admitted. "But I'm still confused."

"Welcome to the club!" Sissy laughed.

Consuela tried a new topic. "So who are you?"

"Me?" Sissy sounded genuinely surprised by the question. "Well, that's simple enough. I am Cecily Amelia Gardner, the one watching over us. The Watcher." She placed French-manicured fingernails against her necklace, a small blue bead on a silver thread.

Consuela hesitated. She didn't mean to be rude, but the meaning of the necklace—if there was any—was lost on her. "What is it?"

"This? This is me." Sissy held the bead up for Consuela to see: a tiny sphere of cobalt glass pockmarked with rough circles of milky white. Like Sissy's eyeball in reverse. "It's Greek," she said. "An 'All-Seeing Eye' bead. Appropriate for a Watcher, don't you think?"

"I'm not sure," Consuela confessed. "Should it be?"

"There's always been a Watcher, like there's always been the Flow," Sissy said matter-of-factly. "People like us have always existed." She crossed her legs primly at the ankles and shook her hair from her face. Consuela noticed that Sissy was missing one ear. "The Flow's been here as long as people have, maybe longer. The animals might have had their own spirit-selves here." She flipped her hair over her shoulder. "Maybe they still do—it would explain Joseph Crow."

Consuela shook her skull. What Sissy said sounded strange, far stranger than walking around without skin. "Who's Joseph Crow?"

Sissy winked playfully. "You'll see when you meet him."

Consuela waited for Sissy to continue, but there was only silence. "Sorry," she said, "but I still don't understand."

"Think of it this way: 'guardian angels' might be too Hallmark or sacrilegious or something, but it's the closest thing I can think of. Spirit guides, maybe." Sissy rested her hand against the keyboard. "I've talked with some of the others, but no one has anything more than vague ideas. Frankly, we can debate until we turn to dust. Me, I choose to accept it and do my job."

"Your job?" Consuela asked.

"Helping people," Sissy said with a smile. "Best job there is."

Consuela appreciated Sissy's answer. Its simplicity was refreshing, although thinking about it made her head hurt. *How do we help people by removing our body parts or skin . . . ?*

Sissy leaned forward in her chair, the leather creaking under her weight. "Can I ask you a question?"

Consuela nodded. "Sure."

"Who are *you*?"

"Consuela Louisa Aguilar Chavez," Consuela said, and lifted her hand, her skeleton shining like pearls under glass. She stared, fascinated. "Bones," she said aloud, then laughed.

"Your last answer was truer," Sissy said.

Consuela turned her hands over, nodding. "Bones, then."

Sissy offered her a slightly awkward left-handed shake. "Welcome to the Flow, Bones."

tHeRe was a crashing and breaking of twigs as he came. He swatted stalks of bamboo out of his way and splintered the crunchy, dead things underfoot. When he hit the clearing, it might as well have been with his fist.

Fish scattered from the surface of the pond, orange and white ghosts vanishing into blackness. Nikki looked up, startled and sad. But then, Nikki was always sad.

Nikki knelt by his dark pool, crying flowers for boys who could not cry for themselves. Tiny pink blossoms fell from his eyes and were carried out to the sunless sea, or taken by the koi fish that brought them somewhere deeper. His hands lay in his lap, his enormous sleeves hung like bells. He made no move to cover his bare chest through his open kimono shirt.

As if indifferent to his guest, Nikki glanced to where the fish had gone, their passage marked only by the ripples of shadow on light.

"I will not do this," he said quietly, licking some of the gloss from his lips. His eyelids dropped, weighed by blue eye shadow and heavy liquid liner. "You are wrong to try and stop it, and I'll aid you no longer."

The interloper drew out a sword, black and pitted from tang to tip.

Nikki neither flinched nor fled, but stood, bowing a fraction—a flowery sort of bravery—before evoking his power. It thrummed under his voice, making it deeper.

"Please, Jason, let me . . ."

Before he could finish, the blade whipped out in a contemptuous arc, severing Nikki's head from his neck.

The thin body crumpled in a pile of sorbet-colored silk. The head rolled into the long grass with an expression of gentle, openmouthed surprise.

The assassin sheathed his sword slick with blood and spinal fluid. He did not want to be called "Jason" nor did he want what Nikki offered. It was an insult. A weakness. He glared at the vacant waters—not one tear shed for *him*.

Walking back the way he'd come, the bamboo forests and carp ponds dissolved into nothingness behind him. Nikki's head lay wide-eyed in the curling mist.

A pink petal fell from his cheek and dried.

chapter three

"Everything in the modern world functions as if death does not exist. Nobody takes it into account, it is suppressed everywhere . . ."

—OCTAVIO PAZ

CONSUELA shouldered her skin of air like an overcoat as she and Sissy said their good-byes. Stepping out into a swirl of color and movement, she whisked herself away

Gliding smoothly through the air, she landed on her own windowsill in no time, feeling impish, like Peter Pan visiting a lost-childhood room. Consuela crawled into the bathroom and wrapped herself in its steamy, familiar warmth. Stepping out of her skin of air was hardly an effort. She strung it on a paper-wrapped hanger and placed it in her bedroom closet, padding back into the bathroom to fetch her own skin before her mother came in to check on her. The Flow was amazing, but she was glad to be home.

Consuela glanced at the tub. She hadn't actually finished enjoying her bath. The air was still thick with lavender and steam. She couldn't've been gone *too* long . . .

The tub quickly filled with the splash and sluice of warm water. Although she doubted she could feel the temperature, there was something soothingly real about the smell of a hot bath. This time, she lowered herself slowly, feeling the water fill every crevice, tiny bubbles of air escaping from the nooks in bone. The slight shadow still held her together, but the water engulfed her as much as the air had blown through her.

Consuela glanced at her toes—no longer buried treasure, but bleached driftwood, sunken ships, and coral bones. She smiled her forever-smile.

Lying back, she wrapped the water around herself, cuddling inside it because she could. Her head stuck out of her liquid poncho, the bath tucked in all around her. Consuela bumped her skull against the inflated bath pillow. *Why was I so worried before? And about such silly things—sickness, school, shopping, clothes?* Without flesh, she had left all her cares behind. She laughed and dunked her head.

The water rushed in through her eye sockets and nose and the crux of her jaw, swimming up her sinuses and between her teeth. She wondered how she'd been speaking to Sissy without a tongue. *I can see without eyes, so why the hell not?* Consuela wondered if she could breathe underwater.

Easier to become the water itself.

Consuela resurfaced, wearing a skin of water. No sealskin or wet suit—skinny-dipping would still be one too many layers to compare—Consuela reveled in the hedonistic feeling of the water, licking ever so slightly with her every move. It was delicious. Decadent. She felt as if she were salivating all over, craving something she couldn't name. Hungry. Eager. It pounded like a drumbeat in her chest.

I could dive down the drain! I could merge with the ocean! I could escape the world entirely and become a cloud of steam . . .

She splashed explosively against the back of the tub, throwing herself aware. She trembled, scaring herself. Consuela huddled into a ball of fluorinated water and pushed away as far as she could go, like she was four all over again and afraid of being sucked down the drain. Except this time, it was real.

I really could fall down the drain! Consuela felt herself

tempted by an elemental pull. *If I'm not careful. If I'm not thinking, I could lose myself in this.*

Between one blink of her eyes and the next, it clicked.

The world snapped open.

The world snapped shut.

The fear melted away, replaced by purpose.

She leaped and, like a needle-borne thread, she spun, funneling down the drain.

past the pipes and the processing plant, the alum and sand, fluoride and grates, Consuela swiveled in a direction she could feel at her core—a spinal column compass inside her liquid skin.

Water into water, she emerged; the temperature changing dramatically, the immense feeling of being one with the lake. Consuela felt all that was skirting in and around her muddy edge: plants and algae, fish and frogs, eggs and spawn and pollywogs, water bugs kissing the surface, birds dipping their beaks—everything, everywhere, held within her. *Life.* To be water was to be alive.

The ruffled-feather, splashing, plinking, diving motion tickled in ripples and soothed her in waves, except for one spot on the edge of her tasting sight.

There.

She felt the tug draw her closer. She swam without thought.

Skimming the surface, disturbing dragonflies as she passed, Consuela sank below the tumult, looking up from within. He was a skinny boy of eight or nine, twiggy legs and arms, wildly thrashing; a dark bluish-black blur against the reflection of the sky. The boy was doing a poor job keeping afloat. His limbs were barely twitching now, the spasms hardly kicks. His round head began sinking, tiny pearls of air nesting in his close-cut curls like a crown. His eyes closed. His face relaxed.

No, she thought. *It is not your time.*

She cupped herself like a net beneath him and, bending backward, pushed him up toward the light. He broke through the water and hung there. She could feel his fleshy weight, still slack against her frame.

Breathe! she commanded as she flattened with him on her surface. Flipping over, she hugged him to her. *Breathe!*

Nothing. A gentle panic seized her. *Was she too late?*

Consuela tightened herself around him, wringing his soggy chest in undulations and waves. His mouth slid open, a pool wobbled behind his teeth.

I'm coming, she thought, and touched a finger to his tongue, reaching deep into his throat and lungs and *pulled.*

Lake water sprayed from his purpled lips as Consuela flung it away. The child rolled over and coughed up a great bubble of wet. He hacked hoarsely, filling his lungs with air. Gasping, he started to cry.

Consuela relaxed into her element, letting him sink against her water skin until he could touch the silty shore with one outstretched foot. He crawled onto the bank, heaving and sobbing. Consuela glanced at the little lakeside cabin in the wan yellow light. It was still early morning.

The boy gave a whining moan. Lights came on. Shouts.

I did it! Consuela thought with a secret grin.

She exploded in a geyser and hit the storm drain like a gong.

SHe landed on the floor of her shower with a slap, uncertain of how she'd gotten there or how long it had been.

Consuela blinked up weakly from the tiles. The realization of where she was, what she was, and what she had done without a second thought quivered through her water and quaked along her skin.

What's happening? What am I doing? Becoming? Thinking?

Consuela hugged herself, feeling her fingers melt seamlessly into her arm. *Enough of the Flow. I'm home.*

She dragged herself from the shower, her body sloshing with surface tension but failing to leave wet foot-prints on the floor. Consuela yanked off the water skin, dropping the strange, silvery-blue pool on the tiles. She watched it from the edge of the tub in case it moved on its own, its innocent shimmer betraying nothing of its true nature.

Beautiful. Powerful. Terrible. It's so much bigger than me.

She gingerly picked it up and carried it to her closet, hanging it next to her thin skin of air. The two impossible things looked eerily beautiful together, as if she should have a wardrobe full of unlikely things. It drew her and chilled her.

She found a garment bag and stuffed the skins inside, zipping it closed. She shut the closet door and pushed her desk chair up against the knob.

Consuela changed into her own skin, adding another layer of underwear and flannel pajamas, tucking herself into cool sheets, warm comforters, and familiar feather pillows. She willed herself into an unsettled sleep, waiting for Mom, or Dad, or morning, to come.

It was impossible to tell whether she was awake or in a dream. Or if she had been dreaming that she'd been asleep, and she was only waking up now.

She lost her train of thought like a helium balloon.

She was in her room—or the dream of her room—inspecting her bedroom door. It sounded like there was a party going on downstairs, whispering with voices and music and the shuffle of feet on hardwood floors. It was hard to hear from where she was. She felt like a kid put to bed early while the grown-ups stayed up late.

Consuela pressed her face flat against the crack under the door and listened. There was something elusive, whispering enticingly at the edge of her senses. She strained to hear what could almost be heard, tried to follow a flicker of what might have been shadows down the hall, could almost smell something like chafing-dish smoke or identify a snatch of conversation made by voices she ought to have recognized. Consuela tried, but she couldn't place any detail—it haunted her like a lingering taste of anise and orange peel, something half remembered from childhood. For some reason, she never thought to open the door.

She pressed herself deeper into the carpet until the fibers stung her cheek and the tip of her nose wedged beneath the lip of the door. It was no good.

Sighing, she stood up and returned to bed, tucking herself into the dream-within-dreaming, wrapped in an unrequited feel of *almost*.

// Bones. //

Consuela couldn't tell if she'd woken up in the world or in a dream. She wondered if she was beginning to lose the distinction between the two.

She pulled off the covers and sat up, straining to hear. Nothing. She relaxed.

// Bones. //

Consuela's hair stood on end. She didn't believe in ghosts, but she believed in burglars. Although the voice had an ethereal, unreal quality—as if electric violins formed whispered words. *Where had she heard it before?* She couldn't think about it now; there was someone in the house!

She looked for what she might use as a weapon. A chair? Her old soccer trophies? She tried remembering her freshman-year gym class on personal safety, but she was full of gibbering thoughts. *Panic,* she recognized. *Not good.*

Afraid to move in case someone was listening, Consuela had frozen half off the bed, her calf muscle spasming in its awkward pose. *This is crazy. I'm imagining things. I'm still sleeping. I've been asleep since yesterday. I've drowned in the tub. I'm anesthetized in the hospital and am having a CAT scan on my head.* This was some nightmarish hallucination. Nothing seemed quite real. She wondered if cell phones and cable TV really did affect your brain.

// Bones. //

Consuela fell onto the carpet. It took her a second

to realize what had happened: her legs had given out in fright and she'd collapsed onto the floor. *I thought that only happened in movies.*

She grasped for her necklace, her tiny topaz cross. A present from her father. She wanted him here, but didn't dare shout. *Are Mom and Dad awake? Did they hear that? Could this be real . . . ?*

// Bones. //

"STOP IT!" she screamed, frightening herself with the sudden sound. Her throat stung in the aftermath. She swallowed. It hurt.

Silence.

She wanted to wake up, because then she would have known she'd been sleeping. Then this all could be unreal. She had to know . . . She felt for the soft lump on her neck. *Still there.*

The confirmation brought no comfort.

Consuela pulled one of her blankets off her bed and wrapped it tightly around her body, right there on the floor. She felt like a tiny anthill about to get stomped . . . waiting for the universe's other shoe to fall.

Consuela kept listening. Nothing.

She surprised herself: she prayed.

There was nothing else to do.

He left after that. Now that he knew for sure.

What was she doing here?

He flicked the lighter crisply on and off, birthing and killing its single star in the dark.

He'd have to keep an eye on her, ask the Watcher, wait and see.

Obviously, he hadn't saved her yet.

chapter four

"In every man there is the possibility of his being—or, to be more exact, his becoming once again—another man."
—OCTAVIO PAZ

HER phone rang.

Adolescent instincts took over. She picked it up without thinking.

"Hello?"

"Isn't this convenient?" Sissy's voice chirped. "You're listed in the book!"

Consuela fumbled for words, cohesive thought, something. The clock said 11:19, but it felt later. She fiddled with her cross, rubbing her fingertips over the stones.

"Hi, Sissy."

"I wanted to invite you over—have any other plans?"

Consuela could hardly think through the just-got-up fog. "None that I know of," she admitted.

"Then grab your favorite skin or come as you are, we're pretty informal around here." Consuela could hear the casual humor in Sissy's voice, but couldn't dredge up the energy to match it. She was tired. *Bone tired?* She thought of skeletons and drainage pipes and bedroom doors and eyeball beads.

"I'll be there in a minute," Consuela croaked. "Did you call me before?"

"This is the first time I've dialed your number."

"No," Consuela said. "I mean . . . out loud." She scratched her fingernails over her scalp. She felt filthy. "I thought I heard someone calling my name." *The one you nicknamed me.*

"No," Sissy answered, "but that could've been anyone, really. Anybody drop by for a visit yet?"

"No."

"Don't worry. They will. You're the new kid in town. *Everyone* wants to meet you!"

"Huh?" Consuela still felt vaguely unsure of where she was, when she was, and what was going on.

"So are you coming?" Sissy pressed.

"I'll be there," Consuela said, if only to get out of her room. She wasn't up for entertaining visitors. She didn't know how she'd introduce anyone like Sissy to Mom and Dad. *Where are they, anyway? Had there really been a party last night while we waited to see if I had to go to the ER?* That was so wrong.

"Don't dally, then." Sissy's voice rang clear as a bell, not like the soft hum of echoed strings. *Like an electric angel.* Consuela wondered where she'd heard it before, or if she'd ever hear it again.

"Later, Bones," Sissy said.

Consuela hung up, still in a daze. Sissy's wasn't the voice that had spoken before. It was as if her last name had been said with steel-stringed violins. A chord that formed her new name as a word. It buzzed through her memory in low harmonics.

She stood in the shower while hot water ran over her scalp. *What does it mean?* She soaped up her hair, scrubbing hard. She was glad she'd grabbed the phone before her parents had. *How am I going to explain this to them? Mom? Dad? Allison?* Consuela dunked her face under the jetting stream. *I can't imagine. I can't believe it. And* I'm *the one living it!*

She wasn't certain of anything, but she showered quickly and draped the towel and her skin over the glass door to dry.

WHEN Consuela arrived at Sissy's office, there was another person there—a guy. Somehow he managed to look scruffy and greasy at the same time, like a lost dog who'd been living in Dumpsters and trash.

His hair was brown and raggedly cut, his face pointy and thin with an extra-long nose. He wore a black T-shirt and a denim jacket completely covered with novelty pins. His hands, thin and lanky, kept moving, tapping the armrests and the pins and his chin. His foot bounced nervously, crossed over his knee. Sissy's eyes were closed, but her face turned toward Consuela as she stepped into the den. Consuela stood behind the chair, waiting politely to be introduced.

"Hello, Bones, this is Wish." Sissy gestured from one to the other. Wish nodded, but didn't say anything, glancing nervously back at Sissy.

"Bones?" He grinned unsteadily. "Is that a joke?" He sounded unsure whether to laugh or not.

"No," Consuela said. "I Ii."

Wish jumped and gripped the armrests, looking wild. She realized she'd frightened him. She'd never considered herself frightening.

"Why 'Wish'?" Consuela said as a way of breaking the ice.

He settled warily into his seat. "Oh, that." He placed

a finger on one crooked eyetooth. "See this? It's still a baby. Never got another growing in. My mum said that I could wish on baby teeth—that was her game since we were too stint to play tooth fairy, probably figured food stamps under my pillow wouldn't be a big thrill." Wish grinned around his scraggly teeth. "So now I can break it off, make a wish for somebody, and have it come true."

Consuela didn't doubt him. "So you have only one wish to give away to anyone at all?" she asked politely.

"Naw," he said, warming to the topic. His foot stopped bouncing. "That's the best part! It grows back every time. But it's only one wish per customer, so choose carefully." He wagged a finger, all nervousness gone. "When you got a good one, you come see me and I'll blow it true."

She laughed. "'Blow it true?'" The idea tickled her like a little kid with a bubble pipe.

"'S how it works," Wish said. "Watch this . . ."

Sissy groaned. "He loves this bit."

Wish pinched his eyetooth and broke it off with a practiced snap. Consuela cringed, which made him grin wider. Wish ran his pink tongue over the hole and tossed the tiny tooth in his palm.

"Check it out," he said with childish glee. He pursed his lips and blew. She watched the bit of bone dissolve into dust as if it were a magician's trick, swirling and reeling inside his cupped hand, like a snow globe, spun by the gentle pressure of his slow breath. The flurry cloud expanded, growing solid, taking shape. It twitched with a jolt of life and a burbling, crooning coo.

Wish grinned and tossed the handful of white into the air. The startled bird ruffled its wings with a newspaper sound, and flew past Consuela on its way out the door.

She ducked aside to let it pass, staring after it in delight.

"Wow," Consuela said to Wish's obvious pride. "What was it?"

"A dove," Sissy said.

"A wish," he corrected.

Consuela stood, awed, and asked, "Whose?"

"Oh, that one's a freebie," Wish said. "I give those out all the time—a general wish for health or happiness, that sort of thing. It'll go to whomever, wherever, even though they didn't ask. I mean, it's never wasted, right? There's enough to go around." He opened his mouth wide. "See?" Wish pointed to the gap and Consuela could just make out a nub of white bone buried in the tiny sea of red.

"It'll grow in pretty fast, so I'll be good to go." Wish glanced at Sissy, who was shaking her head. "So, that's it, then?" he asked her. "Are we good?"

"We're good," Sissy said. "Thanks, Wish. You'll be okay?"

"I'll be fine," Wish said, though even Consuela could tell he was lying. His nervous twitching had returned.

"Can you do me a favor? Ask V to come by," Sissy said. "I know Bones will want to meet him."

"V?" Wish sounded nervous about the request, but then something clicked; he stared at Consuela with open shock.

"You're . . . ?" He pointed at her questioningly. "You're that girl."

Consuela rested her hands on her hips. "I'm what girl?"

"Wish," Sissy interrupted with more than a hint of warning. "V first."

"Yeah," Wish said uneasily, glancing between the two girls. "Yeah, sure thing." He patted the pins again in rapid succession. He thumbed one that said HEAVEN DOESN'T WANT ME & HELL'S AFRAID I'LL TAKE OVER.

"Nice meeting you, Bones," he managed.

"You, too," Consuela said as Wish scurried out of the office like a dog caught peeing on the rug.

Consuela looked at Sissy, who was blind, both eyeballs gone. "What was that all about?" she asked.

"His real name is Abernathy Squires," Sissy said into space. "He's a bona fide paranoid, obsessive-compulsive sycophant with a major martyrdom complex that borders on the tragic. Welfare kid, DCF, DDS, DSS—a whole long list of Ds." She tweaked the muscles of her face to wink an empty socket and smiled. "But he means well. He's an artist and he's got a good heart."

"How do you know all that?" Consuela asked. It was a ruthless description of someone she didn't know.

Sissy shrugged. "He told me his name and I looked him up," she replied. "My computer works in the other world, too." She typed something expertly into some random document file on-screen as she talked. "If you make a wish, I don't know if God can hear you, but sometimes Wish does." Sissy gave a little smile. Consuela noticed she had a small dimple in her cheek. "Sometimes I think God might be like me, and that Wish is one of his removable ears."

Consuela flinched, half expecting a rumble of thunder at Sissy's arrogance. She said a mental, *Sorry, Jesus,* and quickly switched the subject.

"So who's V?" Consuela asked.

Sissy pursed her lips. "Hmm," she said. "I don't know much about him since he comes and goes a lot. I guess he's not bad, mostly keeps to himself, sort of quiet and broody in that good-looking-guy-lurking-in-the-back kind of way, but he's handy in a pinch. V can walk through mirrors."

"Through mirrors?" Consuela said weakly.

"Uh-huh." Sissy smiled. "It's his power. He can see

into the real world. Says there's a whole other world in between, but I've never seen it."

"So, not everyone removes body parts?" she guessed.

"What? No!" Sissy burst out laughing. "I guess you wouldn't know that given the recent sample, huh? No, we've all got different talents. Yehudah thinks it's inherited, while Wish thinks it's all circumstantial and Joseph thinks it's our totems at work."

Consuela shook her head and folded herself into the nearby armchair. "Who's Yehudah?"

Sissy blushed and smiled, shyly. Without eyes, she couldn't look away. "He's the Yad, which means 'the hand,'" she said while gently touching her own palm. "That's the thing Jews use to read their holy scroll. No one's allowed to actually touch it. Same's true with the Yad."

"I don't get it," Consuela said. "What does his hand have to do with anything?"

Sissy shrugged again. "What do your bones have to do with anything? Or, for that matter, your skin? We all have a power that can cross over from this world into the next. For you, it's your skin. For me, it's my parts. For the Yad, it's his blood. He can draw protective shields of warding with his blood."

"Ew," Consuela said.

"No more 'ew' than walking around without skin." Sissy sounded a little affronted.

Consuela raised a forefinger. "Point taken."

Sissy cooled and clicked on her screen saver.

"Is that why you invited me over?" Consuela asked. "To meet the neighborhood?"

"Well, you've only met Wish." Sissy chuckled. "You haven't met Joseph Crow or V or the Yad—don't offer to shake his hand, by the way . . ."

Consuela didn't have a brow to furrow. "Why?"

"It's a modesty thing. That's what I was talking about. He doesn't touch girls. I mean *at all*." The subject seemed to make Sissy uncomfortable as she hurried on. "Then there's Nikki, he's a cross-dresser from Silicon Valley, you'll like him—he's sweet. Maddy's in hibernation or whatever, right now—*long* story—and I haven't seen William Chang in ages, but he could be holed up in Quantum; he does that sometimes. We call him 'Abacus.'" Sissy's voice slowed. "Then there's Tender."

"'Tender'?" Consuela laughed. "Is that a name?"

Sissy hesitated. "He calls himself Tender because he tends the Flow," she said. "But I think it's more like all those before him were 'pre-Tenders' and he's the real deal."

"So what's he like?" Consuela asked.

"He's not like us," Sissy said, too quickly. "He cleans the Flow. All those dark and unpleasant bits we haul around and leave behind? Tender has to clean them up like a janitor. It's not a great job, but someone's got to do it, otherwise we'd all be knee-deep in karmic hell." She spoke with grudging respect, but Consuela noticed that Sissy slowly wound herself tighter and tighter in her chair, hugging her forearm to her chest. Consuela wished she could look the Watcher in the eye to see what was wrong.

"What?" Consuela asked.

Sissy made a face, nervous, embarrassed, and upset. "It's . . . he *eats* pain. Digests it." She touched her own abdomen almost protectively. "The Flow calls him, and he answers. He takes pride in doing his job—and it *is* really important—still . . ." A shudder slid down her limbs. "When he's called, he's like . . . an animal." Sissy muttered to herself, "A sleek, sharp-toothed animal."

Consuela imagined a young boy with sharp, pointy teeth chewing red-brown waste. A shark in a sewer. Her stomach turned. Or would have.

"The Yad calls him 'Bottom-feeder' and Joseph Crow calls him 'Vulture' for good reason," she murmured. "And he's kind of . . . intense."

So was the awkward silence that followed. Consuela felt she had to break it.

"Anything else I should know?" she asked lightly.

"Yeah," Sissy said. "He'll come looking for you soon."

Consuela stammered. "Me? Why?"

There was a knock at the door. Consuela turned, half expecting teeth.

"V?" Sissy swiveled in her chair. "Come in."

The door opened and a young man walked in. He had black hair and olive skin like an Italian oil painting, his face smooth and serious. His button-up shirt hung open at the neck and Consuela could see the sculpted muscles of his chest. She concentrated on his eyes in case she was staring. They were deep brown.

"Wish said you asked to see . . . "—his eyes locked on Consuela sitting in the armchair and he faltered, mid-stride, his deep voice sliding to a whisper—" . . . me."

He stopped, black boots settling heavily on the floor. He looked at Sissy, then back at Consuela with the oddest expression, almost a plea.

"V, this is Bones," Sissy said. "Bones, this is V."

"Hi." Consuela waved, trying to be friendly. This was clearly an awkward moment, although she wasn't sure why.

V stared at her. Swallowed visibly.

"Hi," he managed.

// Bones.//

Consuela sat up, alarmed, as the last threads of violin-voice faded fast.

"What was that?" she demanded.

V frowned. "What?"

"That . . ." Consuela stared at Sissy. "Did you hear it?"

V stood silent. Sissy paused, unsure.

"I didn't hear anything except you saying hi," she said. "V?"

V shook his head. "No."

"But . . ." Consuela felt stupid, but certain. Déjà vu and the feeling of *almost* echoed inside her. She searched the ceiling, the walls, the floor.

"What did it sound like?" V asked.

Consuela felt his eyes sinking into her sockets. She looked away quickly, straining to hear it again, to put into words the sound of an electrified hum singing her name and prove that she wasn't totally crazy.

"Nothing," she said finally. "I guess this is all a bit much." She didn't even believe her own lame excuse. Neither did V. Sissy rescued her by interrupting.

"Well, I was hoping that V would show you around a bit, offer a few pointers, give you some time to get acquainted," the Watcher said brightly, her closed eyes facing V. "Won't you, V?"

V hung his head as if the weight might pull him straight through the floor. He sighed like he'd been punched. Consuela got the impression he'd rather do anything else, be anywhere else, than with her.

"All right," he said softly. "If that's all right with . . . ?"

"Bones," Sissy reminded him.

"Consuela Chavez, actually," Consuela added.

V nodded. His eyelashes lowered and lifted once. Slowly.

"Right. Consuela Chavez. Bones," he said, stepping back. "After you."

Consuela stood. He watched her move, but pretended not to. She pretended she hadn't noticed right back. *Two could play at this game.*

"See you later, Sissy," Consuela said as casually as she could.

"Ha ha. Funny!" The Watcher jeered, pointing at her empty eye sockets. "It'll be a lot easier when I get these back in." She swiveled in her chair, following their footsteps as they approached the door.

"And V?" Sissy called.

He stopped, hand on the doorknob. He didn't look back. "Yes?"

"Explain things, if you can."

His fingers tightened on the doorknob. Consuela barely heard his answer.

"I'll try," he said, and held the door open like a gentleman, allowing Consuela to go first. She shied from the sudden sun-drenched wildflower field bursting right outside the threshold.

"What's that?" she blurted.

"Echoes of the real," Sissy called tiredly. "Everything bumps up against everything else in the Flow. You'll get used to it." She waved her hand. "Have a nice walk."

V shook his head and Consuela stepped out, crushing flowers underfoot. V closed the door behind them and sighed.

"Okay," V said, more to himself than her. "Where to?"

Consuela glanced around. The mysterious tension made her itchy. "How about a nice, relaxing tromp through Mother Nature?" she quipped. "Got a machete?"

V laughed. It transformed him from brooding to strikingly beautiful. Consuela was strangely happy that she'd caused it.

"Not on me," he said. "And we don't have to stay here. We can go anywhere in the Flow, but it's good to have an end point in mind." He hesitated, then offered his hand, fingers curled like a question. "Step when I step," he said. "Intention is key. Move like you know where you're going. The first one's a rush."

Consuela placed her hand in his. He watched her phalanges slide over his skin, folding them gently in a guitarist's grip.

"Ready?" he asked, keeping his eyes on their fingers.

His tremulous confidence fed hers. "Sure."

Consuela might have imagined him squeezing her hand, but by then they'd taken their first step.

Visions of the Flow flew by, a hundred scenes reduced to smears of color. Her mind reeled trying to follow it. Four steps and they stopped.

"Wow," she said.

"Dizzy?" V asked.

"A little," she confessed. They were in a small kitchen, retro-tiled like a fifties diner. A red-checkered potholder stood out against the yellow countertop. The silver stovetop gleamed.

"Give it a second. It's like a roller coaster," V explained.

"I love roller coasters," Consuela said, mildly giddy.

He gave a sort of half smile. "Me, too."

"Can we do it again?"

V chuckled. "Sure. Hold on."

They marched forward. This time, she was ready for it: stepping out into the Flow, knowing they could walk through space, doors, walls. V stopped abruptly in a town green. There was a redbrick church between two lazy country roads, a flagpole in the courtyard, and a gazebo strung with Christmas lights in the middle of what looked like a June afternoon.

Consuela swayed with delayed vertigo.

"I've got you," he said, steadying her spine, then pulled away quickly as if he'd accidentally touched her breast.

"Thanks," she said, covering his unease. "I think I've had enough for one ride."

"All right," he said gratefully. "Want to sit?"

She nodded.

They walked through the emerald grass. Black boots thumped and tiny bones clicked against the worn wood of the gazebo steps. The benches were peeling black paint and the rails were peeling white. There was an abandoned bird's nest tucked under one corner of the roof and a few tired cobwebs hung in the rafters. The air was soft and still.

V placed his foot on the octagonal bench and Consuela hugged her knees to her ribs, preparing herself for whatever was coming next. V rubbed his fingers hard against his sternum, his knuckles turning white.

"You okay?" Consuela asked.

"Yeah," V said, adjusting his collar. "It happens sometimes." He flexed his fingers in and out of fists. "Okay," he began, "So. You can cross into a place called the Flow . . ."

"I know that much," Consuela said, waving off the intro. "Sissy told me."

"The Watcher. Right." V paused. "Well, we're each called to our assignments—people who we're compelled to save—to stop them from dying before their time." Consuela nodded. He continued. "Sometimes we have to save them from something or someone or simply keep them from being in the wrong place at the wrong time. Other times, it's personal—something about them." He tapped on his chest. "Something inside that has to decide to live."

V cleared his throat and shifted position. "After a while, you'll notice there'll be a pattern to your assignments, a certain type of person that you're drawn to protect." He stretched for the words. "But these people are all important, destined to do great things, huge things, help lots of people—more than you or I could ever . . ." He was leaning forward, facing her, his eyes full and earnest. Consuela hung on his speech and the look in his eyes. Startled, he backed away, circling the floor, caught in the belly of the gazebo.

She watched him pace, her silence a question.

"Sorry," he muttered, and wiped his hands on his pockets. "It's just . . . it's hard seeing you here."

That caught her attention. "Me?" she said. "Why?"

"You . . ." V said. "You are not supposed to be here. You are not supposed to"—he gestured at her naked bones—". . . look like this." He shook his head. "This wasn't supposed to happen."

Nerves bubbled along her limbs. "What?"

"And it's my fault," V said in a rush. "It's my fault and I'm sorry."

"Your fault?" Consuela struggled to understand. "And you're sorry?"

He tapped his fist against his lower lip. "I promise, I'll fix it."

"What are you talking about?" Consuela said, standing.

"I'll fix it," V insisted.

"Fix what?" Consuela snapped, strangely insulted. "This is me."

"No, it isn't," V said patiently. "It's a mistake."

"A *mistake*?!"

"*My* mistake, all right?" V retreated, storming in circles. "I get it! I screwed up, okay?" he shouted while flicking his hand in the air. "I know it happens, but it's never happened to *me* before! And no one's ever shown up here . . . !"

"Will you stop?!" Consuela shouted. She took a deep breath the way her father always told her to do, tempering the Aguilar temper.

"Listen. You brought me here? You made me this way?" She laughed a little. "Fine. I forgive you, okay? It's amazing. It's . . . indescribable!"

V deflated, stricken. "Don't . . ."

"No," she insisted. "It's wonderful!" She spread her arms, showing their glory—sunlight dancing on her luminous skeleton. "Thank you."

"Don't thank me!" V said, horrified. "*Madre di Dio,* please don't thank me." He ran his hand over his eyes and closed it in a fist, beating it lightly against his forehead. "You. Shouldn't. Be. Here."

"Well, I *am* here," Consuela said. V retreated. She chased him. He wasn't taking this away from her so soon. "You and Sissy say I get to save people. *Me!*" Consuela touched her own breastbone. "I get to be part of something good. Something real that makes a difference." She had to convince him. She deserved this. She wanted this! "A *huge* difference," Consuela insisted. "Not only for these people, but for hundreds, maybe thousands . . ."

He spun around so fast, she nearly ran into him. His eyes burned.

// Let me save you! //

Consuela heard it, felt it. The sound of electric violins swelled so close, it buzzed along her bones. Echoed inside her skull. Imploring. Impassioned.

It was him. V.

The sound poured off him, but his mouth hadn't moved. He trembled.

"I was supposed to save you," he whispered. "But you couldn't hear me."

61

I can hear you, she thought. *I still hear you.* But the words wouldn't come. She wanted to understand. Ached for it. They stared at each other, speaking without words.

"I will make things right," he said solemnly. "I promise."

V launched out of the gazebo, down the stairs and onto the lawn, the grass flattening under his boots and the Flow bending around him as he strode into nothing. His final stanza hung in the air.

// I can save you. //

V's footfalls erased themselves from the grass as if they'd never been.

SHe returned to her room, drew on her skin, her U-of-I sweatshirt and jeans, and took some familiar comfort in making her bed. If Mom was going to let her sleep in for the day, she was going to do it in straightened sheets.

There was a hard rapping at her window. A black bird hovered outside.

Consuela quickly slid open the pane, praying nobody saw, and the bird settled itself on the sill as if waiting politely to be let in.

"Hello," said the bird. "I am Joseph Crow."

A lot of what Sissy had said now made sense.

"Hi," she said, keeping her voice down. "I'm Consuela Chavez."

The bird dipped its beak in a tight approximation of a bow. "I saw when you flew in to see the Watcher," clicked the crow. "You looked different, then."

"I was wearing a skin of air," she said, taking a seat on her bed. "This is how I normally look."

"Ah." Joseph Crow nodded sagely, his beak clacking as he talked. "I understand. This is my totem form; I am human back in my tent."

Consuela remembered Sissy's etiquette, politeness trumping the worry that her parents might walk in and see her talking to a bird. "Would you like to come in and change forms?" The words sounded odd in her mouth.

The crow hopped a couple of quick steps right and left. "Thank you, no," he said with mild amusement. "I need white sage to shift. Can you switch skins so easily?"

"I guess so," Consuela said, picking at the pilling on her bedspread. "I just . . . feel the need to make one, and before I know it, I put it on and go."

"Really?" The crow sounded impressed.

"Yep," she said. "Although not the water skin. I made

that on a whim, but I ended up going, anyway. To save someone from drowning."

A shiver fluffed the crow's feathers from nostrils to tail. "A water skin, a skin of air . . . how many skins do you have?"

"Just those two," she answered. "So far."

"Multiple skins," he said, preening with quick stabs of his beak. The erratic motions reminded her of Wish. "Like the snake," he added.

"Excuse me?"

"The snake. It's a powerful totem: acceptance, self-reliance, flexibility, rebirth," he said. "Do all your skins have power?"

Consuela thought about the things hanging fantastically in her closet. To ride the winds, to rush down the drain. "I guess so."

"What does this one do?" he asked, pointing a wing at her.

She touched her face as if checking which pair of earrings she had on. "This?" she said, surprised. "Nothing. This one's just me."

Joseph Crow cackled drily through his beak. "That didn't answer my question." He taunted gently. She'd meant to say that this was the skin she'd been born with, not made; it was nothing special. Just her.

He flexed his wings and turned toward the suburban neighborhood outside. "Come visit me later and we'll see what the smoke says." The invitation was half request, half command.

"All right," she agreed. "But how will I find you?"

Joseph Crow cocked his head over one winged shoulder. "Once you've made contact, you can find someone in the Flow easily enough. It's much like instinct," he said. "You know this as you know when it's time to make a new skin."

True, but I don't like being a slave to blind instinct.

Consuela stood next to the open window.

"Okay, well, thanks for coming by," she said, growing anxious. "It was nice meeting you."

"And you as well, Consuela Chavez."

Consuela stared at the talking crow. "Bones," she corrected.

He bobbed his head. "Bones."

He blinked into the lazy breeze and launched, letting himself fall before a few quick flaps swooped him higher. She watched him climb, but instead of fading into the distance, Joseph Crow slipped between a curtain of telephone wires and oak leaves, folded impossibly, and disappeared.

O-kay.

Consuela slid her window closed and drew the curtains for good measure.

WISH was fairly sure he could find him, being one of the few who could. Tender had tucked himself away in one of the many hospital rooms, his hand halfway through a fissure he'd drawn in the wall, peering through the Flow as if through backstage curtains.

"I met her," Wish said.

"Really?" Tender drawled, still glancing through the rift. "What's she like?"

It seemed like a simple question. Wish struggled to form his first impressions—words swam inside his open mouth like fish in a bowl.

"Um . . . Tough to say," he finally managed. Tender glanced at him in disgust. Wish started tapping. "Seriously. I've seen a lot of weird shit, okay? But never anything like that before."

Tender snorted derisively. "Like a girl?"

Wish flipped him off. "Yeah, well, you haven't seen her."

Thumbing his long bangs from his eyes, Tender turned back to his peephole. He ran soft fingers over his belt buckle. "What is she? Beautiful? Terrible? Freaky?"

"All three," Wish confirmed.

"Powerful?" Tender asked.

"Hell, yeah."

"Game changer," Tender muttered as he withdrew his fingers. The Flow oozed closed. He sounded mildly interested for someone so dead. "Well, that means I'll have to step up the plan."

Wish stopped cold. "What plan?"

Tender lingered on the edge of the privacy curtain before the Flow parted, allowing his exit.

"Wish," he said contemptuously. "I've *always* had a plan."

chapter five

"The word death is not pronounced in New York, in Paris, in London, because it burns the lips. The Mexican, in contrast, is familiar with death, jokes about it, caresses it, sleeps with it, celebrates it; it is one of his favorite toys and his most steadfast love."

—OCTAVIO PAZ

CONSUELA sat on her bed and tried sewing a skin of flame.

She had melted two needles into sad, droopy things before she'd thrown the sheet of fire away in a zip of flash paper. *Vwoop!* She was trying too hard, thinking too much. Consuela wanted to figure this out, but the more she thought about it, or thought about not thinking about it, or telling herself to STOP thinking about it and just let it happen, the further away it got.

She'd done it before, so why was it so hard now? Consuela grabbed double handfuls of her thick black hair and pulled, if only to feel something happen the way that it should. She groaned.

Flopping across her bed, she stared up at the ceiling. *What am I doing?* It had taken a lot just to peek into the closet and see the two skins, shining and real, hanging patiently in a garment bag, defying her doubts. This was real. This was really, really real. Now she wanted to find out "how" if she couldn't yet grasp "why."

V made it sound so . . . accidental. *A mistake.* But she couldn't believe it.

Joseph Crow and Sissy wanted her to give in, but she couldn't go blindly—she had to know more.

She tried replaying the feel of the first skin—the feel of air—and thought about why she had mounted the bathtub like a pirate queen and sailed on an ocean of wind to stop some guy with a knife. *How had I known about that?* It was totally unreal. Maybe she couldn't make it happen again because she couldn't really believe it had happened at all.

She was overanalyzing. Consuela knew that if she tried on a skin again, felt the rush of powerful freedom-thought, she'd understand; but the seduction was like a drug. It frightened and excited her, which made it all the more terrifying. She didn't—and did—like the spinning sense of wonder, the total loss of control. *Could I have really slipped down the drain? Was this a hallucination or a dream?*

She mistrusted what she felt in light of V's warnings, his fear, and his sincerity. Despite everything, she was convinced that he meant what he'd said: he wanted to save her. *But from what? Or who?*

Resting the box of matches against her belly, she shook it, listening to the matchsticks rattling around.

Don't play with matches . . .

She took one out: the artificial, crimson tip bulged off the end, a chemical mix slightly dripping over the edges of compound wood. The match looked like something that *wanted* to burn. That was what it was there for: to turn into incandescent ash and be eaten slowly from end to end.

Is that what I'm here for? To burn until gone? That's what was stopping her, really. She didn't want to burn out. She didn't want her life to ever, ever end, especially not knowing what she was here for, and why. The very thought made her throat tight. Consuela envied those who really believed, like her grandma Celina; people who knew for certain that they would live forever in God's grace. She squirmed, vaguely ashamed and uncomfortable that she still wasn't sure. Even now. Knowing all of this. At seventeen, she didn't know what she believed.

But Consuela knew that she wouldn't burn in a skin of flame, any more than she'd drown when she was in and of the water. While she was in the Flow, her life didn't end. It had meaning and purpose and was full of secret powers. This new, bigger life was just beginning.

Consuela slipped off her body's skin, allowing her eyes to shift out of focus as she became Bones. With delicate fingers, she held the match against the strip of grit and scraped it roughly, watching the firelight hiss and catch.

She stared at the tiny flame. It was hypnotic.

This is fire—the ancient, elemental force that kept humans alive. It can destroy every living thing it touches: a simple matchstick, taken for granted in the age of electric lamps. Consuela turned the match sideways, watching the light eat. *This is the power that beat back the night.*

Entranced, she pushed a fingertip under the blue heart of the flame. A wild djinni unfurled. Fire snaked up her arm. Racing toward her chest, it sank in its teeth and engulfed her.

Consuela erupted.

She was a corona of fire, a coat of flame, burning. She felt no warmth, just a soft, rippling sensation, like gills on a fish, opening and closing and gasping for breath. She was full of little fluttery breaths. Myriads of tiny white-yellow-orange-blue tongues lapped and flickered. She inhaled, exhaled, tasted, ate. As with the water skin, her room remained untouched; the bed unsinged, the carpet unscathed. In the closet mirror, she saw her eyes as disks of amber glass. Through them, she could see heat. Everything in her room was cold, but the candlewicks along the bath shimmered, whispers of wanting—light called to light, two flames becoming one—as simple as two magnets kissing with a click.

And that's when she felt it, an opening like a change purse.

The world snapped open.

The world snapped shut.

Consuela lifted herself up on particles of dust and swallowed them as they expired.

Someone, somewhere, was burning alive.

tHe high-rise was a death trap. Its hollow-eye windows burned bright with hate; its gaping door mouth screamed high, fire-engine whines. The crowd watched as sparks escaped, buoyed by the heat; a nimbus of molten gold against the smoke-filled night.

Consuela was a tiny flag of flame, a kerchief settling unnoticed on the roof.

The moment she touched down, she was absorbed. Consuela was everywhere in the fire—racing, running, reeling, devouring. If she'd had a heartbeat, it would have pounded in her ears, but the noise was a vacuum of heat. Nothing escaped, not even sound.

Consuela felt around her body as if trying to locate where it hurt. She felt how deep the fire had eaten away the supports, how it licked the edges of insulation and drywall, and where the best meals of foam cushions and thick curtains could be found. She kicked from the windows and roared behind doors. She tasted where things had died—mice and insects, two cats and one bird, asphyxiated in its cage and smoldering into a coal-black thing. But no people. *Not yet.* She felt the antlike scurry of rescuers within her and tried to see what they searched for behind their anonymous plastic masks.

She slid along the airways, tripping inside the orange-white light. She'd become an elemental thing of rippling heat, honed to the barest of clues like air and noise. Consuela listened for the tiny whisper of oxygen—life-giving breath for both fire and man.

She found him on the floor of 21B.

There was a man coughing shallowly into the carpet. His wide lips panted dry-spittle breaths. Eyes closed, his face shone with beaded sweat. She felt fear, acceptance, and fresh panic rolling off him in waves.

Consuela saw that he had nowhere to go. The room was blocked by fire through the hall and over the ceiling, dancing maliciously beneath the billowing, black smoke. He was running out of air, slowly cooking in the ambient heat.

He was about to give up.

Consuela stepped sideways out of the wall and onto the floor, reaching for him, but she didn't touch him. As part of the house fire, she'd brought its flames with her—a trail of her footprints burned merrily on the floor.

"Hold on," Consuela whispered urgently under the crackle-popping, hoping he'd hear her. *"Hang on."*

She leaped into the flames again, merging with the blaze, racing to find the nearest person in bulky yellow-striped rubber. A firefighter vaulted the stairs. Consuela couldn't hope that he would hear her through the firestorm and his layers of protective gear, but she had to get him to follow her. She glanced back down the dragon-throat hallway, groping for an answer . . .

A blast of heat funneled past, punching a hole and flattening the flames.

Inspired, Consuela ran-swam-flew through the fire, racing along the walls and ceiling as fast she could go, sucking a path clear. The wind tunnel whipped the flames aside, creating a clear passage through the char.

The firefighter needed no prompting and ran heavily down the hall. Consuela let the fire spring back to life as she braced herself along a door frame, digging herself deep into the molding like a stream of fiery termites. She kept the doorway clear, although it was rimmed like the gates of hell.

The firefighter ran inside, pulled the limp man up under the arms, hefted him once, and dragged him quickly out of the room. Consuela swept their way clear—an escort to the outside, where she perched against the brickwork, snapping from a broken window like a plume. She watched as the encumbered fireman made his way into the herd of ambulances and flashing blue-and-red lights.

She was a thing of the flame. The human beings were safely gone.

She'd done it!

I'm never giving this up.

teNDeR approached the door at the end of the hall uncertainly. The space above the door frame was a thick smear of blood, wet and foreboding, smelling of salt. Stepping a foot over the threshold, he half expected to be pushed back by some invisible force, but he could enter easily enough. He passed under the doorposts into a quiet room of baby powder and plush toys.

Yehudah traced the last line of warding along the edge of the crib. He'd cut the skin between his first two fingers and drawn them like a fountain pen down each rail and every bracket so that the lines shone with a soft dark fire. He did not look up as Tender stepped over to peer into the blankets.

"You can't touch him," the Yad said calmly.

Tender ignored him, checking with detached, professional interest to confirm that there was no break in the ward. "How many bars are in the seal?" he asked.

The Yad nodded approvingly, a scholar's vice. "Thirty-six. Twice eighteen. Double *chai*." He translated the Hebrew: "Double life."

Tender liked numbers. They brought order. He respected them.

He touched himself in the spongy place behind his belt buckle, fingering the black morass in his bowels. It shifted perceptibly with the growl of a hungry animal. He nodded.

"You do good work," Tender said.

"Thank you," the Yad said, wiping his hand on a rag. He tucked it into his pocket behind the long strands of his knotted *tzitzit*.

Tender crossed his arms. "Do you ever fear you do *too* well?" he said.

"I do not fear you, if that's what you mean."

Tender sniffed, scowling. There was no point trying to ruffle a religious man, even a guy barely into his teens. Damned Orthodox. No wiggle room at all.

He slid his hand against his belt loops and waved the walls to dim, marching straight through them on his way back into the Flow. If the Yad watched him go, Tender didn't mind. Let him wonder if he'd won this round. There was more than one way to get at what he wanted. Sometimes, it took subtlety.

In the end, Tender would win. He knew the stakes. He knew it better than any of them.

Tender passed the parents' doorway and let himself smile as he reentered the Flow.

The Yad couldn't protect them all.

CONSUeLa had intended to go home. Instead, she'd reappeared at Sissy's door. She shook the last vestiges of foreign fire from her hands. Bright little ashes rolled up and died. *Is she even home? What time is it? Maybe she's already asleep?* She paused before knocking, flickering indecision.

"Come in," Sissy's voice beckoned. Consuela turned the doorknob and went in.

Consuela walked carefully, oddly incongruous for a figure of flame. Sissy smiled from her chair. She had both eyes, but one of her ears was still missing and, strangely, one leg. Consuela frowned. *What good could one leg do anyone?*

As if reading her mind, Sissy glanced down and laughed.

"Some folks just need a good kick in the pants," she said. Consuela, surprised, laughed, too. She noticed that Sissy typed much faster with both hands attached. "What can I do for you, Bones?"

Consuela wasn't sure if Sissy could see her shrug. "I guess I wanted to ask you something . . ." She hadn't realized until just that moment why she'd come. It was as if her feet knew what her head hadn't bothered to tell her yet.

"Sure, fire away!" Sissy said, grinning, but her face changed as she watched Consuela struggle. The Watcher looked like she wanted to hug her, clearly understanding how impossible it was. Instead, she sat and waited.

"Is it always like this?" Consuela asked finally.

"Like what?" Sissy said.

"This." Consuela sighed. "A vague feeling grabbing you and hauling you off somewhere to save somebody you've never met. Looking like this." She gestured to herself. "Like tonight. You saw?" She shucked off her skin as if coming home after a long day of work, hanging it neatly in the closet, and curling into the den chair as the fire-skin flickered its gold and ruby light.

"In a manner of speaking," Sissy admitted, pointing at her face. "I've got both eyes in, but I couldn't help noticing the ten o'clock news." She brushed a stray curl off of her cheek. "But if you're asking about the Flow, what we do here . . . ?" Sissy said quietly, turning away from the computer. "Then, yes, it's always like that."

Sissy tipped her pretty face to the ceiling and recited: 'Never ending, never changing. Always beginning, ever changing.'" She glanced back at Consuela. "No one knows the author. There is a lot of poetry in this place."

The Watcher leaned forward, peering into Consuela's empty sockets as if searching for her friend. "Remember my advice? Learn to live with it," she said with emphasis. "Accept it. What we're doing is important; our lives *mean* something here." Something passed over Sissy's face. "Besides, we really don't have any other choice."

The way she said it chilled Consuela to the marrow. Deeper. Maybe outside the flames, everything felt cold.

"What do you mean?" she asked.

"We live here until we disappear," Sissy said patiently. "Maybe we don't really die over here." Her voice sounded wistful. "Maybe, when we're gone, we get to go home."

Consuela stopped, stunned. A strange swirling blurred the edges of her vision. She heard a rushing in her ears, even though she had no ears.

"I thought we were at your home . . . ?"

"No." Sissy sat back with deep leather creaks. "This room is how I remember it—my dad's office in the basement, where I did my homework and chatted online." She stroked the armrest, tracing the tiny spiderwebs of cracked, weathered hide. "It's just how I remember it . . ." Her glance at Consuela was both pitying and gentle. ". . . *Exactly* how I remember it, the moment the seizures started. Multiple organ failure," she said quietly. "Just like how you remember your room, where you first crossed over into the Flow. It's only a memory, Bones. It isn't real."

Consuela stopped. Her throat locked. She felt hot, even without the skin of fire. Then she felt cold and wanted it on. She had to say something. Anything.

But Sissy's words came again, and what they said was, "It isn't real," but they sounded like "I'm sorry."

Launching out of the chair, Consuela yanked open the closet, grabbed her skin, and went for the door.

"Bones . . ." Sissy said.

Consuela didn't listen. *I have to go. I have to get out of here . . .*

"Consuela?"

She dragged at the door handle, pulling herself out, willing herself away.

"Consuela!"

Consuela felt the wind whip by, a torrent of light and color and almost-sound. She spun into the fondness of her bedroom, closing the door behind her in a comforting clack of painted pine and bronze hardware. *Whooooosh-snick.*

She's wrong!

Consuela stood in the middle of her room. *This is real. This is my room. I couldn't possibly make this all up!* She turned in place, taking it all in. *I can't have remembered every little detail in my head like that! Every stuffed animal? Every crack in the ceiling? Every scrap of paper on the desk? Impossible. There's no way.* She felt sorry that Sissy had somehow convinced herself that she was in an imaginary basement, but she, Consuela, was home. This was home. Her home. It even smelled like home . . . Not *"like home,"* she reprimanded herself. *It IS home! This is my house! My room!*

She dropped her armload of fire-skin onto the floor. It didn't burn, but sat crackling in a little campfire heap. Consuela ran to her closet. All her clothes, her shoes, boxes of photos, even the two other skins, both silvery in the garment bag—everything was here. She rushed to her bathroom. *It's still warm,* she thought. *I couldn't have been gone long . . .*

And that's when it hit her.

The bathroom was still foggy with steam, warm and welcoming, perfumed with soap. The scent of lavender clung to the room. Instead of soothing her, she felt afraid. *It shouldn't be like this. It should have dissipated by now.* Consuela swept her white finger bones against the mirror—she watched the condensation run, a new cloudiness form and, in moments, obscure the glass back to gray. She'd thrown open the windows. She'd filled the bathtub twice. She'd been gone for hours, at least. Days, maybe?

Never ending, never changing. Always beginning, ever changing.

Consuela spun around, looking for something she couldn't see. She wanted something to be different. Something other than how she remembered it.

It hasn't changed! She felt her panic without a pulse. *It hasn't changed one bit since . . .*

Since the bath.

The lump.

And her skin on the floor.

Crashing into bed, Consuela burst into tears. Pulling the pillow hard against her mouth, she screamed. She tried to swallow the muffled sounds and unmake them. Never happen. Never have happened. She screamed over and over—wordless, wrenching screams—crying until she fell quiet, spent.

The sounds all meant: *I want my mom!*

He watched her—he always watched over her now—but he did not like to watch her cry.

He moved his hand as if to smooth her hair, but let it fall back into silver.

She didn't need him.

He sat vigil as she slept.

chapter six

"Tell me how you die and I will tell you who you are."
—OCTAVIO PAZ

SHe was dreaming. Maybe.

As she stepped out into the hallway, bright pillar candles sprang to life, bathing the hall in a warm, chili-oil glow. The top quarters shone, soft and waxy white like shafts of moonlight topped in gold. Tall candles and orange flowers lined the hall, the scent a weird mixture of autumn and home.

Taking another step was like passing into Oz. The colors flipped suddenly into golds and russet reds; white softened to corn yellow and black became plum. Sound pressed a thick blanket against her ears, smothering everything save the deep drumbeat of her pulse. That she could hear clearly. A clock in her heart.

Squinting at one of the candles, Consuela saw something move inside the light. She bent closer to look. Inside the heart of each flame and flower, there was a tiny sort of stick figure, dancing. Skeletons—every one of them—dressed in clothes as she dressed in skins, dancing merrily to a tune she could almost hear.

The men tapped in the candle flames, heels snapping and kicking smartly on the white-hot wick. Proud and joyful, some wore suits or unbuttoned vests, while others pranced in wildly striped ponchos and stiff, wide-brimmed hats. One dancer in particular caught her eye— a mustache curled impossibly over his bony grimace and his sombrero winked as the light caught its silver thread. Consuela felt her face crinkle in a smile as he, undeniably, smiled back.

Skeletal women whirled within the hearts of marigolds, petals blending into their shawls and layered skirts as they twirled, hands on their hips, stepping in time with their bony, bare feet. They were beautiful, equally proud of their richly colored finery and familiarity with the rollicking tune.

All of them smiled, all of them beckoned, welcoming Consuela to the thousand souls' revelry, inviting her to dance.

Consuela gazed at their beauty, the power of their

motions, as the petals slowly rotated and the firelight wove in the breeze. She envied the carefree spirits with their sharp boot heels and their cascading hems.

Día de los Muertos, she marveled. It was as gorgeous as she'd imagined. As a little girl, Consuela had often daydreamed about what the fiesta would be like—only having the words of her grandma Celina to guide her since her parents no longer celebrated. Consuela knew her father missed it, the Day of the Dead. She'd always wished she'd had this growing up, to feel the spirits surround her like old friends and family, not like something scary, but something wonderful and free. *To really feel part of something. To feel safe. To believe.* Consuela swept giddily down the hall, happiness bubbling out the soles of her feet.

Generations spun and snapped, jostled and turned, danced and cavorted in the sunset glow. The hallway stretched out into space, its candles and blooms fading into a purpled distance. It was impossible to see where it led, but something in the shadows looked familiar where the candlelight kissed its details: a handle hung in the night space, slight hints of rectangles, three hinges . . . a door.

Her bedroom door.

It pulled at her. She walked forward in the palpable

rhythm of unheard music, the golden perfumes thick in her head and grand, crimson costumes snagged at her eyes . . . Consuela lifted her hand out to touch the door's handle, feeling its silvery coolness, its indigo weight.

One moment, her hand was on the handle, swinging the door open, and then she half woke with her hand on the handle, clicking it closed.

Consuela stepped back into her room in a sort of bewildered fog. Backpedaling softly, her mind whirling like skirts, she pushed herself up against the solid oak of her dresser, giving the door plenty of room.

She blinked, trying to orient herself, but gave up. Willingly. Gratefully. Full reverse.

She crawled slowly into bed, eyes still on the door. Consuela was filled with the childish dread and wonder that behind that door might be nothing familiar, and that anything at all could happen if she tried to step outside.

Cautious, curious, and vaguely suspicious, Consuela closed her eyes and pretended she'd been asleep all along.

At least one part of her wasn't fooled.

SHE lay on the bed, fetal with shock. Her muscles were puddles. Her puddles were tears. Consuela had layered herself in herself—her skin, her pajamas, and her fuzzy slippers—and crawled under the covers, melting her mind to blank.

She was tired. So tired. Weighted to the bed like cold oatmeal. She had no will to move or breathe or blink, but she couldn't sleep. Or maybe she had. She couldn't tell.

Consuela stared, seeing nothing, annoyed by the little things like the cotton gingham sheets catching the fine hairs on her cheek. But not enough to care.

Her eyes slipped in and out of focus, one moment seeing the clock on the nightstand, the next noticing the sharp curve of one of her long hairs on the bed. Fuzzing in, fuzzing out. It was with distant horror that she realized the clock always read 11:19. She blinked. It never changed.

That one thing might make her go mad.

But it took too much energy to go mad—she was exhausted. She was simply too tired to do anything but lie there, thinking of nothing, and pretending that life didn't exist. Life or the Flow—she didn't care which.

Maybe this is death; or worse, hell.

Consuela never considered herself a sinful person, worthy of damnation, but she supposed that those who were damned never truly saw themselves that way.

But then why did the skin give her such a feeling of

powerful completeness? She felt such worthy, effortless energy when she rode the air, such an amazing rush of pure purpose in the flames. *And I did good things, didn't I? Or were those people supposed to die? Am I defying God's will? Or following a false one? Is Sissy a fallen angel? A demon? Maybe she doesn't know. Maybe I don't either. How can anyone really know if they're evil or good or not? Do the ends justify the means? And if you're crazy, logical or not, aren't you just as insane?*

There was a subtle sound. A television in the distance, a cat by the curtains, but Consuela didn't own a TV or cat.

// Sorry. //

Consuela sat up and threw off the covers.

"V," she whispered. Her heart slammed and flushed her cheeks. *He'd known! He'd tried to tell me!*

"V!" she shouted.

Save me! her mind screamed.

She launched out of bed. "I know you're there," Consuela said, although she didn't see him. "V!" She stepped up to her full-length mirror and slammed it with the flat of her hand, leaving a sweaty print on its surface. *"V!"*

As hard as she glared, she saw only her own face, helpless and angry. She spun away, feeling stupid. Stupid and lost and far from home.

Cupping her hands over her face, she took a deep

breath. Her forehead burned. Her eyes ached from crying, the skin puffy and raw. She saw her window reflected in the mirror under the smudge of her handprint.

And she remembered: she didn't have to wait. Joseph Crow said she could find anyone in the Flow. Anyone at all.

Turning discreetly away from the mirror, she shucked her clothes and her skin and left them in a pile on the bed. Bare-boned, Consuela headed for the door.

She stopped suddenly with an odd sense of foreboding.

She'd dreamed this—a series of dreams—but she couldn't hold on to the images, only the feelings. A wild, chaotic spinning sensation and the familiar smell of oil, orange peels, and smoke.

Consuela hesitated, then threw open the door . . .

There was nothing there. No hallway. No carpet. No family portrait. No walls. No floor. A misty, shifting no-color cascaded, achingly slow, as if she had opened her bedroom door inside of a cloud. But it was thicker, with flashes of light and muffled rainbows in the gray. Consuela stared at the raw, fathomless Flow, too awed to scream. It was as if that necessary piece was back in her natural skin.

She considered the awfulness, feeling around for what to do next.

The void stayed outside her door. She seemed safe in her room. Safe, but trapped. If she was going to leave, she'd have to brave the nothingness. She had found Sissy by simply wanting to see her. V said that intention was key. There was only one way to find out and she wasn't eager to try it, but she didn't want to stay cooped up in her room either.

Consuela lifted her foot off the carpet, leaned into the first step purposefully, thinking of finding V . . .

Her foot came down. She felt the air whoosh apart.

. . . and swirled into a wide, wooden temple painted a dull bronze, resplendent with an ancient gong. Consuela looked back. Her bedroom door wasn't there. *That wasn't so bad.* An unfamiliar silence pushed on her eardrums, an odd, smothering Zen. Even the air felt heavier here. She had no idea where she was, but it was nowhere she had been before. Consuela tiptoed to the base of an altar featuring a gorgeous Buddha lovingly nestled in a field of incense sticks. She explored an empty prayer room and stepped outside. She touched the smooth trunk pendulum of the giant gong, pulled back its creaking rope, and rang a single, full-throated note, scattering small birds out of the eaves. But no one came to greet her. Consuela took a deep breath and stepped purposefully . . .

. . . onto a rocky beach with no stone smaller than

a baby's fist. Cold wind tugged at her hair and the sky was a washed-pale slate blue. A low-hanging lip˙of some forgotten cave beckoned and Consuela ducked inside. Kneeling down, she saw a natural pocket in the porous rock; sharp, black holes that looked like Swiss cheese. The nook held little-boy treasures—metal jacks, a ball of salty-dry twine, and a tiny toy car made of painted steel, missing one of the front tires and a passenger door. She laid them gently back in their hollowed-out notch and crawled out into the wind. Consuela scanned the beach, empty and vast; she seemed the only person in a world filled with no-longer people and their last memories. *No one's here.* She didn't mind exploring the Flow, but right now she had to find V. *Get out. Get home.* She tried to picture the idea, the "feeling" of V . . .

. . . and swirled onto a grass-lined sidewalk running along a chain-link fence. Across the street was an entrance to a redbrick high school, its glass doors shiny and wide. The school was empty, as were the streets and the concrete steps. She walked over to the lone figure propped up against a crab-apple tree. Wish didn't even turn to look.

"Hi," Consuela said wearily. "Is V here?"

Wish squinted as if looking into the sun. "Nope. Just left."

She felt better now that she was closer. "Which way?"

Wish shook his head. "You won't find him. He's in the Mirror Realm."

"Oh, I'll find him."

Wish snorted. "Not in the Mirror Realm." He threw a pebble off to one side. It bounced into the street and lay still. "It's not part of the Flow." Wish picked up another.

Consuela crossed her arms at the edge of the pavement, seething, desperate. The wind brushed the tree leaves. Another pebble danced across the road.

"You ever go to high school?" Wish asked.

She nodded, looking out across the street. "Sure," she admitted in defeat. "I'm a junior at Jefferson. Getting ready for college applications."

"Huh," he muttered. "I didn't think you were a teenager. I mean, most of us are, but you seem, I don't know, timeless. Ageless."

She laughed humorlessly, holding out her arms. "Yeah, well, looks can be deceiving."

He glanced at her skeleton. "Yeah," he said. "Guess so."

Their silence fell flat. Wish began tapping, rattling the novelty pins on his sleeves.

She'd made him uncomfortable, which made her feel guilty. Consuela sighed, considering the thin, scraggly boy in the grass.

"Do you mind if I sit?" she asked.

Wish shrugged, knees bouncing. "It's a free country."

It wasn't a yes or a no, but Consuela settled herself down. She read a blue button near his collar that said I DON'T CARE TO BELONG TO ANY CLUB THAT WILL HAVE ME AS A MEMBER.—GROUCHO MARX.

She tried to break the ice. "Nice pins."

"Yeah?" Wish said, looking at the Marx quote. "They were a collection that kinda took over. You know how it is. Something to do." He held up the pin by its backing: CRAZY IS AS CRAZY DOES.

Consuela rested her ulnas against her knees. "You think we're all crazy?"

"Well, I can't speak for you," he said, "but being crazy would make a lot more sense than knowing that this was real. Still, when we're like this"—he pointed to himself and her—"we're not like that, you know?" Wish gestured vaguely at the high school. She could almost imagine the babble of petty talk, the bus exhaust, the lunchroom politics, the hallway runways, and the locker-room drama. The Flow was definitely different.

"I know." She nodded. "We're more . . ." She struggled for a word, but failed to find a good one.

"Ourselves," Wish supplied. "We're more ourselves and more than ourselves . . ." He jutted his chin. "This is more who we really are than when we were playing it safe, back there. Like this reality matters more than the real one. Know what I mean?"

"Sort of," Consuela admitted, nodding. "Yeah."

Wish's thin-lipped grin tugged at his crooked eye-teeth. "So this is really you?"

She didn't need to grin back. "Yes."

"Sure. See? I'm really me when I can make folks' wishes come true. It's the best!" he said. "What do you do?"

Fly out of windows? Fall down the drain? Burn in buildings?

"I save people from dying," she said. "Before their time."

Wish blew a raspberry, his fingers still tapping erratic, staccato rhythms on his arms. "Well, duh, yeah. We all do that. But I meant how?"

"Oh." Consuela thought about it. "Um . . . I can take off my skin and make new ones out of things like air, water . . ."

"No shit?" Wish sat up. "Sorry. I mean, really? You don't normally look like this?"

Consuela laughed, surprised. "No! I have a face and hair and eyes and everything."

"Huh." He tugged absently at his ear and the tips of his hair. She wondered if he realized that he was doing it. "So what do you look normally like?"

She thought about embellishing a little, but why bother? Who did she have to impress?

"Short," she admitted. "Round, dark. Brown hair, brown eyes, brown skin. I'm Mexican."

"Really? You don't look it." They both laughed at that. "I meant that you don't sound like it."

Her mood shifted.

"Excuse me?" she said.

Wish immediately dropped his eyes and scratched a spot of acne on his cheek. "I meant you got no accent."

Consuela didn't know what to think. No one had ever thought of her as anything but Mexican American. She'd never been mistaken for Caucasian, but without skin . . . skeletons all looked the same. *He thought I was white, like him. Big deal.* But that was supposed to be, what, a compliment? Or was it just something everybody assumed when they didn't know for sure—that people looked like them by default?

"I said I was Mexican," she said. "Not that I was from Mexico."

"Right," he said quickly. "Sorry."

A frigid silence fell under the crab-apple canopy. Wish shrank into a tight, miserable ball.

"Hell," he muttered. "Some things don't change in either world. I can still piss people off right from the start," he said. "Talent I've had since I was a kid. Sissy can still be popular and V can still be cool and Tender can still be a total head case, but someone you gotta have around . . ."

96

"Tender," Consuela said. "What is it about this guy?" She turned, spinning on her coccyx. "Sissy seemed totally freaked out by him."

"She should be," Wish said simply. "You should be. I should be. Heck, I *am* and I'm, like, best friends with the guy."

"Really?" Consuela said.

"Sure. I even made a wish for him once." Wish unwound a little from his self-protective hunch. "Tender's been here years and years. There are all sorts of people who've come and gone, but Tender's role and what he does is something that has been part of the Flow for, like, ever. He *gets* things, right?" His eyes had a sort of wicked spark to them, like when kids tell each other gruesome secrets or ghost stories in the dark. "Sissy tell you what he does?"

"He eats pain," she said back.

"Yeah, right. He digests it. Eats it right up," Wish said. "He can take the darkness inside him and chew it up or spit it out. That's what Sissy doesn't get. That Tender's been here long enough that he knows the Flow inside and out. She thinks he's trash and that she's got his number, but she doesn't. Not really." He sat back with a strange sort of pride in his voice. "That's why she has to listen to me. I know Tender best. He trusts me."

"Do you trust him?" Consuela asked.

"Hell no, but I don't pity him, which he appreciates more than anything," Wish said. "I don't spit on him either. Tender's got a short fuse when it comes to respect. He cares a lot about what he does—knows it's a tough-ugly job, but also dead necessary. Useful." He gestured again at the two of them. "Folks like you and me? We're temps. Dime a dozen. But there's always been a guy like Tender in the Flow. Just like there's always been a Watcher like Sissy. Yin and yang. Either one of them goes, there'll be another one soon enough. There's got to be or the Flow doesn't. Isn't." He drummed his fingers against his knee. "Some think the Watcher and Tender are the same person, the same soul, recycled, you know? Reborn and returning over and over."

Consuela felt a ripple of nausea like goose bumps on her nonexistent skin.

"Sounds horrible," she confessed.

Wish shrugged. "Tender seems to deal with it well enough," he said. "He likes being a big guy. Like my mum says, 'He wears it well.'"

Cradling her jaw, Consuela watched Wish unconsciously tapping his buttons and scabs. "So if I meet Tender . . ."

"*When* you meet Tender," Wish corrected.

". . . *when* I meet him," Consuela allowed. "Anything I should keep in mind?"

Wish leaned back on his hands, his thin chest concave under his denim jacket. "Don't feel sad for him, or pity him, or piss him off. He's a real bastard, but that's how he's drawn," he said. "You have to be tough to do what he does. He has to take it all in." He ran a spindly hand over the patchy grass and the knobby trunk of the tree. He knocked on the wood. "Someone's got to feel it all, you know?"

Consuela placed a skeletal hand against the bark. Without skin, she might be powerful, even immortal, but she could hardly *feel* a thing. She looked at the school building, large, empty and lifeless, too distant and strangely difficult to recall what it might have been like before. She felt numb here, behind glass. Without her skin, she was dead to the world.

"Is it real?"

Wish snorted and jutted his chin at the school. "It may not be real, but it's a lot realer than that."

Consuela stared at the high school, suddenly homesick. She felt tears on her cheekbones, dripping off of her chin—somehow, she could feel those.

"I want to go home," she whispered.

"Hey, hey," Wish said, a little alarmed. His hands moved like butterflies, unsure where to land. He placed a palm against her flat shoulder blade. Consuela leaned into his awkward, one-armed hug. He tried to sound soothing, "It's okay . . ."

"It's *not* okay!"

"No, you're right," he said. "It's not okay."

They sat under the crab-apple tree, the wind playing lazily with the thumbprint-shaped leaves while Consuela rattled against Wish's buttons as she cried. One caught in the curve of her eye socket as she wiped her face. It read I PLEAD CONTEMPORARY INSANITY. He removed his hand from her shoulder joint.

"I'm not supposed to be here," she said.

"I know," Wish said. "But it's not impossible to get back, you know? You hear things . . . if you listen for it." He shrugged. Consuela suddenly understood that Wish liked it here, but was too embarrassed to admit it. She couldn't imagine preferring this crazy half-life to reality. *Family. Home.*

"It's not impossible?" Consuela said. "Then why didn't Sissy . . . ?"

Wish evaded her eyes. "Maybe you should ask her."

He said it like a hint. Consuela debated taking it.

"Maybe I should," she said, and pushed herself up. His eyes followed her, surprised. She paused in a half crouch, a tangle of bones. "Thanks, Wish."

He might have blushed when he shrugged again,

looking down, tapping his buttons and shoes.

"No problem," he muttered. She stood and stretched. Nothing popped.

"I've got to find V," she said, and thought, *I've got to get home.*

"Yeah, well, just remember," Wish said. "This is the Flow. Nothing's impossible."

"No," Consuela agreed. "Just highly, highly improbable."

Wish snorted and threw another small stone, watching it bounce. "Got that right."

And although they watched the school steps for a long, long while, no one ever came out.

WHEN Consuela appeared at Sissy's door, she had a plan. There was only one master of probability in the Flow.

"Come in," Sissy called in answer to her knocking. Consuela tried to ignore the nervous thumping of a heart that wasn't there, yet her voice was tense without vocal cords.

"Can you take me to Abacus?" she asked.

Sissy hadn't turned, intent on her monitor. "Not right now," she said slowly. "I'm a little . . . busy?" She said the last word like a question, like she wasn't sure.

Sissy spared a glance over her shoulder. "Nikki didn't show up."

"Was he supposed to be here?" Consuela asked.

"Not here," Sissy said. "He didn't show up for his assignment."

"Oh." Consuela walked over to the desk and squinted at the screen. It was full of open windows like a vertical pile of scattered papers. "What happened?"

"Same thing that happens every time one of us fails," Sissy said quietly. "His assignment died." She blew out a long breath and tilted her head to Consuela. "Although," Sissy eyed Consuela meaningfully, "I do know of one exception."

She leaned forward and grabbed her cell phone. "I can let you borrow my phone. Abacus has a beeper. The signal will lead you to him, like you did coming here." Sissy tossed it to Consuela, who cupped both hands to catch it.

"Star seven," Sissy advised. "And be sure to bring it back." She resumed typing.

Consuela turned the phone on. "Thanks."

The scrabble of keyboard keys stilled. Sissy turned.

"Can you forgive me?" the Watcher asked.

Sighing, Consuela shifted from foot to foot, long bones settling like toothpicks against the carpet. *For telling me that I'm doomed? For not telling me everything? For*

not saying that none of this was real from the start? For killing
all hope? For not being okay with that?

"Ask me later."

"No," Sissy said. "Let me tell you something my father told me coming from a long line of early stroke victims: You never know how long you have—there might not *be* a later—so don't let things go unsaid or unforgiven." She looked a little embarrassed, scared. She readied herself. "So forgive me now, or don't."

It was true, but no one said those things aloud. The mortal truths. You always assumed there would be time, but there wasn't. Consuela knew it. They all knew it. The Flow knew it, too.

She nodded.

"I forgive you now," Consuela said.

The blond girl smiled a tiny bit. "Good. Great. Now let me get back to work."

CONSUELA appeared on the edge of a hill. The ground was patchy with grass and rocks, above was a picture-perfect puff-cloud sky, and between them stood a structure that made her head hurt.

Fractal images and impossible planes shot up in jagged, defiant directions, reminding Consuela of crystal formations grown under time-lapse film. Hints of reverse-rainbow colors and ultraviolet bands sliced along the sharp edges of . . . whatever it was. If this jumble of jeweled obelisks somehow formed a building, she had no idea how to find the door.

Consulting her cell-phone receiver did nothing—the yellow marker wove itself into a helix.

"Damn," she muttered under her breath.

"Hello?" a voice called from out of sight.

"Hello?" Consuela called back.

"In a minute."

Consuela glanced around, trying to guess where the sound came from, but gave up.

". . . Roughly seventy seconds, or its nearest equivalent . . ." A smiling face appeared through an Escher-angled wall. Abacus adjusted his rimless glasses as he stepped forward. " . . . depending on your relative space-time," he said. "Hi."

"Hi," Consuela said. "I'm guessing you're Abacus."

"And you must be Bones." He offered a handshake, which she accepted. William Chang shook her collection of tarsals without a trace of embarrassment or hesitation. He wore his smile comfortably, like an old shirt; his actual shirt was maroon and tugged at a noticeable paunch.

"Consuela Chavez, aka Bones," he said again. "I've

been looking forward to meeting you." He looked her over appreciatively. "Wow! You're really something, if you don't mind me saying so." His eyes twinkled. "Come on inside. Let me show you around."

He waved toward his mass of towers. Consuela squinted up.

"I'm trying to get home," she said as she tried to follow the lines of the building. The light bent and wobbled, trailing prism colors. Consuela's phantom eyes traced the aurora effect as it climbed.

"Well," he said, "you've come to the right place."

"This is quite the place," she said with a smile in her voice. "If you don't mind me saying so."

Abacus laughed. "Isn't it? I call it 'Quantum' and I can honestly say I made it all by myself. I think it's the only permanent artificial construction created within the Flow." He rubbed his hands together gleefully and gave a mad-scientist laugh. "And it's mine, all mine!"

Consuela burst out laughing. "Well, can we go inside?" she asked.

"Sure," he said.

Standing at the base of the structure, she touched the smooth, quicksilver walls. "How?" she asked.

"I could show off and try to explain the math, but it's simpler to say that I took surreality and bent it to my will. Fun, huh? This way." He stepped one foot dramatically through the wall and held it there. "You might want to swallow before entering, the transition can throw off your inner ear, and you still have those—smallest bones in the body." He winked. "Ready?"

"As ever," Consuela said, swallowed, and stepped through the wall. She tilted suddenly upward and to the right, flipping something inside her skull that resettled into almost the same position. She clapped a hand to her forehead with a clack.

"Ow," she muttered.

"I warned you." Abacus chuckled.

"You did."

"But isn't this totally worth it?" Abacus said proudly as Consuela blinked up at the faceted walls. Whorls of formulae swirled over its surfaces, arcing spirals of numbers and symbols in Greek. The writing changed color as it moved, reflecting its opposite, while incredibly thin lines joined and split, connecting tiny points of light like jewels in an invisible chandelier. Abacus reached up and touched one point of light and, with an encouraging push, coaxed it into a small constellation of similar stars.

"Welcome to the Flow," he said, grinning. "My map of it, anyway."

"Wow," Consuela breathed.

"Tell me about it." Abacus laughed.

Consuela looked around, hoping to find what would get her home fast. "So where's your computer?" she asked.

"Here," he said, tapping his temple. "And here." He scooped something off of a hook. Dark wooden beads rattled on the frame.

As she saw the ancient calculator, William Chang's nickname suddenly made sense. Consuela crossed her arms. "You're kidding."

"Nope." He gloated. "It's a *suanpan*. Faster than a computer. They've clocked it. Now look over here. I think this is what you wanted." He led the way to one of the side towers leaning at a sharp angle to the ground. Consuela ducked when he did and knelt where he bent to enter a new direction. She crept forward, knowing she'd never find her way out of this place if she lost sight of him. Excitement tingled along her limbs. She felt sorry for leaving Sissy and V and Wish without so much as saying good-bye.

They wound deeper in dizzying directions. Fortunately, Abacus waited for her at every turn, a smile crinkling his eyes. When he stopped, she stood up too soon and banged her head on a corner. She might have bit her tongue if she'd had one.

"All right back there?"

She rubbed her skull. "You couldn't imagine a place with right angles?"

"Had to work within parameters," he apologized. "Here we are." He took her hand and guided her to stand. "Look up."

She did. The chamber was full of sparkling lights and alphanumerics spinning in Milky Way computations. Before she could ask, Abacus was already pointing out areas of interest.

"This is one of my pet projects. I have been trying to map causality in the Flow, trying to piece together a pattern based on who we are and who our assignments have been; how it all fits together." Abacus tapped one area and spun his hand around, circling the spiral of proofs and theorems. "Tender's been helping, which is a real plus. He has a knack for inferential outcomes, and I'll admit that I'm pretty good at graphing predictability . . ." He cocked his head and gave her a charming smile. "Well, I *was*. Before you showed up." He knocked a knuckle against the wall. "I thought I had the rules of this place figured out, but, oh well." He placed his hands on his hips and sighed dramatically. "I'll have to scrap the whole thing, of course."

Consuela stepped back. "What?" she said. "Why?"

"Oh, don't worry—I love it!" Abacus laughed easily.

"I mean, it's awesome meeting you: you're a real anomaly. I've checked, and nowhere has anyone left any record of this sort of thing ever happening before." He bounced on his heels like a kid. "You're like your own comet!" he said. "And I saw you first—or, at least, the possibility of you."

Consuela tried to follow his meaning while being distracted by his work. "But why am I so different?" she asked. "Why can't I just go home?"

"It's not a question of whether you can or can't," Abacus said. "What I mean is that the regular rules don't apply to you, or perhaps they never applied to anyone, really. That's the difference between theories and facts. What makes you different is that you"—he indicated a point over his head with a thick finger—"were on *that* side of the Flow and now"—he dragged the spot of light over like a cursor under his forefinger and placed it in a new location on the wall, tapping it—"you're on *this* side." The entire diagram split and roiled clockwise, trying to adapt. The design kept shifting, attempting to compensate while rippling outward. Abacus watched the chaos burn holes in his orderly pinwheel. "See? Throws the whole thing out of whack." He looked pleased with himself.

She crossed her radii against her growing uncertainty. "But people cross over all the time . . ."

109

"Oh sure," he said. "Regular folks do. But I've never heard of someone who was an *assignment* crossing over into the Flow." Abacus shook his head, still smiling at a private joke. "It's never happened before."

A little trickle ran over her skull, the feeling of all eyes on her.

An assignment?

Counsuela failed to say the words; something held her back, maybe fear.

I was an assignment.

An assignment that crossed over.

"Never?" she whispered.

"Well, it's a long 'ever,'" Abacus admitted. "But let's say close enough for grenades. But there's always a chance. We can figure out something." He turned and looked at her bones, glittering under the play of light and crystal colors. His voice slid into a bedtime quiet. "You know how sometimes, late at night, you lie awake and think that maybe the whole universe revolves around you?" Abacus asked, and waved his hand; a thread of numbers followed. The cascade danced across the wall, throwing more order atop the chaos. The vortex kept fracturing, breaking down. More galaxies of twinkling light were pulled into the hole. He winked at her. "Well, in your case, you might be right."

Walking slowly in front of his unfolding universe projection, Abacus shrugged his shoulders with casual glee.

"You see, it no longer makes sense," he said quietly as his work bulged in places and collapsed in others. "Save this one thing . . ." He tapped a handful of points. "Assignments, on average, affect exponentially more lives than normal people do. Ergo, these are important people who we're saving, meant to do great things in the world. Ergo . . ." Abacus nodded like a salute. "You *are* important to the world. And you don't belong here."

"That's what V said," Consuela confirmed.

"Giovanni. Yes. I told him that when he asked me," Abacus said. "It was the first time he'd ever shown any interest in any of this. Or me, frankly. Still, I'm glad you two talked, I know he's been anxious about meeting you."

Consuela frowned. "What do you mean?"

His eyes widened under Quantum's collapsing stars.

"Didn't you know?" Abacus said gently, "You were V's assignment."

chapter seven

"The important thing is to go out, open a way, get drunk on noise, people, colors . . . this fiesta, shot through with lightning and delirium, is the brilliant reverse to our silence and apathy, our reticence and gloom."

—OCTAVIO PAZ

CONSUELA ran-swam-flew, honing herself like a tuning fork, searching for V in the Flow. This time, she found him. And when she found him, she struck like lightning.

"You!" She didn't have the words to express everything she felt—it was the one sound that had surfaced. The only word in the world.

V glanced over his shoulder, his chin scraping against the crisp collar of his shirt. He watched her come charging across the Maine harbor sand.

// *Bones.* //

"You did this!" Consuela said.

"I did," he said.

// *I'm sorry.* //

She ignored the violin-voice, clean and pure in sorrow.

"Why!" she cried.

V held his hands behind him as if offering the perfect shot. The breeze off the water ruffled his hair.

"It wasn't as if I had a choice, finding you," he said. "I had to." Consuela knew what he meant—the compulsion, the pull—but the way he said it made it sound different. Like a confession. Something secret. It threw her anger into confusion.

"I should have done something else," he added. "I should have said something else . . ." Consuela's emotional momentum had nowhere to go. She nearly vibrated in place, energy buzzing along her bones. V tilted his face down to look into the deep shadows of her empty eyes. " . . . I don't know what happened." // *I'm sorry.* //

As he spoke, the musical voice slipped in between his words. "In the mirror, I can stand behind someone's eyes // *Bones* // and say the words that they needed to hear. That's how my power works." Consuela shook her head, trying to remember those split seconds between hangers and mirrors and orange juice and floor.

V's voice—his real one—grew more insistent. "When

113

you take a long look at yourself, stare deep into your own eyes—try to talk yourself into something, or out of something, or steel yourself for something about to happen // *pain/fear/love/choice* //," V's voice fell to a whisper, a sound matched to the hush of waves. "That's when I can whisper // *heart to heart, soul to soul* // and people can hear me."

She crossed and uncrossed her arms, struggling with what to say, what to think. Soothing crashes lulled behind her. A buoy bell rang softly in the distance.

Know thyself.

"That was you," she said, finally. On the changing room floor, in her bathroom mirror, in the Flow.

V nodded once. "That was me."

The air smelled of salt and wet, green things.

"Why were you there?" she asked.

He sighed, disappointed. "You know why I was there," V said. "I *had* to be there to try to save you. You weren't supposed to—"

"Cross over," Consuela interrupted. Fear crept up her insides and scattered her breath. "So what happened?" she whispered.

V's hands fell to his sides, useless, defeated.

"I don't know," he said again. "I was there. I saw you fall. I saw you look into the mirror and you saw *beyond* it. Beyond the glass and the foil. Like . . ." He ground his teeth, rubbed his face, and tapped his fist against his lips.

// *Like you could see me.* //

". . . like you were hallucinating," V finished.

Consuela took a tentative step forward. Her own voice was lost, absorbed by the sea and the drum in her ears. "That wasn't what you were going to say."

V shifted on his feet, dropped his eyes. "No," he said. "I thought you could see me."

// *I hoped/wondered/wished.* //

She closed the distance; knuckles of tension popping one by one.

"And could that be what brought me here?" she asked.

// *Me?* //

V stared at her. Anguish raked his face like his worst fears confirmed.

// *No, please, no.* //

"I hope not," he said.

// *Is it my fault?/Are there accidents?/Is it all meant to be the way it has to be?* //

The Flow strummed on V's electric currents, crackling the salty air between them. It felt almost impossible to Consuela that they stood this close and didn't shatter. It was as if all of time compressed so that this moment could happen.

Consuela gave the barest of nods, the ice on her insides beginning to thaw. V wavered, uncertain.

"I forgive you now."

He started breathing, half surprised that he had stopped.

In unspoken agreement, they started walking. Their feet made soft whispers in the shush of the sand. They walked closer to the shoreline, leaving smears of footprints that were erased by the water's edge.

"So you are my angel," Consuela said casually.

V slid his hands into his pockets. "Something like that."

Grandma Celina had once told her that everyone had angels to watch over them, protect them, and listen with love. Consuela decided V deserved the chance to do his job.

"I have to go back," she said. "I *need* to go back. But Abacus didn't know how."

"I know. You're 'an anomaly,'" V quoted. "If he'd stop getting so excited about the math, he'd get how much it doesn't help being an exception to the rules."

They walked together in the silence.

"So what was supposed to happen to me?" she said.

After a long moment, he answered. "I should have saved you," V said. "Right there on the floor."

"From what?" she asked.

"I don't know," V said. "But when I saw you again after you crossed over, all I could think of was how you were just like that first time // *bright/beautiful/laughing/alive* // and it reminded me of . . . something." He scuffed long tracks in the sand.

Consuela couldn't tell which words struck her more: the things that V said or what he said without knowing it.

V shrugged. "Whenever I've saved someone, saying 'No, not yet' or 'I'm not going to die' usually works. Simple and direct. The mind tells the body, and the body obeys. You know it. You believe it. You are *not* going to die." He spoke harshly, as if convincing himself. "And they don't. That's all it takes. Knowing yourself." // *Know thyself* // He shook his head. "But you? You had all that already," he said through a fan of wind-tossed hair. "You didn't need me, you couldn't even hear me—you picked *yourself* off of that floor." He looked away. // *I just screwed it up.* //

Consuela, embarrassed, inspected her hands; soft hues of pink and blue shimmered along her willowy bones. *It wasn't true.*

"'Know thyself,'" she quoted.

The words hit unexpectedly hard. His eyes swam and she wanted to take it back.

"You heard me," he whispered.

"I heard you," Consuela said, but couldn't add, *I still hear you.* The fact that she could hear his innermost thoughts was an intimacy she couldn't confess.

"Then why . . . ?" V began, but exhaled a long, slow breath and glanced away at many nothings. "After my father left, it was Mama, my four younger sisters, and me," he said. "The man of the house. There were bills to pay and school and protection and rent due and it was . . . more than I could handle." He kicked at the sand.

"Whenever I didn't know what to do, or couldn't choose, or had to play Dad when the girls got wild, Mama would say, 'Know thyself.'" V shook his head, remembering. "It was her answer for everything; like all the answers were already inside me." He sounded wistful. "I never felt like I got it, though. And when I saw you in the mirror . . ." He glanced at her profile at the juncture where the jaw and skull met. "I got it. You had it. You were *huge* with it. You were so completely, obviously you." He spoke with his hands in grand gestures. "It was all I could think about when I saw you. 'Know thyself.' That's what she meant." He scraped his teeth over his bottom lip. "I hadn't meant to say it // *to you* // instead of whatever I should have said. But I thought, maybe, that it might have been enough . . ."

"To save me?" she said.

V nodded. "Yes. But even if I failed, you were never supposed to show up here," he insisted, stopping their

118

walk. "I'm glad you did. And I'm sorry you did. And I'm sure none of that makes any sense." He fumbled the apology, but made an effort to be sincere. "You know what happens when we fail?" he said.

"They die."

"They die," V agreed. "But you *didn't* die. You're here. And that means there's still a chance to get you back," he said. "You'll be exactly who you are and where you belong." // *Meant to do great things.* //

A flash of light passed over him, a slicing shine as if he'd suddenly gone one-dimensional, reflected in a pane of glass. V sighed.

"I've got to go. Next assignment." He placed his hands gently on her clavicle. He spoke like a father, an older brother, a best friend—but her attention was on his thumbs resting softly on the curve of her bones.

"I promise I'll do everything I can to get you home."

She believed him. At that moment, he was the realest thing in the world.

"I know," she said softly. "Thank you."

They stood that way in silence. There was another flash of shorn light, and Consuela was alone on the sand.

teNDeR bowed into the first tower thinking if Abacus was so smart, he should have dismantled the door. He trailed his fingers over its purple-gold surfaces, listening for the tiny mouse sounds of clapping beads.

"Crunching?" he called by way of greeting.

"Like granola," Abacus answered. "I'm up in T3, 24-15-66."

Tender ducked into a sharp corridor and wound his way up an acute-angled wall, hopping into the adjacent tower as naturally as a spider.

"You met the new girl?" he asked.

"Yeah. She's a game changer," Abacus replied from somewhere up ahead.

Tender entered the room where Abacus sat hunched over his calculations. The flat map of stars hung like a blanket over his head; an indoor pup tent for the Chinese Boy Scout.

"Isn't that why you're here?"

"Sure," Abacus said, sliding the *suanpan* clear. "And why are *you* here?"

Six quick excuses danced across Tender's tongue, but none of them fit as nicely or neatly as the math on the wall. Instead of answering, Tender walked over and admired it once again, although parts of the pattern were broken or bulging in gross parodies of their sleek, former design. He touched the calculations, which writhed under his fingertips. He flattened his palm possessively.

"Why are any of us here?" Tender said aloud.

Abacus stood up and hung his namesake on the wall with a slap. "You think you've got something figured out, don't you?" he said, his voice bouncing off the crystal walls. "But you haven't, you know. None of this is true. No solid answers. No grand design. Bones proves that." The young mathematician wiped his hand over the wall and the elaborate constellation erased, swept blank by its uncaring creator. Tender touched the wall in confirmation. Only a smear of fingerprints remained.

"We don't know *anything*," Abacus said, casually pinching out a few errant points of light. He reset his glasses on the bridge of his nose. "If a tree falls in the forest," he quoted, "et cetera and so on."

Tender shook his head with a ripple of laughter. "Oh no," he said. "You're the one who's got it wrong." He relished the flash of momentary confusion in Abacus's eyes before making himself clear. "Here is the grand design: if there are no trees, there is no forest." Tender turned from the wall and ticked off his fingers. "No trees, no forest. Ergo: no us, no Flow."

The Chinese boy paled save for two hot spots on his cheeks.

Tender was glad to see that Abacus understood.

Then he cut his friend down and licked his dark fingers clean.

SHE'D gone as a skeleton down through the Flow, following an odd trail of raked pebbles and smooth bits of glass. Consuela stumbled across the recycled Zen garden while waiting for V, feeling restless and powerless. The worn shards of cobalt, pale blue, and bottle green were like sea-glass stars in a pale gravel sky. The tiny bones of her toes could be any one of those smooth, pink stones.

When she looked up, there was a young man perched on a boulder.

He had thin blond hair that hung long in the front, the edges of his bangs curtaining impossibly thick black eyebrows. He posed like a model, confident and sure, wearing a navy polo shirt and jeans with a wide, stamped silver buckle.

This was undeniably Tender.

Tender gave her a look-over that made her feel more naked than bare. She couldn't believe how she suddenly felt self-conscious as a skeleton. He tossed his bangs out of his eyes and smiled.

"So you're Bones?"

"Yes," she said.

"You do good work," he said.

It was the last thing she'd expected, given all that she'd heard about him. It threw her off balance.

"Thanks," she said warily.

"I've been watching you," he admitted. Consuela felt a flash of panic at his confession. "The Watcher's not the only one, or V, for that matter, but they're curious or guilty or both." Tender let the sentence hang like a guillotine, and then he winked, boyishly mischievous. "Not me."

Consuela cringed at the idea of all those eyes watching her. "And what are you?"

"I'm different. I'm an exception to the rules," Tender said, "like you." He pulled gently at his shirt collar. "I don't have assignments, my duty is here. And the longer you do your job, the better you get." He reclined lazily on the rock and tapped his chest. "And I'm here all the time."

He dropped down from the rock, his boots crunching chaos through the finely raked path. The Flow swirled around him like a Technicolor cape.

"I wanted to talk to you," he said, his voice dipping low. "Out of all the others—and I've known one hundred and thirty-two—I think you might be the one who could best understand."

His face had grown serious, a puckered mark between his brows matching the small cleft in his chin.

"Interested in hearing me out?" he asked, a wry twist at his lips. "Or do you think the Watcher knows all the answers?"

Consuela hesitated, intrigued. Sissy may have accepted her fate, but Consuela wasn't done yet. She was just getting started. She was determined to go home.

"Yeah," she said. "Okay."

"Come." Tender turned and led the way through the Flow, passing quickly through a darkened bar, a tiled bathhouse, and a ruined bathroom stall full of scribbled phone numbers and chipping green paint. Consuela followed, trailing in the wake of the swiftly changing landscape.

"I've been trying to piece together your type, so to speak," he said. "Given what I've seen, I'm guessing you work with strong individuals," he began, but halted. They stood brazenly in someone's cramped dorm room. He shrugged. "Of course, we all do, but yours are exceptional: firm believers with a strong spiritual center. A personal belief system that includes faith in a higher power; it flitters through their thoughts and flavors their fear." He resumed striding through surreality. "And you swoop in to restore that faith, that core belief, the moment *before* they give up, saving both their lives *and* their souls. Am I right?"

Consuela stumbled to keep pace with his words and

his steps. Her mind whirled and burned with new questions unasked.

"I hadn't thought about it that way," she said. "But that sounds right." It *felt* right, too. *Did I save the burning man or the firefighter that night? Was it life or faith or both?* "I save them before they give up."

"Perfect." He smiled brightly and strode on. His teeth were quite normal, but she still thought of sharks. "I have a theory and I want your opinion."

They dove through three consecutive snippets of woodlands, a lake pier, and a garage filled to the brim with junk. Consuela hesitated, keeping in mind Wish's warnings.

"Okay," she tried.

"So, us and the Flow," Tender began. "We are who—and what—we are. We don't have to understand, we just *do*."

It was disturbing how right he was in describing so much of her experience. Maybe being here so long really had taught him something after all. *How long has he been here? Has he ever tried going back?*

"But for some of us, that's not enough." He winked. "For those of us *trying* to understand, the real question is 'Why do we do what we do?' or 'What purpose does it serve?' It's tricky, but it's the key to everything."

He set a mean pace and the Flow warped to allow it. Dizzied by the images flung by the wayside, Consuela worried that she was going deeper into the unknown, wandering farther and farther from folks like Sissy or V. She tried to walk unafraid. Nervousness would be seen as a weakness to someone like Tender.

"Where are we going?" she asked.

"Here," Tender said, but there was nothing to see.

Consuela tried to focus on it, but the Flow flowered open as a colorless mass of roiling, billowing motion. Gray white with swirls of ancient hues, the Flow enveloped the world. It was like space or the Grand Canyon; Consuela felt infinitesimally small. Insignificant. It crushed her under its immense nothingness. After the barrage of different places, the unformed wall of silent froth was deafening. Maddening. It gave her a headache to look at it.

"What is it?" she whispered, thankful for the sound of her own voice.

"We're at the edge of the world." Tender smirked. "Here there be monsters!"

He settled himself into a sitting position and an upholstered chair materialized beneath him. Its twin condensed nearby, and he gestured for her to sit. Hesitating, she folded herself into its cushioned seat, her legs a pentagram of tibias, fibulas, and femurs. She curled away from the beachless tides of endless nothing. Kicking his feet out in front of him, Tender smiled out into the stark, curdling Flow.

Consuela's insides crawled with the need to escape.

"You're here to create change," he said. "I'm sure the Watcher told you as much. You save certain people from an untimely death. We don't exactly know why, and we don't exactly know how, but you do it because you're meant to do it. You are meant to change things for some greater purpose. That's why the Flow, and us, continue to exist."

He shifted a little, brushing his bangs from his eyes. "Now, it's clear that no one really expects massive change to take place one single human life at a time; that would require far more people in the Flow and certainly more time than even time here permits. There are too many people living too many disparate lives to protect each one of them from every foible known to man," he said, scratching his knee. "Therefore, my theory is that we're concentrating our efforts on individuals who happen to have the ability to achieve maximum impact on the maximum number of *other* people around them.

"Oddly enough, these people aren't presidents or priests; assignments are usually ordinary people who simply have the ability or opportunity to affect many more people, disproportionate to most. It's the Ripple Effect. Six Degrees of Separation. Jungian Collective Consciousness. Do you follow me so far?"

The passion in his voice was almost hypnotic. His eyes sparkled as he spoke. He leaned forward into his words, toward her. Tender spoke with a conviction as solid as the chairs. She was surprised at how grateful she was that she had the sound of that confident voice to hang on to out here.

"Yes," she replied.

"Good. Now if the Flow works along these principles," Tender said as he adjusted in his chair, "I believe that we affect these select individuals so that maximum good, for lack of a better term, is achieved. Our actions have a disproportionate outcome comparative to our involvement. Our ends are exponential to our means."

He raised his hand, splaying five fingers. "By saving these chosen individuals, we create a chain of events that affect a mass of people, that eke things toward a larger state of good, more so than could ever be accomplished by attending to each of these people individually." He ticked two fingers. "It's simply a matter of economics and numbers. The Flow admits only so many, and we, in turn, only attune to so many. Therefore, if we are expected to achieve our fullest potential, we have to commit ourselves to impressing that maximum impact during our short windows of opportunity." His eyes grew intense. "Our purpose, therefore, is to create maximum impact upon the real world."

Consuela liked the sound of noble purpose. She straightened in her unreal chair. "Does the Flow . . . know this? Are you saying that the Flow is alive?" She balked. "That the Flow is . . . God?"

"Would God be so cruel to stick us here? Seriously?" he said. "I think it's merely economics again, using available resources." Tender glanced at her sideways. "Feel used?"

Consuela considered it. "Not particularly," she said. "I just want to go home."

"And you will go home," Tender said with conviction. "All it takes is tenacity. Here, in the Flow, the means *do* justify the ends." He sat back in his chair, pale face flushed, radiating warmth like joy.

She almost forgot the looming, unmade universe in the wake of his words. *I will go home.* He sounded so confident, so eloquent, she'd forgotten to be frightened. Out here, Tender didn't seem frightening compared to the oppressive horizon.

"So why are we here?" Consuela asked. "Not 'the Flow' here, but 'here' here, near this." She waved at the oblivion.

"I like it here," he said. "Sometimes I'm so tired of see-ing every little thing, touching every little thing, feeling every inch of it all the time, sometimes it's nice to come here and just . . . not." He shrugged.

She nodded, feeling guilty that she'd misjudged him, that she'd been so easily swayed by gossip about someone she hadn't even met. She squirmed in her chair, embarrassed. *What if I was stuck here and shunned because I had to clean up after everyone else? What if everyone else just decided that they didn't like me and I had nowhere else to go?* Caught between Sissy and Tender, Consuela felt a sort of popularity panic. She shoved it aside, clinging to her hope: *I'm going to go home!*

"I see," she murmured.

"Do you?" Tender sounded so eager. She leaned her elbows against her knees.

"Maybe," she said. "What if I did?"

Tender stretched, long-limbed and content. "Then you're somebody that I was hoping to find one day— someone here who understands."

Consuela felt the Flow shift unexpectedly beneath her—a silky and sinister, slippery thing. She felt like she could get easily sucked under if she wasn't careful. Was that the nature of the Flow? Or Tender?

"Someone who understands what you're saying?" she asked. "Or someone who understands you?"

Tender gave another winning smile, boyishly hand-some under his featherlight hair. Only his thick, black eyebrows made him look devilish. Wickedly amused.

"What's the difference, really? Who am I beyond what I say that I am? Not to be overly philosophical, but here—especially here—what you say is who you are. My words, my beliefs, are all that I have." Tender shrugged. "Of course, I have to be willing to back them up with action or it's all just hollow propaganda. If I cease to be reliable, I cease to be. In a world where we literally cause things to happen"—he rapped the chair's armrest—"I better *mean* what I say. After we die, what's left, really?" He gestured to her body. "Not even bones, I'm afraid. The only thing left is the memory of us—what we've left behind, what we've done, and how we're remembered. *That* is the mark of a life well lived, one that is remembered after it has passed. Our words, our actions, are our epitaph."

Consuela shook her head. *Who uses words like "epitaph"?* Although their conversation was interesting, it was smothering, pressing down on her; she didn't know how to contribute or how to get out.

Tender took pity on her by shifting gears. "Listen, Bones, not many will speak of death here in the Flow. I think the others believe that they can cheat death if they stay." Consuela self-consciously hugged her limbs tighter. "They create pecking orders or a higher society or whatever it is to convince themselves otherwise, but it's all the same," he confided. "They're hiding. I'm not."

He squeezed the ends of his armrests and grinned. "I'm content with death, but that's because I choose to live fully—with maximum impact—doing what I need to do right here. Right now." He stabbed the wood with his forefinger. His voice carried his passion and contempt in equal amounts. Consuela only listened with half an ear. Most of her was itching to leave.

Tender gestured contemptuously to the great beyond, waving off eddies and billows of Flow. "They are all caught up in why we're here and what does it mean. I say, who cares? This is the highest calling, no matter who spent the quarter to dial me up. This is our second chance and I'm going to milk it for all it's worth." He looked at her over a fist near his chin. "And, I suspect, you're the very same way."

They had a stretched-moment staring contest. Consuela, having no eyes, won.

"You're not scared, are you, Bones?"

Consuela wanted to say yes, that she wasn't scared of her power, but she was scared of death, that she wasn't scared of being in between, but she was scared of not getting home, and that she wasn't scared of him, exactly, but that she was a little scared of *everyone* she'd met in the Flow. She was scared of the Flow. She didn't like being here. She hated feeling frightened and confused, hated not knowing where to place her faith when the only people she knew were phantoms and the world around them was an uncertain, unreal place. She hated knowing that she could be whisked away at any moment by an unseen force that could pluck her up and spit her out anytime, anywhere. She wanted to be in control of herself, and she wanted to go home, and she wanted someone to tell her that it would all be okay.

What she said was "No."

"Well then," Tender said, standing up, the Flow dispersing around him and the chair unmaking itself into mist. "That's all I wanted to say. To introduce myself, let you know a little about me, and what I am all about since we're going to be together for some time. And that there's more to me than my role in the Flow, despite what the others may think." The way he said it, it was clear he'd meant Sissy. *Sissy, Wish, and V.* Consuela bristled, wondering if she'd be on that list, unsure of where her loyalties lay or why she had to choose sides at all.

Tender twitched his hair off his thick eyebrows. "Thanks for taking the time."

"No problem," Consuela said as she got to her feet, her own chair dissolving only after she'd left it. She wobbled on the lip of raw Flow, fighting the urge to run. The whole conversation had left her dizzy and confused. She was glad to have it end.

Tender waved a hole through the universe, leading them into a strange, null space—a tiny closet without walls. It felt small, enclosed, and Consuela pressed against him unexpectedly. His smile faltered and he pushed to one side; the space swung wide like a door. Tender held it politely as Consuela stepped onto the crosswalk of an empty city street of clean asphalt and tinted glass.

"Next time, come with me and I'll show you more," he said. "Nice meeting you, Bones." He grinned wolfishly and waved the Flow into folds, swallowing itself and him with it.

After a long moment, Consuela shook herself from skull to toes, rattling what was inside her, as if checking to make certain that it was all still there.

SHe ran. Consuela tried to outpace her thoughts and her fears of the churning oblivion and its clever puppetmaster. She thought of Sissy and V, but she wanted to be comforted by someone uninvolved, someone outside the Flow. She wanted to talk to Allison. Mom. Dad. Anyone real. She wanted to go home. She wanted to get *away*.

She flew through the world, unable to hold a solid picture in her mind of where she wanted, what she wanted, so she kept racing through flip pages of space. She dove through the Flow and into fog, the difference measured only by the thinness of the air and the heavy scent of wet nettles.

Gasping, she stopped. It was a misty-morning backyard grove, the white fog curled thickly around a candy-striped metal swing set and a three-season porch. Consuela swallowed, hearing her own sounds too loudly. Her breathing puffed in the air. Dewdrops wet her edges.

Exposed, she was suddenly too scared to move. She tried holding her breath, but it made her head swim. Shifting slowly in the grass, hearing every crackle and break, Consuela tried to make out the shadowy shapes in the mist.

She froze.

Someone stood on the edge of the hosta. The fog rolled and unfurled around a round, pale girl with dark, lazy eyes and limp black hair. She was the shape of a nesting doll, hunched and half awake, all but obscured in bluish-gray mist. She set Consuela's instincts on edge.

Consuela wanted to run. She knew she mustn't run.

Mustn't move.

Mustn't make a sound.

Winding tendrils played through her ribs. Moments ticked by, full of questions, while Consuela waited, trembling, uncertain whether she was predator or prey.

The girl's nostrils flared, painting swirls in the mist. Squinting her puffy eyes, she laboriously turned and ambled off into the trees. The snap and crunch of footsteps disappeared between a fourth step and a fifth.

Consuela started breathing at what would have been the eleventh step.

She rushed forward, the ground-dwelling clouds scattering, extending her senses to find her way out before the person in the mist came back. She wanted to feel safe— the feeling of home—and she ran for the next best thing.

Her bedroom door closed behind her before she even registered the knob under her hand and she tumbled into the comfort of her own soft bed. She hugged the pillows against her smooth surfaces and clawed her fingers deep into down. It smelled of home and she breathed it in deep, trying to fill that space inside her that had emptied ever since she'd learned that she was nowhere near her real home.

Consuela stood up and threw back the curtains, opening the window to let in the sunlight and the last of a half-remembered breeze. *Home.* She held the idea like spun glass. This was where she'd last felt safe. This is where she belonged.

She sat heavily on her bed and fell back against the covers.

Sprawled on her back, feet dangling on the floor, Consuela eyed the cracks in the ceiling, remembering Quantum's walls. It was all connected. They were all connected. She saw the tiny light being pushed by Abacus in her mind's eye and thought about what V had said, and Tender, too: she hadn't died. She could still get home. All she needed to do was find the way back from one side of the constellation to the next, the path that connected the dots from the Flow back into the world.

She knew what she needed to do, but not how to do it.

Consuela felt, rather than saw, the minuscule brush of fluff. Sitting up, she moved her foot aside and saw a single feather caught in the carpet. She picked it up, twirling it slowly between her finger bones. It was stiff and black, but when it caught the sun, a bright band of greenish blue sheared its surface, a crisp prism of negative light.

It must be one of Joseph Crow's.

Spinning the stiff quill in her fingers, Consuela wondered if he needed it back, if it would transform into a finger or something, or whether he molted feathers like people shed dead skin cells.

She used to examine feathers under her plastic microscope when she was little and Dad wanted her to be a microbiologist. He said he'd wanted to give her the world, down to the littlest things. She used to play with her dollhouse for hours: little tables, little chairs, little books, little lamps, little baskets of bread. Still, nothing man-made was quite like a feather. Nature's symmetry was like a puzzle and Consuela loved the minutiae of detail.

Consuela admired the feather's simple precision and wished that she could pluck the barbs apart and count them, one by one. Try to peek inside and figure out its secret. It was a secret she was looking for, the secret to the Flow. If she could just figure it out, she could find her way home.

She ran the feather along her wrist and watched it ripple and re-form.

She lost the moment when fascination became compulsion.

It flittered in.

Her left hand lifted of its own accord and plucked another feather right out of the air. Consuela was surprised to find it there. She reached up and grabbed another—this time watching as it wafted in on a lazy pillow of air. She plucked another, and another, flicking her wrist just so, clicking her thumb and forefinger together like chopsticks catching flies. The universe answered her will.

Five blue-black feathers had fastened to her fingertips, extending outward in an exotic fan. She unfurled her fingers, watching the mirage of motion, a dark hummingbird dance.

And Consuela knew.

Placing a finger against the back of her wrist, she traced a line up her arm. A flurry of feathers materialized, whirling out of the world, filing through her window to follow her lead. A sound like the shuffle of cards filled her room under the sudden torrent of pinfeathers, breast feathers, contours, and down. They funneled in from everywhere—lining up like keyboard keys wherever she trailed one finger, then the other, drawing herself tattoo lines of wings and skin.

Blue-green-black and shiny as oil, soft as fluff and paper stiff; her skin whispered with the beat of wings and hollow bones.

Yes. She thought, *Beneath it all, we're just bones.*

The world snapped open.

The world snapped shut.

Consuela bunched her legs beneath her and lifted her ruffled chin. Eyes upcast, she unfolded her magnificent wings and flew.

the woman stumbled through the field, weaving in and out of cornstalks as if they were strangers at a bar.

Her hair was a curtain of dirt blond and dirt. Her knees were muddy; she'd fallen more than once.

The glass bottle in her hand was her counterweight. Its caramel-colored contents sloshed, swinging her from one furrowed ditch to the next. Dead, choppy stalks cracked underfoot, and her shoes sucked mud like a whiskeyed kiss.

She tripped. It was the final fall. She knew it before she hit the ground.

Her cheek slapped hard, registering "cold" and "wet" as the mud pressed against her eyelid and plugged her left nostril. She tried to sit up, but thought that, perhaps, she was ready to reenter the earth once again.

Instincts thought otherwise. The woman coughed into a puddle, gagging and sputtering against the taste of silt. She tried to catch her breath, but the soft earth rushed into her nose and mouth.

Her coughing became bubbles. Consciousness winked fireflies. If she closed her eyes, it would be for the last time.

Consuela plucked her up like a hawk.

The thin woman weighed nothing, as if she were made of silk scarves. Consuela climbed with her quarry caught in taloned feet. Four beats like a wild heart, each chamber getting its due, and they soared past the face of a waning moon.

The smell penetrated Consuela's head with twin scents

of sick and self-loathing. She climbed higher, shaking these things loose in the whipping wind. Her mad rattling revived the woman, somewhat. The older woman wiped at her face, smearing brown filth across her nose and cheek while still clutching the bottle. Consuela frowned and squeezed the woman's shoulder. The hand jerked. Glass shattered fantastically on the asphalt below.

A series of quick, fanning thrums lifted them higher, where the air was cleaner and cold. Death faded behind them like old perfume. The woman laughed in delight and slurred something coherent.

"I'm alive!"

Only then did Consuela permit them to sink into the warmer currents rippling up from the earth.

Perhaps she was supposed to feel omnipotent or benevolent or some otherworldly, compassionate thing, but all Consuela felt was an odd mix of disgust, a sort of parental worry, and relief that she'd made it in time. She wanted to tuck this woman in a safe place to heal, nested and comfortable and far away from here. Consuela caught a flat image of a battered orange hideaway bed seen through broken blinds, plastic flamingos, and a tangle of half-dead purple begonias.

Home, she thought, although certainly not her own. *Safe.* Consuela's thoughts were animalistic and pure. She adjusted her pincer grip and banked into the east. A trailer park reeled into focus, speeding under her charge's dangling, mud-encrusted shoes.

The woman looked up.

"Angel!" she crooned.

Hardly, thought Consuela as she dropped her burden unceremoniously onto a bare patch of lawn to sleep it off.

"aṇɡeL!" Consuela crooned as she and Sissy broke out laughing.

"To be fair, what did you expect her to say?" Sissy asked. "I mean, just look at you!" The Watcher gestured with both hands. "Show me those wings!"

Consuela tried, but they wouldn't fit. Folded inside Sissy's basement office, she realized how impressive she must look. V was still out on assignment and she crackled with unspent energy. It made her giddy. She didn't want to be alone. And she wanted to show off her skin.

"Sorry, can't," Consuela said, shrugging. "I didn't realize that she could see me."

"Usually they don't," Sissy said. "Or, at least, if they do, they don't tell. But I've long suspected that behind every angel sighting, fairy sighting, Elvis sighting, or alien abduction is just one of us doing our job." She ran a hand over the flutter of Consuela's elongated humerus bone. Consuela felt every feather bend and spring back. "You must have, like, a twenty-foot wingspan," Sissy murmured, walking behind Consuela like a dressmaker. "How can your arms bend like that?"

"The same way you can remove your eyeballs," Consuela said.

"Fair enough."

Consuela rippled her arms in a shiver of joy remembered. "I could fly with these things—I *flew!*"

Sissy poked her in the bicep. "You've flown before," she said. "Remember Rodriguez in the park?"

"That wasn't the same." Consuela struggled to recall. It was hard to think back to when she'd stopped living in the moment. "That was more like standing on a moving sidewalk or skating on ice. Not much effort involved," she said, brightening with renewed laughter. "But, boy are my arms TIRED!"

Both laughed so hard, Sissy had tears on her cheeks.

"Wait, wait, wait—this deserves a toast!" Sissy ducked under one enormous wing and bounced toward a built-in bookcase in the corner. She removed a giant leather-bound edition of the *Webster's Dictionary* and flipped it open, revealing stiff pages that had been glued together and a wide bottle hidden inside. Sissy winked.

"Once Dad realized that we could look up everything online, I think he decided to put this to good use." She lifted the heavy bottle and plopped the hollowed-out tome on the desk. "The best part is, in accordance with the Flow, this thing literally never runs dry." She spun the top off with a practiced twist and lifted it high. "To Bones: the Flow's fluffiest angel!"

"You're kidding me," Consuela said uncertainly. The smell of whiskey and puke still clung inside her nose, yet Consuela was intrigued. "You've got everlasting Scotch?"

"Nineteen forty-six Macallan. Read it and weep," Sissy said, offering the bottle until she realized Consuela was without hands. "You want me to pour you a bowl or something?"

"No," Consuela said. "Let me take it off . . ." Not quite sure what to expect, she kneaded the back of her neck with the knobs of her thumbs, and feeling the telltale loosening and kiss of air, she shrugged her shoulders and shot her arms outward—the feather skin collapsed with a dramatic *flump* onto the floor.

"Wow!" Sissy cried. "Burlesque!" She handed over the bottle. "Here."

Consuela sniffed the liquor with her senses cleared, not knowing if her body could eat or drink. The liquor's perfume penetrated through the roof of her palate and danced in her sinus caves. The smell—earthy and vibrant—whispered in a voice that could carry across a crowded room. It smelled familiar, a warm presence of pipe smoke and old wood.

"This was your father's," Consuela said wondrously. Sissy smiled with nostalgic pride. Consuela watched the liquid play catch-can with slivers of bronze-gold light. "My father didn't like to drink," she said, "but he loved his cigars."

Consuela inhaled, trying to catch a whiff of memory; that wonderful mix of scratchy, cherry-rich tobacco smoke. Her hand moved to touch the topaz cross that was not at her throat. It was back with her skin and clothes. She let her hand fall.

She called me "angel." Consuela mused happily to herself. *Mom and Dad would be proud.*

"To angels," she said, and drank. It felt elegant and numbed like fire.

"To angels!" Sissy crooned in mock worship.

"To you." Consuela tipped and swallowed. "And me."

They spent the rest of the night sipping phantom Scotch, tying spare bedsheets around their wrists and taking turns jumping off of the stately chair, spinning and leaping and playing at being angels until they wound, tumbling, down.

chapter eight

"Death is a mirror which reflects the vain gesticulations of the living."

—OCTAVIO PAZ

CONSUELA woke tucked in a warm, cotton chrysalis on Sissy's floor. She could feel the well-laundered blanket curled around her, protecting her against noise and light. She rubbed her fingers over her smooth skull and into the sockets, her knucklebones slipping deep into her sphenoids.

She was alone in the basement. A sort of lazy trust infused her. She'd forgotten how much fun late-night talks and laughter could be. It had been a long time since her last sleepover party. It made her miss Allison something awful.

She didn't know where Sissy had gone, but she knew

her own way out and spied her enormous, flowing cape of inky feathers hanging magnificently on the closet door.

Consuela politely folded the borrowed blanket, stacking it neatly on a decorative pillow lying flat upon the chair. The large computer screen was active and displaying a message in fourteen-point font:

At O'Sheas. New configuration = 126. Stop by? Yad

Uncertain whether the words were meant for Sissy or her, Consuela read the strange message again. She was intrigued by the invitation, but even more by the author—the Yad. If she was going to get home, she had to meet everybody, explore every option, and the Yad was someone new.

Toeing the limp feathers aside and sliding the closet door shut, Consuela headed for little Killian O'Shea's room in Roxbury.

a young man stood precariously on a stool, his hands over his head, painting a long line over the door. He was formally dressed in black vest and pants, a long-sleeved white shirt rolled to the elbows, and a white undershirt that was strangely frayed, knotted strings hanging long past his pockets. Consuela watched him slowly trail his fingers from right to left, singing softly under his breath. She didn't want to disturb him. It looked suspiciously like prayer.

He hummed to silence and cracked an eye open. "Hello," he said.

"Hi," Consuela said, uncertainly.

"It's a ward," the Jewish youth said, stepping down. "To protect the boy inside against the Angel of Death, as it is said." He wiped his fingers on a rag. It was then she realized that the ink was really blood.

"Not to die before their time," she finished.

"Exactly. Mine is to protect firstborn sons," he said. "You must be Bones. I'm Yehudah Rosen, also known as the Yad—" He held up two fingers smeared with blood. "The 'hand,'" he translated.

"Nice to meet you . . ."

"I don't shake hands," he said.

She dropped hers, recalling Sissy's warning a bit too late.

He smiled. "It's a respect thing. *Shomer negiah*," Yehudah said politely. "I'll only touch four women in my life: my mother, my sisters, my wife, and my daughters."

"You have a wife?" Consuela squeaked. "And daughters?" The Yad looked all of sixteen.

"Not yet," he said. "Someday, God willing, when I return home."

Consuela nodded, looking up at the ward. It was powerful, she could tell. She was drawn to this spot almost against her will.

"That's sort of what I wanted to talk to you about," she said. "I'm not supposed to be here. I have to go home."

"Well, if it's any comfort, I believe that if you weren't meant to be here, you wouldn't be," the Yad said, adjusting a skullcap on his thick, curly hair. "Sorry, I don't mean to sound flippant. I wish I could help." He held up a waiting palm with a shy smile. "*But* since we know that some things can cross back, I don't see why you couldn't."

"Things?" Consuela asked. "What things?"

"Well, I have this." He reached up and removed the hairpin that held the circle of suede on his head. She wondered if he was joking. He smirked. "No, really. We all bring something with us that can cross from this world into the next. It's usually something personally significant or associated with something personally significant. Cecily has her computer, Giovanni has his cigarette lighter, Wish has his paints." He considered the tiny piece of wire. "Amazingly, it's come in very useful."

She laughed. "For picking locks?"

"Only when there isn't a key," the Yad said, looking back over his handiwork; his thoughts seemed to stir like a swirl of ink or blood. "But I've found that there is always more than one way to get at what you want."

149

"Well, I want to go home," Consuela said, surprising herself with her vehemence. She checked to see the Yad's reaction. He simply listened. "Sissy said it can't be done, but Wish said it can. V told me that intention is key and Tender tried to explain something about the power of the mind or words or whatever." She tried to remember the shape of Tender's speech against the vacuum roar of the Flow. "He said that if you're willing to stand for something, it could become real."

"Really?" the Yad said, intrigued. "He said that?"

"He said a lot more," Consuela answered. "But most of it went right over my head."

The Yad nodded. "Tender is very . . . intellectual. Although to hear him say that there is manifestation in our words, that we can speak things into being—well, that is a profound insight into the nature of truth. Words and numbers have considerable power."

Consuela knelt down on the carpeted floor and peered up into the Yad's faraway stare. Sissy said he'd studied the Bible, or something close to it.

"So you think he's right?" she asked.

"Possibly," he said. "I wouldn't say that he's wrong."

The concept crushed her like a soda can.

"What is it?" he asked.

She tucked her hands beneath her knees, hunched into a ball. "So . . . did I do this?" she said, voicing something she hadn't meant to admit. "To myself, I mean? By being so . . . afraid . . . ?" *Of dying. Of living. Of doing it wrong.* Consuela couldn't finish. She massaged one bony foot, watching the tiny, round anklebones shift and slide.

The Yad squatted across the hall and crossed his arms in thought. She felt oddly honored by his silence, his not rushing to answer or joke. His was a long, careful contemplation. She had never considered her thoughts that important before.

"Perhaps you have it backward," he said finally. "Perhaps this power was within you all along and only now manifests itself in the Flow." He pointed at her skeleton almost without meaning to. "Before, it came through your thoughts and dreams and fears. As one of the Flow, you become yourself, pure and simple. Literal. Black fire against white."

Consuela examined the floor. "Joseph Crow said something like that," she muttered. "Wish, too."

"There are many ways to say the same truth," said the Yad. "And Wish wears a lot of them."

A moment of silence stretched like the line of blood burning over the door.

"I'm sorry. I'm staring," the Yad said. "It's rude." She hadn't realized that he had been. He grinned ruefully. "I've never seen anything like you. When Cecily told me, I'd thought maybe a dybbuk? But you're not a ghost.

More like an angel. An anti–Angel of Death—an Angel of Life." Yehudah dug a knuckle in his cheek, tilting his head as he grinned. "I wonder if the hand that stayed Abraham's might have looked like yours? If it was one of us sent to make known that it was not Isaac's time to die?" he said. "An Angel of God."

Consuela chuckled, strangely flattered. "You know, you're the second person to call me 'Angel' today."

The Yad smiled. "Maybe, then, it's true."

She didn't feel very angelic. Mostly she felt scared, a tittering nervousness that stayed buried as long as she was moving. As long as she could hide in her skin. Like this, she felt naked—all guards down. In some ways, she felt stronger, braver; yet in others, totally vulnerable. She missed her old skin, folded, lonely and abandoned in her room.

Who am I when I'm iridescent bone? Who is Consuela? Who is Bones?

She scratched the patella floating in the shadow of her knee.

"Don't you worry that you'll never get back?" she blurted. "Never get to find your wife and have kids? Grow up? Have a life?"

The Yad stood up slowly and Consuela straightened, too.

"We are granted the life given to us," the Yad said. "It

is up to us to choose what to do with it." He inspected his ward as if it underlined his words. "The Rebbe said, 'Instead of "Why me?" think, "What should I learn from this?"' If this is my life, I'll live it to the best of my ability and know in my heart that it is enough."

He wiped at his hands as he and Consuela walked down the hall, which faded into the nothingness of the Flow. It bent and wobbled like a soap bubble to admit them.

Consuela stopped, glancing back, her heel on the threshold between two worlds. There was something she'd forgotten—a nagging tug like a half-remembered tune, an unfinished sentence, the feeling of something unintentionally left undone. She hovered on the hardwood, uncertain of what it was.

"It was nice meeting you." The Yad waved as he turned aside.

"Same here," she said vaguely. "See you later."

Alone and unable to place the source of her unease, Consuela reentered the Flow.

SHE'D retrieved her feathered skin, trailing it like a Brazilian wedding dress, and tucked it into the garment bag before dressing herself in flesh. Consuela returned to the closet. The black, iridescent feathers had settled darkly against fire, air, and liquid light. It was a tight fit. This was becoming less a fashion statement and more a bizarre haute couture collection.

Consuela touched each one briefly and wondered how many skins she'd eventually have. Maybe she should pack her normal clothes into her winter chest to make more room? There'd be no reason for dry cleaning in the Flow. No reason for laundry. No reason for clothes without skin.

She smoothed the sleeve of her favorite blouse, the one she wore to church on Sundays, dimly realizing that her fingers were trembling. She stared at them as if they belonged to someone else.

11:19.

Something sane and solid snapped. She collapsed to the floor, coughing jagged sobs.

How long can this go on?

How long will I be here?

How long before I . . . ?

The sentence wouldn't complete itself before drowning behind a wall of fresh tears. Consuela curled up in misery, alone and scared to death.

She thought she'd become powerful as Bones— invincible, elemental—but she was weak, a fake, more vulnerable than ever. She wasn't dead, but where was she?

Do they know that I am gone?

Will I die here?

Where will I go?

Am I being punished? Rewarded? Given a second chance?

Where is God when I need Him most?

She lay on the floor, keening, praying, overwhelmed by skins and mirrors, bloody smears and toothless wishes, eyeless prophets and handsome angels. Her skull throbbed, her ribs shuddered, she could feel each vertebra pressed against the wall. Even in her own skin, she could feel the power inside her—the truth of who she was. She could sit in her room and her skin and pretend, but there was no escape. Consuela hugged herself small.

// *I'm sorry.* // The choral voice whispered from somewhere overhead, echoing in the central air ducts like Mozart playing downstairs. V was somewhere, whispering to her heart. // *Try to sleep.* //

"I can't . . ." She shook her head, blubbering. "I can't . . ."

// *I know,* // the voice hummed. // *It will get better. Sleep.* //

She couldn't. She couldn't stop crying. It sounded so sorry, her disembodied angel.

// *I promise,* // the violins hummed on steel wires.

// I'll help you. I promise. // The litany became a song. Consuela stared at herself in the full-length mirror.

She edged closer, uncurling across the carpet. Still sobbing, she reached out her hand and pressed it against the glass. Another hand materialized beneath hers, surfacing in the silver, mirroring her reflection—she couldn't feel it, but could see the echo of it there.

"V." The name slipped beneath her tears.

// I'm here. //

Their fingers shifted slightly and threaded through the glass, his becoming real as they settled against her skin. Consuela cried harder, in release and relief, pulling him through. V emerged, crouched to meet her, and folded her in his arms.

// I'm sorry. I'm sorry. I'm sorry. //

She cried helplessly into his shirt. His arms enfolded her like a heavy cloak, a kind, protective wall against the outside world. Her hand bunched in his sleeve, she clung to him like a child. He stroked her hair. Her breathing faltered, choking on sobs.

"Consuela . . ." he said aloud, and couldn't seem to find more words to say. He brushed the hair from her face and placed a kiss at her hairline. She buried deeper into his chest and the edge of his lips caught the side of her cheek. He placed another kiss there. Her tears stopped. The moment caught like a breath. She was afraid to guess. Afraid to move.

// Please. //

One arm unwound, letting the light and him in.

He kissed her softly on the lips. One shared gasp, and they both tasted the warm salt of her tears. Mouths opened. Kissed again. Her fingers wound tighter as he combed through her hair. Her head bumped the wall and he pillowed her against his palm. Pressing, pulling harder, they fell into each other, feeding the ember enough air to burn.

They burned like a matchstick, flaring then gone.

The kiss ended with a sigh. They broke apart slowly.

Consuela wiped at her face. Feeling shy and embarrassed, she took stock: V was shoved against her wooden shoe rack, her legs tangled underneath her, both of them huddled on her closet floor. His shirt was a wreck. She was a wreck. Consuela tried to breathe through her nose, which was stuffed. She kept her head down.

"Sorry," she muttered, and made an attempt to pull away.

"That's my line," V said, and stubbornly held her against his chest. Consuela could feel the rumble of his voice beneath her cheek. His heart had been singing the whole time. Only now was it quiet like a hush of settled leaves.

V shifted next to her, keeping her close.

"You're exhausted," he said. The words were puffs of breath she felt on her temple. She was too tired to say anything back.

They rocked quietly in a comfortable silence.

"I've been thinking . . . about something the Yad said—" She broke off, hesitating to speak and ruin this moment. V waited. "If I wasn't meant to be here, I wouldn't be." She settled her hand against V's arm. "Maybe I'm *meant* to be here . . . ?"

V shook his head. "You don't belong here."

"Then I wouldn't be," Consuela said. "Don't get me wrong, I want to go home. I *have* to go home." She hoped V believed her and could help make the wish come true. "But maybe here, now, for this little while, I'm supposed to be here." She tried the words on aloud, testing their fit. "Maybe I'm the only one who can save someone important. Maybe it has to be me."

V grunted and stood up. Consuela did, too, suddenly neither one touching.

// You're not supposed to be here. //

He held his breath and moved with a stitch, like his leg had fallen asleep. Standing, he looked fragile.

"Are you okay?" she asked. He nodded and squeezed her shoulder.

"It . . ." He stalled.

". . . happens sometimes," Consuela finished for him.

"Knock knock!" called a familiar voice from around the corner. V dropped his hand. Consuela stepped out of the closet, V trailing close behind. Tender leaned half into the room, hanging off the doorknob. His wide smile faded when he saw her tears.

"Hey. Are you all right?" he asked, stepping in. He flashed a stern glance at V.

"I'm fine," Consuela said, which no one believed.

"I was just stopping by, but I see you already have a visitor," Tender said. "Hello, V."

"Tender."

V spat the word, flat and robotic. Tender's eyebrows quirked.

"I'm not interrupting anything, am I?" Tender asked.

V glared.

"No," Consuela said quickly. "V's just . . . I'm just freaking out."

"I know," Tender said. "You're sad. I can smell it. Like vanilla." He took a long, gentle sniff to prove it. "Anything I can do?"

V spoke first. "No." He glanced at Consuela and added, "Thank you."

Tender chuckled and leaned with one hand against the wall. "Oh, come on, V. I help *you* all the time. There's more than enough of me to go around." His eyes flicked to Consuela. "It's what I'm here for. Like Sissy."

"The Watcher," V corrected.

Tender rolled his eyes. "Whatever," he said. "It's a sincere offer."

Consuela frowned at the familiar, edged banter. "Do you two work together or something?"

"No," snapped V.

"Cleanup crew." Tender pointed to himself. "When V can't handle it." V turned still as stone, eyes burning. Tender ignored him and grinned magnanimously at Consuela. "Don't mind us. We're *old* friends," he assured her. "We actually have a lot in common, but we approach things differently, that's all. Don't worry, you're in good hands—he's one of the good guys. Best *intentions* and all." V said nothing, but melted back a step. Tender raised his thick eyebrows, a dare on his lips. "Need any help today, V?"

"No, thank you," V said. Forced politeness was hardly politeness at all.

Tender gave Consuela another long, appraising look like he had when she'd been all Bones.

"Are you sure about that?" Tender asked quietly.

"I said, 'No. Thank you.'" V overenunciated to make his point.

"I heard what you said." Tender mocked him like a child. "Fine, then." He pushed off the wall with a shrug. Taking one long step toward Consuela, he effectively cut V out of her sight. "But remember," he said sing-song, "devils may dance where angels fear to tread." He winked and touched her arm lightly. "I'll see you around." He nodded once to V and let himself out. V shut the door and pressed his back against it.

Consuela set her hands on her hips. "What was that all about?"

V drummed the flat of his fists lightly against the wood. He didn't look her in the eyes.

"Let me tell you something about Tender," V muttered. "He's a constant reminder that without him, we drown. And he's not above flaunting it. Or rubbing it in." His deep voice dipped lower. "And we all know he can make things 'unpleasant' if he doesn't get his way."

Consuela frowned. "How?"

"You know what Tender does here in the Flow?"

Consuela nodded. "He cleans it," she said. "He eats pain."

V rested his head against the door with a loud thunk, and looked at Consuela through low-lidded eyes. "Yes, well, I don't like pain," he said. "And some of us carry around a lot more pain than others."

His violin-voice added something unspoken:

// Not everyone is as strong as you. //

She glanced away, feeling the uncomfortable weight of his words. He thought too much of her. She thought too much about him. He stepped toward her, a slight stumble with the stitch in his hip, his boot heels soft in the carpet. She tipped her eyes to meet his.

"You don't need him," V said. "And you don't need me. You don't need anyone, really, but I'm going to help you all I can."

They stared at one another, the echo of their kiss in their eyes and on their lips. His eyes—dark, chocolate brown, like hers—searched for something she wasn't sure she had or knew how to give. Consuela hung on the edge of him, wondering, waiting. It was a moment when anything could happen.

The phone rang.

chapter nine

"Time is no longer succession, and becomes what it originally was and is: the present, in which past and future are reconciled."

—OCTAVIO PAZ

SISSY'S cell phone buzzed on the bookshelf near the door. Consuela had forgotten all about it. Hurrying over, she flipped it on.

"Hello?"

"Bones!" Sissy snapped with something like relief. "You still have my phone."

"Sorry," she said, and meant it. V frowned a question. Consuela shook her head.

"It doesn't matter. I'm glad you're there. Bring it and come over." Each command sounded like a gunshot in the dark.

Consuela gripped the phone. "You okay?"

"No," Sissy said. "But I'm glad *you're* okay. Just come over now. Please?"

"I'm on my way," Consuela said, and hung up.

"What is it?" V asked.

"I don't know. Sissy's scared. She sounded scared," Consuela said while walking to her closet, turning and stopping V from following her in.

"What are you doing?" he said anxiously.

Consuela sighed. "She asked for Bones."

Closing the door and smoothing the goose bumps over her arms, she pulled her skin free from her skeleton in one tug. She hung it up, trading it for her skin of air, feeling less vulnerable: cool, clean, and untouchable.

She opened the door and shimmered in the light. V moved awkwardly, trying to catch a glimpse of her. He held Sissy's phone in both hands.

"You don't have to come with," she said.

"I'm going."

"You're hurt."

V frowned. "It's nothing," he said. "Really. It happens all the time."

Neither wanted to push it and panic trumped the unsaid.

"Come on, then," she said quickly. "Let's go."

Something in Sissy's voice plucked at her nerves. Consuela couldn't shake the feeling as she and V strode through the Flow.

Her knucklebones, hard puffs of air, rapped against Sissy's door.

"Bones? Is that you?"

"I'm here," she said. "So's V."

Consuela heard the lock click open, not realizing until that moment that Sissy's door could be locked.

"Thank God. I called V, too." Sissy waved a small pocket mirror by way of explanation. There were words written across its surface in neat script. "I didn't know if you'd see it in time. I had to talk to you now. I can't reach the others as quickly." She spoke in rapid, official patter.

"What is it?" Consuela asked her.

"It's Nikki," Sissy said. "He's dead."

"Dead?" Consuela didn't know who said it first, her or V.

"It's why he never showed up," Sissy said. "I went to find him and . . ." She shook her head, swallowing.

"He's gone?" Consuela asked softly, suddenly sorry she never met him.

"People go all the time," V said. "When it's time."

Sissy's eyes blazed. "No! He's not *gone*—he's *dead*. Not disappeared or 'moved on.' Dead-dead. And death in

165

the Flow is the same as death back home." She shook her head, loath to say it. "He cut off his head."

V fell into the chair.

"WHAT?" Consuela shouted. "That's not possible, that's . . ."

// Tender! //

Dumbfounded, she stared at V. His head was down, held in clenched fists.

"Tender?" Consuela whispered.

"Tender?" Sissy repeated. "No. Tender's creepy and arrogant as hell, but there's a big difference between being a jerk and being a murderer." She scratched her own arm, leaving red tracks. "You can't just *say* things like that, Bones," she whispered harshly. "You're new. You don't know . . ." She shook her head. "All I know is what I saw. I'm not jumping to conclusions. No one should. But I still want to make sure that everyone's safe."

"But . . ." Consuela struggled to understand all the disparate facts. "How can someone behead themselves?" Suicide was a sin. She felt it more now than she had with Rodriguez. "That's . . ." She couldn't say "impossible" either. Not here in the Flow. Her helplessness spiraled as language failed.

"You've never been to Nikki's end of the Flow," Sissy said. "He crossed over watching anime and it flowed over with him. Anything ridiculously cinematic was possible there." She kicked the leg of her chair methodically. "And Nikki was . . . melodramatic. Over-the-top and very, very sad. He cried all the time—that was his power, after all. But I didn't know he had a sword."

Her words barely registered. Consuela concentrated on V; only one word reverberated in his brain:

// TenderTenderTender //

"Can you help me tell the others? You can send them to me, but I can't do it all by myself. New arrivals could appear at any moment," Sissy said, heedless of the violin shriek. "Bones, can you tell Abacus? And V, tell Wish. I'll tell Yehudah and Tender."

// Tender/No!/Tender! //

V still hadn't said anything—anything aloud. Anger, fear, pain, rose off him in waves. Consuela could almost feel it buffeting against her. Consuela wished he'd say something because she didn't dare say it for him; too embarrassed or too frightened about what it might reveal.

"Bones?" Sissy repeated. "Is that okay?"

Consuela snapped back to the moment, mute with indecision.

"What about Maddy?" V muttered.

Sissy sighed. "Maddy's hibernating. I'll have to tell her when she wakes up."

That snagged Consuela's attention.

"I think she's already up," Consuela said. "I think I saw her in the Flow."

The others stared and she wondered what she'd said wrong.

"No," Sissy said dully. "That can't be right. She can't be awake. Not yet." She squinted at Consuela as if making her out from a distance. "Are you sure?"

"Big girl, dark hair, kinda Asian, wide nose?" Consuela said. "She was standing somewhere in the mist, surrounded by woods. Sniffing."

V and Sissy said nothing. Their long pause confirmed it.

"She only wakes early when something's bad," Sissy said. "When something's really, really bad." She massaged the back of her hand with a hard thumb. She looked at the two of them, eyes wide. "So that means something's really bad, right?"

// Tender //

V retreated to a corner of the bookcase. Consuela glared after him, hating the fact that he was avoiding something, hiding something. *Coward!* He was supposed to be brave. *He's supposed to get me out of this. He's supposed to get me home!* Now people were dying in the Flow? No one mentioned that could happen!

V pretended to read the spines of old books.

"Well, if Maddy's up, I'll find her," Sissy said. "But she'll be grumpy. Hopefully, I can steer her back to bed."

Consuela blew past them in a gust, not looking at V; flowing over the carpet, she coalesced by the door. She knew the way to Abacus and wanted to go, get out, get far away from here. And V. She paused at the exit.

"What about Joseph Crow?" she asked.

"Joseph Crow knows," Sissy said. "Somehow, he always knows."

"And you don't find that suspicious?" Consuela asked.

Sissy pursed her lips angrily. "Again, I don't 'suspect' anyone," she said. "And neither should you. Nothing like this has ever happened before. Sound familiar?" Her voice quivered. "Think about *that* before you accuse anyone else of anything else."

Consuela flushed invisibly. Her palms felt hot and moist. Just when she thought she understood something, someone, everything changed.

"Fine. I'm on it," she muttered, and flung herself through the field.

She would do her part, for now. But Abacus also happened to be the only one who had a map of both worlds.

She didn't have to wait to talk to him. She was going right now.

One way or another, she was going home.

QUANTUM hurt her brain. She winced against its bizarre majesty and kept her head down. Why couldn't she appear at the front door or, better still, inside? The Flow worked in ways that were less mysterious than annoying.

Abacus hadn't come out to meet her and she didn't know how to get in. Tapping the crystalline spires failed to produce a door. Knocking made no difference and hardly any sound. It was like rapping on concrete: dull and dead.

"Damn," she muttered under her breath.

"Hello?" a familiar voice called. "Hey, there you are!" Tender shook out his bangs and emerged from behind some random corner. Consuela knew he hadn't been there before. "You look . . . amazing," he said, the confession apparently surprising them both. "What did you do to yourself?"

"I'm wearing a skin of air," Consuela said dismissively. She didn't want to talk to Tender. She hadn't expected to see him here and V's unspoken worry still echoed in her head.

"Huh," Tender said, impressed. "So are you made up of air or do you wear air? Is air a part of you, or vice versa?"

"I don't know," Consuela said. "I'm looking for Abacus."

"Chang? He's not here," Tender said. "I was hoping that he'd help me out with something, but nobody's home."

Consuela was secretly relieved. At least she didn't have to be the one to tell him about Nikki's death. But she was selfishly disappointed she couldn't ask the friendly mathematician more about the possibility of crossing over and getting out right now.

"Are you sure?" she asked.

"Yes," Tender said, pointing. "You can tell by the *suan-pan*." He knelt down to show Consuela the old hardwood frame with ten metal rods; the small, redwood beads were arranged in random intervals. It looked more like an abacus than an answering machine.

"What do you mean?"

"It's a message." Tender laughed. "In a conversion code Chang likes to use. It's a bi-quinary system of base-two and base-five for decimal and hexadecimal computations corresponding with . . ." He trailed off as he noticed her drifting. He smiled apologetically. "It says he's gone out," Tender finished.

Consuela could have left it at that, but something held her back. She felt . . . unfinished. Almost like she had when she last saw the Yad. *You never know how long you have—there might not be a later.* It bothered her enough to say what was on her mind.

"Nikki's dead," she said.

Tender nodded. "I know. I was there."

"What?" Consuela felt an eerie rush along her limbs.

"I had to go clean it up," he said. "I had to . . ."

Consuela flinched, horrified. Her mind swam with slasher-movie gore.

Tender read her thoughts like splashed canvas.

"It's not like that!" he said hastily. "I don't *eat* people, just the karmic backwash. The black aura. The shadow. The feelings left behind." Tender sighed and tucked his thumbs behind his belt buckle.

"Violence and pain taint the Flow, and us, and everything. Gunks it up." For a moment, he deflated, as if his explanation were a confession. "I *have* to keep it clean; it's what I do." His voice dipped to a whisper. "Besides, I get hungry."

"Hungry?" she said, shivering, an all-over ripple.

"Yeah," he said. "That's *my* compulsion. I have about as much choice as you do. It's a need—you know that." That was true, she did, but she didn't like thinking of it as a hunger.

172

Tender saw her discomfort and shrugged. "You haven't been here long enough to get shadow," he said. "When you do, you'll need me. Then you will understand."

What Consuela needed was an excuse to leave. Now. To stay here felt dangerous, wrong, sliding on the edge of something sharp. But she wasn't going to leave this unfinished. She'd come to help, she'd see it through.

"Right now I need to leave a message for Abacus to go see Sissy," she said. "Right away."

Tender looked at her approximate face. "No problem." He picked up the ancient calculator and began snapping the beads about, rearranging the *suanpan* with quick flicks and clicks before setting it down again. "There. That says for him to go see Sissy ASAP. He'll see it first thing when he gets back." Tender smiled. "So that's that. You ready?"

Consuela balked. "For what?"

"Don't you remember?" he chided. "Last time we took a walk you said you might want to know more. See more. Still interested?"

"Not right now," Consuela said. "I should get back to Siss—the Watcher. Tell her I left a message. Maybe later."

Tender's eyes grew dark and daring. "She'd be the first to tell you, there may not *be* a later," he said. "If you don't come now, we may never know."

What hung between them could have been a promise or a threat.

She remembered // *TenderTenderTender* // and felt her chances slipping away.

"Okay," Consuela said, uncertain as a fly on a spider's thread. "Sure."

Tender tried to search her face. "Are you certain?" he asked graciously.

"Yeah. Why?"

He shrugged. "I can't tell," he said. "No face, no facial expressions, no eyes to the soul. Right now you're omnipotent—it's spooky."

She laughed. She couldn't help it. "I've been walking around this whole time as a skeleton, and that's the first time anyone's called me spooky!"

"Well, you're not spooky, then," he said. "You're exquisite."

The word trilled down her spine like a xylophone, every one of her hidden vertebrae a different key. She didn't know what to make of it.

"What did you want to show me?" she asked to cover her embarrassment.

Gallantly, he conceded. "Follow me."

He moved left and the Flow bowed to admit him into another piece of its world. Stepping directly through its bubbling, shifting mass was nothing like the flip-book montage she'd seen while walking with V. It was less like they were traveling along its surface than punching straight through it.

When she and Tender emerged, Consuela recognized where they were.

"This is Wish's place," she said, standing on the long sidewalk by the high school fence and its familiar crab-apple tree.

Tender kept walking, boots shifting on gritty concrete. "Just the edge of it. Anyway, it'll do." He started searching the edges of the sidewalk with his eyes, his long blond bangs pointing straight down. "Just remember, Bones, none of this is real."

The disclaimer didn't soothe her sense of foreboding. She wasn't certain what he was looking for, but she felt strangely guilty trespassing on Wish's turf. She glanced at the crab-apple tree and shrank inside. *We shouldn't be here. Not without Wish. Or his permission, at least. We shouldn't be doing whatever Tender's planning on doing . . .* But she didn't know what to say or how to say it to make it stop. It was as close to breaking and entering as she'd ever been.

"There," Tender said triumphantly.

"What?" Consuela said. "Where?"

"Right there, look," he said, pointing.

Consuela frowned. *"Ants?"* she asked, feeling like the butt of a prank.

"Look closely." Tender's finger traced the small trail of tiny black insects picking their way over a mound of sand pellets in the crack between two sidewalk squares. "How many worker ants would you guess are in there?"

"I don't know," Consuela said, vaguely, attempting to guess the trick. "Twenty?"

Tender looked disappointed. "I'd say closer to forty-two—it's the answer to everything—but I've done this before." He sighed and shook his head. "Anyway, let's say this represents, oh, about one forty-seventh of the active colony—workers, males, and one or more egg-laying queens, skipping over the eggs, grubs, and larvae. Now, that's one thousand nine hundred and seventy-four ants scurrying around, keeping things in order so that this colony has the maximum chance of overall survival." He held up a single finger in the middle of his lecture. "Now, here's the interesting question: who do you think has the largest impact on the colony as a whole?"

Consuela thought about it. "The queen?" she said.

Tender smiled wickedly. "No. Me."

He stomped one boot, flattening the mound of sand, stepping back to smile over the scattering tumult of terrified insects and broken bodies that lay twitching in the dirt. Consuela rippled in the breeze. It struck her as such a little thing and such a huge thing all at once. She cringed at the mad excitement that flushed Tender's face.

Tender tapped himself in the chest.

"Maximum. Impact."

She stared at him, horrified in one thousand nine hundred and seventy-four tiny little ways, but Tender dismissed the almost palpable accusation.

"Sometimes you have to think outside the box, then the answer becomes obvious," he said. "What are you willing to do to save someone, Bones? What sacrifices are you willing to make to achieve your objective? Hmm?" Tender's eyebrows shot up a question that she couldn't answer. Her stunned silence pleased him. "Think about it. Lesson one's over. Let's go."

Consuela kept staring at the undying ants. Tender glanced over his shoulder when he noticed her shimmer hadn't followed. Consuela couldn't seem to find the words to express what she felt. She drifted, feeling lost. He sighed dramatically.

"No actual ants were harmed in the making of this film," he said, chuckling, but it broke off in a snap. The black shutters behind his eyes slammed down. She floated back a step.

"Don't disappoint me, Bones."

A strange, feral growl upset the silence. Tender paused and touched the space above his belt buckle.

"Ah. Now I'm hungry again," he said. "Excuse me—you know how it is." He paused as if about to say more, but decided against it, his voice tight with struggle. "Either obey like a sheep, or go like a hound set free." His eyes said it all: *which do you choose?* "Later, Bones." He nodded and turned in a quick twist, his next footstep blurring into the ether of the Flow. It warped and banked around his exiting tread. Two quick movements, and he was gone.

Consuela stared, shaken and confused. *What just happened?* Her brain couldn't register the half of it, but grasped one thing: Tender had gone to feed.

Feeding. Off the pain of the Flow. *Bottom-feeder. Vulture. Tender.* She thought of Nikki and V and Sissy's fingers trembling in her lap. This private compulsion left him as vulnerable and naked as she'd ever been, slave to the powerful pull of whatever called her across into the real world. She knew that she could learn something if she went after him; something nobody was supposed to witness or know—Tender at his most tender moment. *His weakest. His weakness.* She'd know more if she were willing to be brave.

I'm not a coward.

Consuela considered Tender's scent lingering like a fading note on the echo of his trail. All she'd have to do was follow it.

It was only fair. He deserved it for Wish, for the ants, for scaring me . . .

"You've been talking to him."

Consuela swirled around. Wish stood right behind her. She had no idea how long he had been there, watching, listening. She felt a flash of guilt for trespassing and another that he'd guessed right.

Wish fiddled with his pins. But while his hands fluttered, his eyes stayed solid, boring into space. She didn't need to ask whom he had meant; his words were less an accusation than a statement of fact.

"Yes," she said. What else was there to say?

"Don't," he said flatly.

"'Don't?'" Consuela echoed back. "That's it? Just 'don't'?"

"Yeah," Wish said. "Don't."

Consuela moved to brush past him, but he crossed his arms and stood his ground.

"We were just talking," she said. It sounded petulant, even to her.

"That's the most dangerous thing you can do, talking

to him," Wish said as he picked the acne scabs on his cheek. "He can talk circles around you, like rope, and you don't know how tied up you are until it's a noose around your neck." He clicked his bitten fingernails against a pin that said THERE'S NOTHING WRONG WITH YOUR EYES, THIS IS HOW I REALLY LOOK. "I think Tender's real power is in his talking—he can get you to do anything. *Anything.* And then, later, thinking back on it, you think it must have been your idea all along, like you were going to do it anyway. But you weren't, and you wouldn't, before he started talking and making it all sound like it makes sense . . ." Wish gazed into the shimmering rift in the Flow. ". . . but it doesn't. None of it makes sense."

Consuela was about to say that Wish was the one not making sense, but was too distracted while trying to hone in on Tender's whereabouts. It was so easy if she didn't stop to think about how to do it, like a smell or a taste just out of memory's reach.

"Don't," Wish said, moving to catch her arm. She didn't think anyone could touch her, but his fingers gave a little resistance on the edge of her skin before passing through. She didn't feel it.

"Don't follow him," he said in an almost-plea.

Consuela wanted to ask him why, but the expression on his face was composed of many things: terror, disgust, fear, and a strange protectiveness. She wasn't sure if Wish wanted to protect Tender or her.

She was sick of people telling her what she should or shouldn't do.

"I won't," she said, pulling back. Wish stared at her grimly. He watched her go.

Consuela pushed herself outward so she wouldn't have to look back.

She felt bad about the lie.

CONSUELA went to see Tender feed.

Following him had been easy. Maybe she knew where to look, or maybe she could still taste his scent in the air she was in.

He was shirtless, alone on his knees in the middle of a rich man's deserted hallway, almost as if he were kneeling in prayer. Legs buried in wine-colored carpet, Tender bowed his head while electric sconces flickered coppery light against black-and-white photos in gilded frames. It felt old, musty, and expensive here. Consuela pushed herself around a dark corner and watched him from the shadows. He was buried in the task, oblivious to anything else. Like her.

Tender took long, deep breaths, priming himself for something.

Eyes closed, he shook his head like a dog, slowly, then

building speed, and with a quick, wrenching noise, un-hinged his jaw. Consuela winced. Tender's mouth lolled open, held on solely by the skin of his face. His tongue flapped like a landed fish.

Tender bent forward, his back undulating as if he were about to vomit, but—like retching in reverse—his long body began to heave, sucking in dark fumes like a giant vacuum.

It curled off of everything: the walls and the floor, the lightbulbs, the doorknobs, the display shelf and even—or especially—the photographs in their frames. It was as if a film lifted from a lens, an abiding grayness gone.

He drank. His body fought against his thirst, his hands pushed back, arms rigid. Even as his face bent far-ther forward, his fingers raked against the carpet, trying to resist.

The end came like a rubber band snapped. He stopped, rocking on all fours in recoil.

Staggering, Tender trembled on his hands and knees, breathing hoarsely through his gaping maw. His tongue hung loosely in his head. His chest buckled. His pale shoulders shone with sweat.

Blinking hard, he placed both hands firmly against chin and cheek, and, with a grunt, wrenched his jaw back into place with a loud bone crack.

Groaning, Tender struggled to sit. Leaning back on

his knees with a look of relief and regret, he swallowed. Tilting his face up to the ceiling, blinking back tears, he couldn't see Consuela staring at him in horror. He bent farther backwards, and Consuela saw the sudden squirming motion like a bag of wet cats where Tender's stomach should be.

There was a loud gurgling. She could hear it from here.

He inhaled sharply and screamed.

Reappearing somewhere in the Flow, Consuela realized that she'd flown in a random direction and now she was lost. Being vapor meant she didn't have to gasp for breath, but instinctive fear pummeled her chest like hail.

The look on Tender's face had burned itself on the backs of her eyes. The sound—that inhuman, impossible sound—scrabbled around her brain on sharp, needled claws. That wasn't the brazen, brilliant egomaniac she'd met, that was . . . she didn't know what Tender had been just then. *Terrible. Enslaved. Martyred.* It was the closest thing she could get to pitying him. She wondered why she still didn't.

Tender eats pain. He hates it. It hurts him. But he can't help himself; he's hungry. The next synapse fired an awful certainty: *This is who I am and that was Tender. That is who he is.*

It made her sick and sad and sorry and no small part grateful that it was him, and not her, who had the burden of maintaining the Flow. How could he stand it? *Could God be so cruel?* Tender's words haunted her. Consuela had often wondered the same thing, reading the paper or listening to the news, things were not so different in the Flow. There were still victims and predators, cruelty and fate.

And still, she couldn't pity him. Or admire him. She was just glad she *wasn't* him.

Disgusted with herself and what she'd witnessed, Consuela's skin felt like a layer of sewer-soaked clothes or unexpectedly bloodied underwear at that time of month. She tore the lump behind her neck and ripped off the skin, violently pushing it from her. It fell limply in a pile, one empty arm drifting like a swirl of campfire smoke. Consuela hugged her skeletal arms, clacking them against her breastbone and ribs. She ran her hands up and down her radii as if trying to get warm. At least she felt better; at least she was still wholesome and whole.

Her body glowed gently with its muted pink-blue-pearl light and she took comfort that she was still her, inside. She was still Consuela—Bones—and being in the Flow hadn't changed that. It just made her more herself, like Wish said. And the Yad. It made more sense to her now.

Draping her cast-off skin over one arm, Consuela concentrated on finding her way to her room.

Or, at least, the memory of her room.

She closed her eyes against the strain and saw a flash image of Tender's loose jaw. She opened her eyes again— no good. If she thought too much about it, she'd never get anywhere. *Go,* she urged herself. *Just go.*

Trusting that her feet knew the way, Consuela stepped sideways through the Flow's tesseract doors and onto the soft carpeting of her own floor. She stumbled and righted herself, almost surprised to have gotten there so easily.

Feeling the air skin against her body, she flinched at its closeness. She never wanted to wear it again.

Never again, she thought, and tossed it aside.

The skin pinpricked into its own black hole.

Consuela stared after it. Or the place where it wasn't. She stepped forward, reaching out to test the air. Nothing. She spun in place with the disorienting feeling of having had her keys a moment ago and now being unable to remember where she'd put them.

Consuela got down on her hands and knees, her sharp patellas poking into the plush carpet, sweeping the surface as if searching for a lost contact lens. It felt strangely like a dream. Her fingers stippled over the carpet yarn.

Nothing. Her skin of air was gone.

Pushing herself up, she wondered with a thrill of excitement and dread whether she could ever make another one again. Or was it like Wish's tooth wishes? Only one, then gone?

Consuela padded into her bathroom and unbolted the window. Climbing into the tub and stepping onto its edge, she sat upon the windowsill, feet dangling in the air. But the feeling wasn't the same. There was no urgent *need* to make windswept footie pajamas, and without the internal tug, she didn't feel like testing the theory by falling three stories and crashing to pieces on the back deck if she were wrong.

She crawled back out of the window and into the empty tub, racing back to her closet. She grabbed the water skin off its hanger and marched back into her bathroom. Holding it over the tub, she thought it *undone*.

The skin fell through her fingers, splashing against the porcelain, spinning and gurgling as it slipped down the drain. Tiny droplets of water clung to her finger bones, threatening to fall like tears.

Were the skins reverting to their original components or did they simply cease to exist? Between her last two skins, only one held the answer.

She scooped up her trailing gown of inky feathers and spread it over her bed. Carefully tucking all the stray ends onto the comforter, Consuela smoothed her hands through its tucks and folds, burying her fingers in its dramatic sheen. Closing her eyes, she willed it *unmade.*

A soft *pluff* sound and a great loosening collapsed the skin into a pile of loose feathers. She picked up a few and let them spiral down. Separated, alone, they were nothing like the skin of the dark, winged angel who'd rescued a muddy drunk. She gathered up the corners of her bedspread and, unbolting the double-paned glass, Consuela pushed the bundle out the window, letting two of the corners fall. A great cloud of feathers exploded, beating at the window, obscuring the view, before pinwheeling out into the fathomless "wherever" that existed beyond her make-believe room. She shook the bedspread with vicious snaps, pulling it back in only after she'd dislodged the last bit of downy fluff. She snapped the window shut and threw the comforter on her bed. It was a violent release, a daring game, playing chicken with the Flow.

Consuela considered her last victim crackling merrily in its garment bag, tongues of yellow-orange flame licking the inside of the clear plastic. She stood in the closet doorway, the gold light playing merrily over her bones. Would undoing this last skin free her from the Flow? Or would it make her powerless, trapped as a living skeleton, forever, without any skins? Would it kill her, making herself "undone"? Would it do none of these things and simply curl into a zip of warm nothingness, leaving only a touch of ash—if that—behind?

Could it free her? Kill her? Bring her closer to the end? A real end, like Nikki's: death in both worlds.

The fire skin hung by a crackling thread.

The real question was: was she willing to risk it?

She rotated that last question around in her mind.

No.

Consuela took her own skin, unfolding it gently like an heirloom quilt, and stepped into herself slowly, welcoming it on like an old friend. She felt her spine slide closed, soft orbs settling into her sockets, the itch of her scalp as it tightened against her skull, and the comforting weight of her fatty curves as they nuzzled over her ribs and hips. Consuela lifted her head, looked at herself in the mirror, and recognized the full-lipped, high school grin.

I know you, she thought at herself. *This is me.*

chapter ten

"To us, a realist is always a pessimist. And an ingenious person would not remain so for very long if he truly contemplated life realistically."

—OCTAVIO PAZ

WISH whimpered as he stumbled on a stretch of nothing, slipping through the infinite space of the Flow. Dodging between islands of other people's pasts, he cursed for the millionth time the fact that he couldn't be selfish if he tried.

He ran wildly, tripping over his long shoelaces. He could sense murder coming like a storm.

Perhaps he imagined it—not the killer, *that* was real—but the echo of footsteps, sharp and sure like marching soldiers. Damn boots should make a sound outside his head! He couldn't have been seen, not yet anyway, or the footfalls would've gotten faster, right? Anyone human would start running him down. Then again, Wish wondered if there was anything human in there anymore.

Wish bounced off of something solid, the edge of familiar territory, but whatever it was retreated before he could get a grip on it and yank himself into freedom. *No trespassing. Doomed in the empty.* Probably Joseph Crow's trickster-coyote trapdoor.

"Shit!" he swore, spun to his feet, and kept on running, fast.

The somewhat-sounds were coming closer, and Wish felt a desperate clawing-bile-panic need to escape. He was good at wishful thinking, but he was much better at hiding.

Wish sat down, curling into a fetal ball on the nothingness floor. He rolled up—whimpering—and ground fists in his hair. The un-noise kept ticking like a grandfather clock.

Wish teetered on his seat, pulling his jacket full of novelty pins like an umbrella over his head. He shook, back turned toward the imaginary echo, feeling the cold on his crack where his shirt lifted from his briefs. Ducking his face into the hot hollow between his chest and legs, he squeezed his eyes shut, openmouthed-breathing, hiding the animal sounds coming out of his throat.

It wasn't my wish, so this should work . . . Wish clenched his hands tighter. *No, no, no—it HAS to work! It wasn't mine. It HAS to work . . . !*

He kept his weird prayer spinning in his head, forming a sort of convincing cocoon, winding a thread of hope to cover him whole.

The marching came closer.

He has to have seen me . . .

The sounds were steady and even.

Inhuman robot prick!

The footsteps never faltered, driven like a steady hammer to nail, gunshots at a firing range. It was almost upon him—the press of hot, dampened Flow pushing everything out of its wake. Wish cowered, waiting. He didn't want to die, but couldn't help wondering what it'd feel like if he did. He wondered if it'd take long. He wondered if it was happening now. Was the sword hanging over his head? He couldn't stand not knowing. He looked.

Wish peeked over his collar under the cover of his hair at the bright black boots stalking by. The young psychopath's strides ate up the Flow and spat it back like some parasitic worm. He didn't see Wish, didn't even pause to sneer; the Angel of Death kept walking, storming toward somewhere else in space. Wish watched him go, refusing to breathe.

It was an old, familiar terror: too scared to speak, too scared to tell, and no one ever believed him, anyway.

The boots walked into the nothing as Wish sat unnoticed, sculpted in fear.

He unwound only when his muscles began to burn, when his knuckles shook with strain and sharp spasms bit the base of his spine. Uncurling like a hedgehog, meek and cautious, Wish kept expecting the inevitable predator-pain.

He couldn't believe it—it worked! He'd passed within inches, if that.

Relief crashed through him with the promise of a major migraine. *Paranoid, am I?* Wish smirked. *Then what the hell was that?!*

He wiped his hands on his pants and headed elsewhere. His laughter, when it escaped, bubbled out in spurts of maniacal soda-can froth. *Piece of cake;* he giggled. Should he try to warn the others? Sissy was a goner, for sure. Bones, too, probably. He couldn't risk it. There wasn't time. Maybe he could find Abacus or Maddy and hide out with them. Wish might not be the only one left, after all.

Smarter than the average bear, Wish congratulated himself.

It was tough to hide in a world where nothing really

existed, so he'd tucked himself behind somebody else's wish, and waited for the threat to walk right on by.

tHIS time, there was no knock, no warning, Tender walked right through her bedroom wall with a secret smile on his face. Consuela jumped up from her desk, cold with fear. Had he known that she'd been spying on him? Had Wish said anything? *Tender's going to kill me!*

He was as confident and cool as ever, as if he'd never once cracked open his mouth and swallowed layers of black pain from the Flow.

"Hello, Bones," he said. "Sorry to intrude, but I knew this couldn't wait." He flicked his head to move his bangs from his eyes. "I figured out your problem and—as promised—I'm here to help!"

The creepy, numbing buzz hadn't left her limbs, which tingled awake without having fallen asleep first. She remembered the ants. And Tender's screaming. She was proud that her voice sounded calmer than she felt.

"Help?" she asked warily. "With what?"

Tender grinned as if they shared a joke. "Oh, come now. V wanted to do it all by himself—right past wrongs, that sort of thing. Make it up to you," he said. "And we all gave him his space and ample time, but I think you've had enough and would rather just get out, right?"

Consuela stammered, "Get out?"

"Get. Out." Tender overenunciated. "Go home. Go back to your life. That is what you want, isn't it?"

Her head spun, thoughts twisting one-eighty. *"What?"*

"I asked," Tender said smoothly, stepping forward and looking pleased with himself, "if you wanted to go home?"

She blinked up at him.

"Home." She repeated the word, visions of her parents and Allison and her car swam to the surface; school and pizza and walking out of her room and away and away and away . . .

Consuela was hopeful enough to ask.

"How?"

Tender clapped his hands as if he'd been waiting for that question. "Well," he said theatrically, "let's see what our lucky contestant can find behind Door Number One." He grabbed her bedroom door handle and cranked it down, pulling it open with a flourish. Consuela stared.

There were hardwood floors, cream-colored walls, the worn, Indonesian runner, and the framed family portrait at the end of the hall.

Home. Her mouth felt dry. She forgot to breathe.

Tender stepped aside.

"How about here and now?" he said.

She was afraid to move, afraid to blink, afraid to believe it. Her feet were glued to the floor.

"That wasn't there before," she whispered.

"Of course not," he said. "But this is the Flow, which can be anywhere at any time and right now it is at your house, on the second floor, just outside your room." Tender leaned on the door with a self-satisfied smirk. "Now you say, 'Thank you,' and kiss me good-bye."

Consuela stared at him and was surprised when he glanced away, embarrassed; a flush brightened his throat, but hadn't made it to his cheeks.

"The kiss is optional, of course," he said. "But I thought you'd be grateful."

I am, aren't I? She was too nervous to be sure. Suspicion blinded her. It didn't seem possible, but then nothing had seemed that way since she'd found the lump. More to the point, it didn't seem *right*—but she couldn't figure out why. She kept staring at the framed photograph down the hall, willing the image sharper, proving itself real, knowing it would look clearer if she stepped forward. She remained where she was. *Why can't I just go?*

"That's real?" she asked, stalling for time to think. "That's the real world?"

"As real as it gets," Tender said gently.

Consuela almost frowned as a thought occurred to her. "Why me?"

Tender paused. "Excuse me?"

"If this is real, if the Flow can go anywhere," she asked carefully, "why don't you use it to go back?"

Something in his eyes flattened and his proud smile grew stiff.

"You presume that I *want* to go back," he said through his teeth. "I don't *ever* want to go back."

"But the others . . . ?"

"Neither Sissy or V or Joseph or Wish want to go back either—despite what they say out loud to convince one another how much they miss home. They know their lives are no longer pretty or *they're* no longer pretty—" He shook his head. "But we all *want* to stay here in the Flow, otherwise we wouldn't be here." He tapped his chest and winked. "Maximum impact, remember? We do better here. But you—" He lifted his hand to touch hers; she flinched. "You don't belong here. V's said it a thousand times. You've said it yourself. You have to go back. V is being stubborn and selfish by making you wait when all he had to do was swallow his pride and ask for help." He glanced at her under his thick black eyebrows. "You should never be afraid to ask for help." His eyes quirked, full of double meanings. She gazed out the door to a familiar world.

"And I could just go now?" She said. "Just walk out the door and close it and be home?"

Tender looked out with her, saying nothing, leaning against the jamb.

"It's up to you, Bones," he said finally. "It looks like a nice life."

Home.

"What are you waiting for?" he whispered.

Home. Don't piss him off. TenderTenderTender.

What am I waiting for?

What am I waiting for?

I'm waiting for . . . ?

She searched for it. It was something. Unfinished.

"It's not my time," Consuela said quietly, not quite believing that she'd said it. It was as true as she could make it, although it seemed as if they were both saddened by her answer. Tender pressed his belt buckle slowly, a gentle pressure. Consuela didn't dare blink as he weighed something behind his eyes.

"Okay," Tender said flatly, and closed the door with aching slowness. The latch caught with a sliding click. He let the handle go with a showman's regret. "Have it your way." He waved his hand and her window smeared open, punctured by the Flow. Tender walked toward it.

"If you change your mind, come find me." His voice lilted, almost mocking. "When the time is right."

She watched the Flow slip closed behind him, her window coalescing back to normal and the volatile feeling passing like rain. Consuela's hand hovered above the door handle but she withdrew it and glanced at herself in the mirror, half wanting V to be there, spying, half wanting to privately convince herself she'd done the right thing.

She searched the reflection of her eyes, but she found no answers there.

She heard Sissy's crying through the door, artless and broken. Consuela hesitated, not wanting to intrude on grief—she thought of mourning as a private thing done with wringing hands and tugging hair. She didn't know Sissy well enough for that. But she still had to tell her Abacus was out and that she'd left a message. Correction: Tender left the message. She only hoped it said what she'd told him to say.

She was conscious of lurking outside the door.

Knocking cautiously, Consuela let herself in. There was only splintered crying. She had no idea that Sissy had been so close to this guy, Nikki.

The Watcher's chair was empty and the sounds came from around a corner. Consuela crept carefully past the bookshelves, noticing the great, gaping hole where the dictionary had been. She was somewhat prepared when she found Sissy on the floor, propped up against the wainscoting, her hair hanging down over her dripping face and the bottle clutched in her hand. The Watcher sniffled thickly, limp tremors shaking her body. She looked like a marionette with all its strings cut.

"Sissy?" Consuela got down on her hands and knees and touched the girl's shoulder. Her face came up—full and whole, but red and swollen. Consuela could see the pink on the insides of her lids, loose around bloodshot eyes.

"Bones?" Sissy said, then burst into fresh tears, pulling Consuela into an awkward hug. Consuela tried to comfort Sissy's raw hysteria with a confused sort of patting. Sissy was damp and smelled like a warm chemical spill.

Consuela tucked her chin over Sissy's skull and rocked her almost roughly, like a kind slap to clear the senses. She couldn't help thinking that both Wish and V were better at this.

"Shh," she said helplessly. "Shh. Shh."

"N-n-n—" Sissy burbled, trying to speak. Her crying was so hard it choked her. She gagged.

"What is it?" Consuela felt the uneasiness return. She had an icy premonition. "This isn't about Nikki." It wasn't even a question. Sissy shook her head violently. The bottle thunked against the carpet with mute anger.

Consuela couldn't feel her hands. *Isn't that weird?* In her own skin, she should feel everything, but the world had gone dead and cold in a sort of slow-motion moment. She felt that she knew the answer even before asking, but she had to say it. She had to hear it said out loud.

"Who?" she asked quietly.

"YEHUDAH!" Sissy screamed, fell sideways, and vomited on the floor. Consuela grabbed her shoulder and tried to hold back her hair, like the time after Allison tried chugging her brother's beer. Consuela's hands shook along with Sissy's and the two of them crouched over the acidic puddle of puke.

Sissy convulsed weakly in three quick bursts, but nothing more came up. She cried louder through a cracking throat.

"They killed him!" she spat at the floor. "They killed Yehudah!"

Consuela went all pins and needles. "They who?"

"It! Him! Her! They!" Sissy wailed. "I don't know!"

"Sissy . . ." Consuela pleaded.

"Killed him!" she cried. "Killed Nikki! Someone's out there killing us!"

Consuela tugged her friend sideways, away from the mess, scooting them across the floor. She snagged a box of everlasting tissues and pressed a handful against Sissy's blue eyes. Her tremors were contagious. Consuela could feel them in her chest.

Tender?

"Yehudah's dead?" Consuela repeated, thinking of the dark-haired boy on the chair and the smell of baby powder. He was too nice to be dead.

"They—" Sissy stumbled over the words as her eyes rolled; her tear ducts failed her, although her eyes still shone in the recessed light. "They chopped him into bits. You wouldn't know it was him except . . ." She shuddered. "Except they left his two fingers together, intact, on the floor." She dry-heaved against Consuela, whose heart beat like a train.

"Oh God," Consuela stammered, surprising tears filling her eyes.

// *TenderTenderTender* // echoed in her head. *Really? Tender? But then, why didn't he kill me? He even showed me the way home . . .* She remembered Tender feeding on the hallway floor. Panic lurched. *Or did he?*

"How could they have gotten him?" Sissy babbled helplessly. Her breath sounded like a stick dragged across a picket fence. "His wards were impenetrable. No one could pierce them in either world. Killian O'Shea was proof of that."

Consuela shook her head, ignoring her own fear, trying to wrap her brain around someone being there one moment and not the next. She knew it happened but not that it could be happening now. She squeezed Sissy's shoulders.

"Maybe he was like Wish," Consuela said slowly. "Maybe he could only do things for others, but not for himself."

"No," Sissy said. "He warded the two of us dozens of times . . . so we could talk together." She wiped her face with her hands and the wad of Kleenex. "It's the only way he would speak with me *unchaperoned*." Something about the way she said the word brought fresh tears to her worn eyes, capillary pink against the blue. Consuela wondered why there'd been no wards between her and the Yad that one time at the O'Sheas'. As Bones, was she no longer considered female? Or human? Or alive?

He'd called her an Angel of God.

"Wish," Sissy whispered urgently. "Did V find Wish? Did you tell Abacus?"

"No," she confessed. She'd found Tender instead. *Was Abacus even alive?* "I left a message."

"We have to find them," Sissy hissed, trying to get up. "We have to get Maddy . . ."

"Wait." Consuela got her own feet beneath her and tried to push-pull Sissy up. It wasn't easy, even with her weighing a good forty pounds more than her friend.

"Come on," Consuela urged. "Let's get you cleaned up first."

She took Sissy under the shoulder and threaded their hands together, brown and white fingers tangled like stripes. Consuela pushed through the door, ignoring the stink of fear and puke, and stepped purposefully through the blur of the Flow. One, two, three, four. The last step swirled into her bedroom, welcoming them with its clean-cotton smell. She turned a sharp right as they stumbled against the carpet.

Pulling her friend into the cloudy warmth of lavender steam, Consuela lowered her onto the shower floor clothes and all—and cranked the water on.

Sissy sprawled on the tile, limp and surrendering, mewing weak protest behind a lengthening curtain of wet hair. Consuela watched her gentle curls turn into a sheet of tarnished gold, the steam obscuring her tragic face. This strange, melted person looked nothing like the Watcher. Grief shrank Sissy like a deflated balloon.

Consuela grabbed a couple of ibuprofen and a glass of cool water, glaring once at the mirror above the sink, filmed in mourning gray. She sat on the edge of the bathtub, thinking, until Sissy showed signs of being uncomfortable in wet clothes.

Shutting off the water, she wrapped Sissy in a thick bath sheet, tight as a hug.

"Take these," Consuela instructed. Sissy did as she was told, swallowing both pills and draining the glass in long sips. "Now, up." Consuela yanked her to standing and brought her over to the bed. Shivering and silent, Sissy flumped hard. Springs creaked. Consuela grabbed Sissy's ankles and swung her legs sideways, feeling a sickening pliancy as her supernatural joints gave way, almost leaving her delicate, white feet on the floor. Consuela switched her grip as she tucked Sissy into bed, towels and all. For a moment, she wanted to huddle on the floor and be a loyal friend; but that would be hiding from the monsters outside her bed. Consuela wasn't going to hide.

She pushed wet hair out of Sissy's face. There was a dark patch like raccoon shadows over her eyes.

"You stay here and rest. I'll go," Consuela said. "I'll tell the others. I'll be back soon."

Sissy's eyes moved a tick to the left and focused. "Be careful," she said.

"Don't worry."

It was a nothing sort of thing to say, but there was nothing more to say. Nikki was dead. Yehudah was dead. Abacus might be dead. And death in the Flow was real.

Consuela left her room, plowing through the Flow, reaching out to find V. It was like stretching her arm outward, far beyond her body, and grabbing him by the shirt collar, the rest of her body following.

She found him in a pink room full of ruffles and white

furniture. Most of it looked pristine, but the edges were curled black. There were blackened holes on the blanket and in the carpet, like pockmarks on the floor. The curtains ended in shriveled, crusty squiggles and the teddy bear's fur was singed in curly, tight nubs. Small piles of ashes and smears on the desk whispered of things that once were or might have been. The burns tainted things, like the sound of a slowly-turned jack-in-the-box, making everything dark and tinny and wrong.

V turned when she came upon him in a rush. He was relieved and embarrassed when he saw that it was her.

"You found me," he said.

She hit him with the flat of her hands, hard against the solid slab of his chest.

"You!" she accused. "You suspected! You *knew*! And you didn't say anything!" she shouted, surprising them both.

"What . . . ?" he said, half blocking her blows.

"You didn't say *anything* and now they're *dead*!" Consuela screamed. "They're dead, V! Dead!"

"What?!" V shouted, his voice bigger than hers. "Who's dead? Tender?"

The name enraged her. *Now* he could say it? When it was far too late? "You're as bad as him!" she screamed. *"YOU'RE AS BAD AS HIM!"*

Shaking his head, V ignored the assault. "Who was it?"

"The Yad," Consuela said, her arms flopping down. "Yehudah is dead."

// *Yad? No!* //

V staggered, looking wild. She punched him again. The symphonic echo died.

"I can still *hear you!*" Consuela cried, hitting herself in the chest with rigid fingers. "Right here! Right HERE! Heart to heart—soul to soul—'Know thyself,' V! I can hear you!" She was crying, the words coming in stabs. "I can't stop hearing you!"

// *No . . .* //

"Bones," he started, then switched. "Consuela . . ."

"I *trusted* you," she hissed. "I trusted you with everything! I trusted you to get me home. I trusted you to keep us safe. I thought that you . . ." She shook her head, the tears unhindered and unheeded. Consuela shuddered, mortified to admit what she'd felt on the closet floor.

She'd been V's *assignment*! That was it. Nothing more than his embarrassing failure. He wasn't her angel any more than she'd been that drunken woman's dream. Consuela didn't want that to be all it was, but it was.

That was all there was.

The weak, vulnerable feeling warped into a tight ball of fury. V didn't care about *her*—not like that. He had just been compelled to help keep her alive. Get her back. Anything he did could be part of his compulsion, creating the maximum chance of successful completion by whatever was pulling their strings in the Flow. He was a tool. A puppet. A player. A fraud. And she, the idiot dreamer, had believed him.

She was inhumanly glad that she didn't have a violin-voice speaking her thoughts aloud.

"Don't," he whispered.

Anger mixed with embarrassment and curdled. She drew her hands into fists.

"You don't get to tell me what to do anymore!" she said.

// No/I can save you/Get you home/Get you back. //

"STOP IT!" Consuela shrieked, flailing her arms. V grabbed her wrists and held on, restraining her pull, her push, her want to tear everything down. She yanked her shoulders and screamed through her teeth. Her hair stuck to her face in salty patches. V held her safely at a distance as frustration and fear somersaulted in her head.

Her anger finally slaked, she fell against him, sobbing— butting his chest with the top of her head, weak and weary and worn. His arms settled around her shoulders.

"I'm sorry," he said.

// Sorry/Sorry/Sorry/Too late!/I'm sorry. //

"Stop being sorry," she murmured.

They stood together in the burnt-rose room. The crisped teddy bear watched them with flat button eyes.

"Tender showed me the way home," Consuela said. "He said I could go. But I didn't."

V stiffened. "Tender can't . . ." The words bumped against each other, as if struggling to be first. "I'm sorry. I don't know what he said, but he can't take you home."

"I know," Consuela said sadly. Remembering her family portrait, she ran the topaz cross along its chain, feeling its tug at her neck. "But he wanted me to think that he could," she said; a part of her still wondered—*hoped?*— that someone would help her get home. That it could be as easy as walking through her bedroom door.

"He wants something," she added.

"He wants out," V answered. "Like you."

She shook her head. "That isn't it. When I asked why didn't he use the door himself, he said that he didn't ever want to go back. It might not have been a real way out, but I heard it in his voice." Tender didn't want his old life. He was after something else. "He said none of you wanted to go back to an ugly life."

V said nothing, hiding while holding her.

"For some of us, that's true," V said.

She shook her head against wondering what kind of

life she'd find, what kind of body she might return to. *It didn't matter—it would be real. It would be home. Mom. Dad. It would be better than here.*

"Did Tender kill Yehudah?" she whispered urgently. "Did he kill Nikki, too?"

V's arms tightened around her, like a knot. // *I don't know what I know . . .* //

"I've suspected Tender was up to something, but I couldn't tell the Watcher," he said carefully. "I had no proof. I still don't. And we can't go around pointing fingers." A twitch cascaded down V's back; Consuela could feel it jumping and jerking under her palms. He cracked his neck. "It's no secret none of us like him much. He's tough to be around because of who he is and what he does. But it's not that." Consuela wasn't sure if she imagined V's arms growing tighter as he talked or how good it felt to be there. She closed her eyes and listened to his voice under her ear. "In here, we only have the things that cross over; we're all we've got. We can't afford to turn on one another."

Consuela pulled back, needing some distance from his intoxicating skin.

"What proof do you need?" she asked.

"Anything. Evidence. Whatever he's doing, he's been planning it for a while. // *I feel it* //," V said, raising his eyes.

209

"Have you noticed that we all leave a trail, like a feeling or a smell? It's how we find one another. // *How I found you/ How you found me.* // It marks where we've gone, where we've been. His is everywhere when something's gone wrong." He wiped his hands on his jeans. "Like a warning you can feel." V massaged the place where she'd hit him, an echo of pain like the tears drying on her face.

// *Tender* //, the violins sang unheard in the room.

Consuela thought back to the last time she'd seen the Yad, and that feeling of forgetting something, left unfinished.

"What is it?" V asked.

"Nothing," she said. "I was just thinking . . . of the compulsion."

She was still raw inside as her mind whirred, the ripple effects of logic boosting her nerves. Consuela stepped up to V, nearly into his chest. "Do you think we can be called to help one another?" she confided. "Does that ever happen in the Flow?"

He stayed within a breath of her, gazing down into her eyes. "I don't know." He hesitated. "But I've felt it . . ."

"For me." She finished the sentence for him.

"For you," V said, and glanced away. He sighed. "I told you that I saw you see me in the mirror," he confessed. "But I never expected . . . // *You would be you.* // *Here.* // // *Now.* // *Bones.* //" The violins sang softly, and faded.

"I don't know what I can do for you here in the Flow," he confessed. His hand moved as if he meant to touch her hair, but he dropped it, rebuffed by an unasked question.

"I was your assignment," Consuela said. "Maybe I'm still your assignment. Maybe what you feel is . . ." She faltered, trying to speak around the tightness in her throat. She met his eyes."

V's face softened. "No," he said. // *No.* // His music held no doubt. "Consuela, I know the difference," he added quietly. "I know what's real." // *I know myself.* // *Consuela.* // *Bones.* //

Shyly, she nodded. One fear down. "Well, then maybe I'm here for a different reason," she murmured. "Because I think I felt something when I last saw Yehudah. When we were at Killian O'Shea's. I thought it was the ward, but maybe it was something else."

V looked intrigued, impressed . . . and maybe a little, what? Disappointed? Jealous? Then memory hit like a slap.

// *The Yad is dead.* //

"You think we should go there?" V asked under the sad lilting of electric strings. Consuela nodded. V took a deep breath. "Fine. When you get there—"

"When *I* get there?" she interrupted.

"I don't know the way," he said. "Crossing through mirrors isn't the same as going through the Flow. So when you get there, open this." He dug in his back pocket and handed her a shiny silver compact of blush. "It was Sissy's," he said with a tight grin. "She said she didn't need it as much as I did."

"I assume she meant the mirror." Consuela tried to laugh, but it stuck in her throat.

V watched as she opened the shiny bit of plastic and ran a finger along the pressed powder's edge. "When we cross over, the image stays," he said softly. "Like a photograph. Everything we last see there comes over here, too—down to the last speck of dust and lost ballpoint pen." He smoothed the mirror closed, pressing the backs of her fingers. It was a gentle gesture, but his eyes were intense.

"Everything here is precious because we can't go back and touch it again. What we bring over is all that we've got, all that we have, including each other," V said. "If we question it, it can undo everything." He squeezed their fingers together, like a promise or a pact. "Are you willing to do this?"

She kept her eyes on his as she clicked the silver case closed.

"Let's go."

WHat happened here?" Consuela asked V as they entered the dim hallway; she knew the floorboards were cold without needing to feel them. The lights were off, the door was open, and all the photos in the hall were gone. It was as if they'd entered an abandoned building, a before-and-after shot of Casa O'Shea.

Consuela had flipped open the compact, expecting to see V's face staring back—like some sort of *Star Trek* gizmo trick—but a rush of color and matter hurricaned out and left V standing next to her, very much whole. It was both unsettling and cool.

"Is this the right place?" she asked aloud.

"It's the right place," V said as he pointed up. The line of blood still burned.

"The ward's still alive even when . . . ?" Consuela couldn't finish.

// *The Yad is not.* // V's heart spoke the seraphim echo that he, himself, couldn't hear. She knew for a fact that he was hurting. V knew the Yad. They had been friends.

Consuela didn't know the Yad well. She hadn't had the chance.

"He's not here," she said, thankful that there wasn't a body or chopped-up bits in the hall. She'd been half afraid of what they'd find, but the place was empty of everything but dust. "No one's here."

// *But I can smell him. He was here.* //

She heard V, but said nothing; the baby-powder scent was all but gone in the empty room. Cardboard boxes labeled with fat black letters littered the floor: WINTER CLOTHES, TOYS, SAFETY STUFF, LINENS/DRAPES. The walls were bare and the drawers were empty. Everything except the boxes, a roll of packing tape, and the large furniture was gone. The hardwood crib in the corner of the room still burned with flickering, dark fire. Neither of the Yad's wards had been broken, but the baby and his family were gone.

V walked around the room on the empty carpet. "So? Anything?" he asked.

She didn't feel anything, but she was piecing together what she could see.

"They're moving," Consuela said. "And it was unexpected."

V frowned. "How can you tell?"

"Ever had to move a whole house?" She pointed at the boxes, half of which had yet to be taped shut. "It takes forever. This is happening quickly and missing important bits." She pointed at the crib. "Where does Killian sleep?"

"In another crib, somewhere else," V concluded.

"Somewhere unprotected." Consuela said, examining the boxes. "This looks like it's a second load of stuff. The first went out already; clothes, diapers . . ." She glanced at the open box labeled TOYS and a thought slid into place. "It's not his mom."

V peered into the box full of bright-colored junk. "What?"

Consuela felt the chill like a sudden drop in temperature. "Killian's mom didn't pack this," she said. "The stuffed animals and blankets are all tossed in. A mom . . ." She remembered when her family moved to Illinois how her mother had packed every one of her toys with blankets so they wouldn't break, how each of her glass figurines had to be excavated carefully from bubble wrap and towels. Her room had taken the longest to pack because her mom kept telling her stories about every little thing. Consuela's fingers stroked the satiny edge of a yellow blanket.

"Moms like to linger over sentimental stuff," she said softly. "They pack those things with extra care. Baby things, especially."

"You sound as if you know something about it," V observed.

She shrugged and said, "I've got a mom." Her voice cracked.

V coughed uncomfortably. "So the O'Sheas are moving, Mom isn't doing the packing, and the Yad is dead." He waved an open palm at the undone room. "If there's something else here, I don't see it."

"Me either," Consuela admitted. She had no other ideas. She felt for the stale traces of any of them being here, but it wasn't something she could sense. The black lines of blood shone like a command: *Protect them.*

She was an Angel of God, after all.

"Maybe we should ask Sissy where the O'Sheas are going," Consuela said. "It might be good to give her something to do."

"Good idea," V said quietly as he stared at the crib.

// His body's somewhere. // Yad. // It's not fair! // I should have been there/done something . . . //

Consuela self-consciously waved a cardboard flap closed. She could feel the pain spilling off V in waves, rippling through the air. V trembled with a sadness he couldn't express. Not with her here.

"Okay," she said, and walked quickly past him, her passage brushing the black curls from his eyes like a blown kiss.

"I'm sorry," she said.

V nodded and rubbed a hand over his face, massaging the deep shine in his eyes.

He turned away. She turned away. She thought that maybe this was why guys needed someone like Nikki, someone to cry for them when they could not.

Consuela left to find her next grieving friend.

chapter eleven

"Modern man likes to pretend that his thinking is wide-awake. But this wide-awake thinking has led us into the mazes of a nightmare in which the torture chambers are endlessly repeated in the mirrors of reason."

—OCTAVIO PAZ

It was like stepping into an old movie or a bad museum trick. *Animatronics,* Tender thought, *with hidden wiring and lights.* He didn't like things that tried to look alive when they weren't.

Joseph Crow looked like the Ken doll of the Indians. *No way he really looks like that,* Tender figured. Then again, none of them did. Except Wish. *Abe's too stupid to take anything for himself.*

The large man stood bared to the waist, hairless and tan, wearing body piercings and well-worn Levi's jeans.

The jeans looked like they'd gone through the desert, been run over by a pickup truck, and dried while worn after the rain. They were the jeans every other male trouser wanted to be. Those were Joseph Crow's only clothes.

It was hot. *How can he have a fire going in here?* Tender wiped sweat from his eyes and stared at the small hole around the rough, center post. *Air. Fresh air. Hot. I can't breathe! The bastard did this on purpose, dammit.*

"I came to talk," Tender said to Joseph Crow, watching the smoke curl up and out, thinking, *If anyone's escaping, it's going to be me.*

Joseph Crow didn't turn around, which irked him. The giant Native American stared into a corner at a six-pack of cheap beer. The cans had the untouched look of having always been there. Joseph Crow kept staring. Tender thought if this was a contest, the beer might be winning.

"Going to offer me a drink?" he asked.

The big man finally said something: "No."

Tender shrugged and took a step closer. "I have something to ask you."

"No one's keeping you from asking." Joseph said it like a challenge. The silver barbell pierced above his Adam's apple bobbed as he talked. Joseph Crow threw a bundle of gray twigs into the fire and the place grew smoky-sweet.

"Someone's killing in the Flow," Tender said. "Folks are dying."

Joseph said, "I've heard," not making it clear whether he had heard about it secondhand or that he'd overheard it done. The ambiguity made Tender nervous, despite his cocksure grin.

"Do you care?" Tender asked.

Joseph glared at him. "Do you?" From under the wink of two hoops through his left eyebrow, Joseph's eyes were darker than brown.

Tender, annoyed and surprised, said, "Of course I care." He wiped his limp bangs angrily from his face. "I wouldn't be here in your goddamn wigwam if I didn't. How about you?" he accused. "You give a damn?"

Joseph cocked his head sideways as he scratched absently at his chest. There were rough patches of discolored scarring, an inch above each pierced nipple, which Tender thought was pretty homo if he stared at them too long. He kept his eyes up.

"I do," Joseph said finally. "I give exactly one damn." He glared again, rubbing the stud in his ear and fingering its smooth green stone. "Care to guess whose?"

Tender frowned and slipped a hand through hidden ooze and over the hilt.

"Are you threatening me, Red Man?"

He said only, "I am Joseph Crow."

It was not a correction, or another veiled threat; it was as if the bare-chested man were summoning courage or something bigger. More. Tender drew out his pitted sword and held it between him and the flames. Black sludge ran, secreting out the blade's pores to hiss, bubbling, onto the hot coals. The smell in the tent changed from white sage to sick.

Joseph held up two shriveled things on strings: shrunken claws—eagle talons—that he waved above the smoke. Raising his head, he tipped back his chin, nostrils flaring with a deep inhale. He pierced the black points through the scars on both breasts.

He screamed without surprise, a rictus of the familiar, a groan of endurance. Tender stepped back. The sharp nails fished around, jutting points of tented flesh. Meat hooks beneath the skin. They burst like bloodworms out of Joseph Crow's chest.

The wounds poured, bleeding freely. Joseph's eyes rolled back in his head as he swayed in pain, or ecstasy, or both.

As he leaned back, the thongs attaching pole to claws to skin pulled taut. Belt hooks of chest flesh yawned, but held him upright. Tender could see Joseph's black gums against his gnashing white teeth.

"I am Joseph Crow."

Each word pushed a fresh cough of blood onto his chest, streaming to slide under his belt and soak into his jeans. He spread his arms back as if he might fall; a spectral image superimposed itself, flaring out of the smoke. The slicked-back hair smoothed into a crest of feathers, his bear chest blending into stag legs. Hawk eyes blinked, cat-reflective, and huge black wings flapped for balance, whipping through the wan image of arms.

Wind and sparks and stinging ash beat at Tender, who shielded his eyes with one hand.

"*I am Joseph Crow*"—the creature's voice rolled like thunder—"*and all that I am may oppose you here.*"

Tender blinked against the rain of debris. Bits of stone and dirt pelted the sword and stuck.

"Screw this," he muttered, and lowered his blade, sliding it back into its sheath and retreating from the totem knight.

Tender blew through the hide walls as if they were mist, wondering whether he was as afraid or if he'd just seen too many animals at once, like at the zoo.

He hated the zoo, what he remembered of it. No one ever knew how many bars there were on each cage, no one had even bothered to count. Animals behind bars, pacing, stinking . . . contained. Uncontrollable. Intolerable.

Tender knew all about cages.

He'd passed through eight other outcrops in the Flow before he realized his mistake. "Damn," Tender muttered. Joseph Crow had seen the sword. Tender had left the job undone and he'd most likely be barred from Joseph's part of the Flow. It was only a matter of time before the freak job squealed to Sissy. He couldn't let that happen.

Fortunately, Joe would need time to recover. He wouldn't be able to get a message out until then. Tender had other alternatives for just such an occasion and he'd been saving one for a rainy day.

Tender smiled to himself. He was actually looking forward to this . . .

SHe looked better. One eye swollen, the other somewhere hidden, the Watcher stared resolutely at the computer screen, fingers flying over the keys. The cold blue light outlined Sissy's face, making her look more skeletal than Consuela usually did. After the initial fear at finding her bedroom empty, Consuela found Sissy in her dark office, working. Sissy had turned off the lights, plunging the wide basement room into mourning.

"I'm back," Consuela whispered.

"I know," Sissy said. "You're safe?"

"I am."

"Good," she said with an ember of warmth. "Find anything?"

The question was an uncomfortable one. What could she say?

"Maybe," Consuela admitted. "No hints as to what happened, but V and I noticed that Killian's family had gone."

Sissy stopped typing and spoke into her shoulder without turning around.

"Why did you go to the O'Sheas'?" she asked.

Consuela slid into her usual chair, trying to catch Sissy's one eye. They said nothing about what had happened between them; it was as if the incident hadn't happened at all and was verboten to speak of now. That hurt and Consuela moved around it uncomfortably.

"It was the last place I'd seen the Yad," she said uneasily. "I thought, maybe, there'd be . . . I don't know. Something." All her words were suddenly awkward, fragile. "The O'Sheas are moving."

"Correction," said Sissy. "Killian is moving. His parents both mysteriously died in their sleep. The police suspect carbon monoxide poisoning, but that wouldn't account for little Killian being found safe and sound the next morning. There's going to be an insurance investigation." She sounded quivery and tired, the afterburn of grief. "I doubt they're going to find that there was a protective ward drawn around his crib." She swept her flawless hair back from her cheek; it had dried in enviable, sculpted curls. "He's going to live with his legal guardians and I'll have to track him down again. Without the Yad's wards . . ." A sniffle threatened to stutter her sentence, but she got it under control. "Killian's vulnerable and Yehudah knew it."

Consuela nodded. "I saw the note. Why one hundred twenty-six?"

"Seven times eighteen," Sissy said automatically. "A lot of his power was based on Hebraic numerology. It's not unusual; Abacus works on similar principles, although Chang's specialty is crunching numbers to calculate probability." Consuela squirmed. Unaware, Sissy continued to find comfort in talking, her words growing rapid as her single eye burned. "He can triangulate our assignments back in the real world—mathematically predict events and outcomes—all by finding the inherent significance of numbers. Yehudah said everything has a sum since every letter in Hebrew has its own numeric value." She paused, then recited: "Know the name, know its number, know the thing."

Sissy watched her own fingers tap the keys as if they were separate, living things. "The word for 'life' in

Hebrew is *chai*," she said. "The two letters that spell it are numbers eight and ten. Eight plus ten is eighteen. Eighteen equals 'life.'" Sissy made an effort to look Consuela squarely in the face. "I'm eighteen. Doing one hundred and twenty six separate wards would increase the protective life force by a sacred number. The Yad figured that it would make Killian's room impenetrable from harm." She sounded defeated.

"Even from carbon monoxide poisoning," Consuela said. "It saved the boy's life."

"But not his own." Sissy's face grew hard again, the harsh light carving deep, ugly lines by her mouth. "Yehudah suspected something. That's why he went to increase the wards." She swiveled her seat back and forth. "Maybe something that was meant for Killian got his parents instead?" she mused. "Maybe it got Yehudah or maybe it's been after us all along."

Consuela fidgeted in her chair. Should she tell Sissy about Tender? What could she say? V was right—without proof, accusing Tender would just add paranoia. If he was trying to get rid of them, one by one, why did he try to get Consuela to leave voluntarily? Was Tender really capable of *killing* people? She didn't think so. She was caught in silent dread.

Sissy picked up her phone and slammed it down. "I

wish Abacus would answer already," she said. "I'm worried . . ." She let the rest drift off, unspoken. Consuela knew what she was thinking; she herself had been thinking the same thing. *What if Abacus couldn't answer?*

Sissy yawned and knuckled her empty socket. "Oh God, I've *got* to collapse," she said. "I just don't want to dream."

Consuela gave her shoulder a small squeeze.

"Don't drink," she said. "At least, don't drink alone." Consuela tried to inject a little humor as she headed for the door. "I'll be back soon and we can play angels again."

Sissy watched her go. "You'd better."

Consuela nodded and closed the door.

tHERE was a knock on the inside of her bathroom.

"May I come in?"

It was V. Consuela looked up from the mess on her floor. "Sure."

He walked over to Consuela, who was hunched over a pile of papers, books, pens, pins, paper clips, binders, notebooks, mugs, stray photos, bookmarks, string, and loose gadgets. She was inspecting a screwdriver.

"What are you doing?" he asked.

Consuela put the tool down. "Trying to figure out what's the one thing I have that can cross over," she said. "It was one of the last things the Yad told me about, and I thought that I should at least know what mine was." She played with the topaz cross on its chain. She'd hoped that the necklace would have been the key—somehow linking her back to her world, her parents—but so far, nothing. She let it fall against her skin. It felt like her last, desperate attempt to go back was slipping through her fingers.

"Can you take me home?" she whispered.

V sighed. "If I could, right this moment, I would. You know I would."

She stared at the screwdriver. "I told Sissy about the O'Sheas, but she already knew. Now she thinks that something was after Killian and got the parents or the Yad instead." Consuela shook her head sadly. "I didn't know what to say."

V nodded. "I understand," he said as he settled himself onto her pink carpet, fiddling with a red paper clip. "I had an interesting conversation with Joseph Crow," he said darkly. The metallic hum trilled, // *Eerie/Ominous/ Saying nothing* //, while his true voice continued, "I can't find Wish. Sissy couldn't find Maddy. Abacus is out somewhere," he said, nodding to her. "The Watcher's a wreck and Nikki . . ." V cast his eyes to the ceiling. She heard it before he said it.

// Nikki's dead. //

"Nikki's dead," he said, taking the screwdriver from her hand. "But you're safe," he concluded, his accompaniment adding, *// There's still time. //*

Consuela was too aware of his fingers on hers. Was it alarm or excitement that made her heart jump? *It didn't mean anything!* She swore he could see the pulse beating in her wrist. When had she become such a vulnerable, fleshy thing?

He tugged her to stand. "Come on," he said. "I came to show you something and I wanted to see what you think."

"Why me?" Consuela asked.

V grimaced. "Because you seem pretty smart until you say dumb things like that," he retorted.

Her voice flatlined. "'Excuse me?"

"Please tell me you're not one of those girls who thinks they're stupid or pretends to be so just they can hear compliments all day long," he shot back.

Consuela arched her eyebrows, taking back her hand. "Issues much?" she said.

V let go, surprised. "Sorry," he said. "Pet peeve. I have four sisters and they all play dumb. It isn't cute." She rubbed her wrist where he had touched it.

He had the grace to look ashamed, then glanced over

his wide shoulder at her. "You have any brothers or sisters?" he asked.

"Nope," Consuela said, sliding her cross on its chain. "Just my mom, dad, and me."

"Well, you're lucky," he said roughly. "At least there's not as many to miss."

He stopped in front of her full-length mirror and offered his hand, which she took with a boldness that was becoming familiar. "Now keep in contact," he advised. "Don't let go."

And with that, he stepped them through the mirror and beyond.

She'd hoped to see what was in the rumored Mirror Realm, but stumbled, surprised, into a blindingly bright hall with hardly a gasp in between.

They'd exited on the flip side of a large looking glass that had been left propped by a metal door. The floor was anonymous linoleum tile. The door was industrial-grade with a little glass window, crisscrossed with wire. Consuela peered through it, seeing nothing but white.

"Where are we?" she asked.

"I think it's Tender's," V said quietly. "Tender's place in the Flow." They exchanged looks. Consuela opened the door.

Instead of a room, there was a vacuum cloud—a

formless, white nothingness and a chair. It was a cheap chair, metal-framed and plastic-cushioned, the exact bruised-red-orange color of summer tomatoes. The seat was scuffed a little with a slight tear on one corner; a few plastic threads stuck out of an L-shaped hole. Consuela nudged it; it moved easily even though she had the impression that it should have been bolted to the floor.

V circled it warily, trying to make out anything in the eerie dreamscape.

"This is weird," he muttered in his low bass.

// *Unusual.* // *Creepy.* // the violins trilled.

"Really?" Consuela said. "It doesn't seem much weirder than Abacus's place."

"That's different," V said. "Abacus made it that way once he was here; 'the power of possibility,' he called it. He was always a little out there. But when we first come over, the scene freezes in exactly the same way as we left it, down to the dust. I don't see how anything could be like this in the real world."

"Maybe he made this?" Consuela frowned again, thinking of chairs. "He feeds on the Flow," she said. "And he can make things appear."

"He eats," V said, still searching. "And he makes illusions. This is real." He knocked the chair. "Or, as real as it ever was, which is why this doesn't make sense."

She paused, not wanting to argue, but she kept thinking about Quantum—Abacus had made something real out of the Flow. And Tender worked closely with Abacus. If Tender could make something real, what might it be?

V crossed his arms in frustration. "It's not even like a fog machine," he complained, and waved his hand through the air, but nothing swirled or moved. "See?" V kept his hands out like feelers. "But it still *smells* like him—feels like him—traces of it, anyway. Can you sense it?"

Consuela tried to. "No. Sorry." She stood in front of the chair again, the one solid thing in the vaporous room. She stroked the frame, aluminum and cool.

"There's only one thing for it," she said simply. "We'll have to try it out." Consuela gestured to V. "You want to?"

// No. //

"Do you?" // Bones. // Both voices were terrified.

She gathered the strength from her mother-of-pearl soul.

"I guess I will," she said, and before she could hesitate, sat.

// DON'T! //

The last thread of electric warning hung in the air.

Consuela waited, but she only sat in a slightly creaky, uncomfortable chair surrounded by nothing in all directions. She blinked up at V.

"Oh well," she said. "I guess that was pointless."

// Daring. // Brave. //

The correction hung between them. She inspected

231

her cuticles in order not to betray that she kept overhearing his innermost thoughts. He found her brave. That was something. Consuela tried a smile, but his next unsung word stopped her.

// *Beautiful,* // he all but said.

She froze, thoughts reeling. *How could someone like V find me beautiful? Okay, maybe as Bones . . .* She wouldn't deny that in her Flow form she was amazing—even Tender thought so—*but now? Like this?* V was something from a magazine ad, someone for tweens to fawn over at a comfortable, glossy distance.

But she couldn't correct him without admitting what she'd heard. And, knowing that it was his secret voice, what he said was irrefutably true.

Her heart beat thick in her throat. Was it really him or just a compulsion of the Flow? Did he even know what he was feeling? Thinking? Did she?

V stared at her. Consuela, wide-eyed, stared back.

"See anything?" he prompted.

"What? Oh!" Flustered, she blushed and was completely surprised when she did, in fact, see something.

"Wait a minute . . ." she said. Her vision telescoped down, zooming to focus on a pen. She shifted her eyes— the pen disappeared, replaced by a book nearby. She could still see the barest ballpoint tip.

Consuela tilted her head to read the title on the hardcover spine: *Faust*. She looked back to the first spot; the book had disappeared and the pen was back. The faux-wood grain beneath them remained the same. Consuela figured out that she could only spy a four-inch circle of space at a time.

She slowly discovered details, a jigsaw-puzzle picture, enough to piece together that there was a small side table on which there was a book, a pen and reading glasses, an adjustable lamp, a tin of mints, and an otherwise completely unnoteworthy smear of something wet leading up to a take-out coffee cup. TALBOT was handwritten on the cup in black marker. When she saw the plastic lid, the coffee smell hit her with the force of a truck.

Consuela swooned and gagged under the zero-to-eighty French roast filling her nose to the tear ducts and her mouth to the teeth. She pitched forward in the chair. V dove to catch her shoulders.

"Bones?"

At first she wasn't sure which of his voices had spoken. As she blinked back the tears, she thought, maybe, both.

Consuela shook her head and clucked her tongue against the phantom taste. "I'm fine," she said, incredibly aware of V's hands on her body. She wanted to move closer, but pulled herself back.

"Wow," she said, covering the moment.

"What happened?" V asked.

"Coffee." She described the smell as best she could as V tucked his hands into his back pockets.

"Sensory memory," he said quietly. "I've heard of it." Consuela realized she was still reliving the feel of V's hands on her skin, her own sensory memory. He'd also called her brave and beautiful. It was hard to think straight after that.

She glanced back at the chair. Was this really how it had been when Tender crossed over? What had Tender's life been like to be frozen like this?

Consuela reached out for the space that should have held the table and the glasses and the copy of *Faust*, but she walked clear through the white nothingness. She reconsidered the chair, alone on the floor.

"We should tell Sissy," she said.

"The Watcher," V corrected.

"The Watcher." Consuela groaned. "Fine. We should talk to her. She can find where this is. She wanted to get Maddy and . . ." She swooned as her vision plummeted out of focus. V grabbed her again. The movement was less romantic than strong.

"You okay?"

"What?" It hit her like the coffee truck. Her head spun and she all but fell onto the floor. V was there, his arms holding her up. The world was impossibly crooked.

She tried saying something, but the words came out up-side down.

"Hold on," he said, and physically lifted her up, cra-dling Consuela in his arms like he was some sort of Italian Prince Charming. She thought he was probably breaking his back.

"I can . . ." she slurred.

"You can't," V corrected, and sliced them through the ornate mirror in the hall. Her head kept spinning even as he crossed her room and laid her down on the bed, set-tling her softly onto her pillow, where she felt she'd keep sinking into layers of sleep. The pillow was cold and still slightly damp from Sissy's towel.

"Consuela," he whispered, brushing back her hair. His lips didn't say: // *I'll watch over you.* //

She thought she'd said his name, but realized she was already dreaming her dream.

It was dark, purple-dark. The hallway was lined with tall candles and bouquets of autumn blooms. Consuela could see the dancers in their places, hopping and swaying through their cotton-quiet songs. The men in their flames, the women in their flowers, their skeletons weaving poetry their lips could no longer speak.

It was an eerily beautiful sight.

Knowing the door was there, knowing it would end this scene, Consuela ignored it and bent to watch the tiny dancers. She searched for the old *calavera* with the impossible mustache and the brushed-black sombrero, finding him gentlemanly and oddly fetching in his silver-threaded suit. He was on his wax perch halfway down the hall, stamping his shiny boots as if he were big enough to be the only angel dancing atop of his white-hot pin.

He spun for her. Cavorted. Bowed. Brandishing his sombrero like a bullfighter's cape, he swept it grandly in a circle, as if daring her to dance.

Seized by a mischievous impulse, Consuela licked the tip of her finger and plunged it through the flame.

Color exploded like tinsel and paper flowers. Music swelled to life—driving guitars, clacking maracas, and the pleading whine of trumpets—heartbreakingly clear and beautiful. The noble skeleton dancer appeared, full-scale, taking one of her hands in his and placing a guiding palm at her hip. He held her like a grandparent, both proud and frail; Consuela fell into his steps, feeling that she should be in her lace-trimmed *quinceañera* dress with satin ribbons in her hair.

The fiesta burst loud and hot and bright all around them, but he held her protectively through the steps of the dance that popped beneath their feet like coals. Strings of *papel picado* swayed overhead, paper cutouts hanging like portraits in garish hot pink, purple, orange, and green. He pulled her hand up into an expert twirl, handing Consuela to another dancer with a tip of his incredible hat.

A female *calavera* hooked an ulna to Consuela's waist, pulling her wrist flat against where the woman's belly ought to have been. The dancer wore a blazing red gown ruffled in stiff, black lace, a tight bun of hair pinned to the nape of her neck with a tortoiseshell comb. She laughed as they spun, teeth chattering like dice in a cup, before whirling away, clapping her hands over her head, inviting Consuela to do the same. Dance with the dead. Her partner curtsied, leaving Consuela with the impression of plucked, hawkish eyebrows arching up and away.

Consuela swung wildly with young men in dapper kerchiefs and minced daintily with a woman in a tight, fitted dress and an enormous Victorian hat with silk flowers and little, stuffed birds. Consuela tried matching steps with a stooped man in a voluminous, stained poncho and a weather-beaten hat. He had one hand wrapped around a bottle of tequila as he repeatedly pumped his trigger finger, unloading explosive blasts of memory into the air. He leered at her as she whirled away; Consuela noticed that several of his yellowed teeth were missing.

A tall skeleton in a silk tuxedo pressed close against

her, a lit cigarette between his teeth flashing like a fire-fly by her head. A trio of short, squat women encircled her with their hands on their hips, swaying with their shoulders; the fringe of their shawls mimicking batting eyelashes. A child in multilayered skirts and a wreath of paper flowers held Consuela's fingertips and twirled in careful circles until she grew dizzy and fell down. The little girl laughed like a windup toy. Consuela laughed, too, and helped her up. Her tiny party shoes *tap-tap-tapped* away to cuddle against her mother's lap.

And then she was there.

"Grandma," Consuela breathed.

Grandma Celina's skeleton gathered Consuela gently in her arms—the smell of her, like rose water and melons, filled Consuela's memory with sweet, warm, and loving things. Consuela's eyes swam with happy tears and she laughed into what little space hadn't been filled with music and tobacco and clapping.

Grandma Celina still gave the impression of being heavy and solid, flesh packed invisibly onto her bones. She held Consuela's hands as if she were a bird in flight and they danced, their hips and feet mirroring one another, embracing arm in arm. Consuela couldn't take her eyes from the shiny gold cross, the favorite coral brooch, or the rosary wrapped around her grandmother's wrist that she'd last seen buried with her grandma in the earth. It was so good to be with her now, so good to be with family, dozens of generations, hundreds of years . . . so good—*so good!*—to dance, reunited, to be whole once again. Consuela didn't want it to ever ever end.

But Grandma brought her to the midnight door. She mimed the motions, urging Consuela to grasp the handle, to open the door, to step through. Consuela resisted.

"No, Grandma," she whispered. "I want to stay here with you."

The expressionless skull seemed to soften, capturing the forgotten-yet-familiar gesture, cupping her face like a drinking glass and pressing cheek to cheek. The bone was warm against Consuela's cool skin. The moment was so invitingly real, if Consuela closed her eyes, she could see her grandmother's face clearly—full of wrinkles, laugh lines, and dove-gray hair sprayed in place with Aqua Net.

Her grandmother turned Consuela's chin to look upon the shadow door. Purpled layers blossomed outward, revealing a Gypsy's glimpse of a faraway place. The image sharpened. Consuela's heart stopped.

Mom and Dad sat on a picnic blanket weighted down with picture frames; a huge wicker basket lay open at their feet. They were laughing, smiling, waving hello to other people as Dad cranked a corkscrew into a bottle and Mom lit citronella candles with a thin butane lighter.

Consuela watched as they hugged each other close, her father whispering something around the chewed end of his cigar. She could almost smell the burned-cherry smoke, almost taste her mother's roast chicken and the creamy potato salad with dill. There was even a pitcher of tart lemon iced tea—her favorite—beading a little with ice-cubed sweat. She saw three paper plates, three plastic cups, and three folded fabric napkins that matched the basket set. But she was here. *Did they notice? Did they care?* Consuela held out a hand as if to grab the pitcher, but it was too far away.

It hurts. She felt it. *It hurts to be this far away!*

She didn't belong here. Not yet.

I'm not dead! Mom? Dad? I'm here! I'm not gone!

Consuela needed to hold them like an ache, pull them hard against her and feel them close. She needed to be there. She need to be living, breathing, real. It turned her eyes to water and her chest to stone. She felt heavy, sinking—*this is too far away!*

"Grandma . . ." she whispered into the primordial party—food, love, friendship, and music, absorbing and re-forming, spinning into a frenzied pitch. The skeletal hands wrapped in beads were an offering, a benediction, a blessing: *Go on.*

Consuela turned quickly and wrenched open the almost-door, plunging suddenly, deeply, into a familiar quiet.

She was in her room. Her hand on the door handle, she realized that she'd been sleepwalking again. Pushing down, both feeling and hearing the *click-click* of the catch, Consuela hesitated, wondering if this was her last step before death. She wasn't afraid, remembering Grandma's touch and the fiesta of flowers and flame. But she was . . . unfinished. Too restless, yet, to rest in peace. There was too much left to be done. So much more to do.

Mom. Dad.

With a strange, fluttering, all-body sigh, Consuela let go of the door handle and crawled back into bed, returning to herself, asleep.

Only later did she identify the feeling as regret.

V paced the length and breadth of her room, unable to sit still and unwilling to watch her fitful sleep. Without the comfortable distance of silver and glass, it felt like a hospital, like a deathwatch, like he was a voyeur. And if he stared at anything too long, it felt uncomfortably like prying.

V coiled around the worry and the room. If he stopped, he might touch her. If he touched her, he might wake her. If he woke her, he wasn't sure what he would do. It was best to keep moving, trying to ignore the smell of her skin and clean sheets.

He didn't realize the moment when he stopped walking. He didn't realize that he'd marched past her as she twisted sleepily in the bed. He didn't see the mirror or feel the slicing transition as he walked through, answering a familiar pull of invisible threads.

He was gone before he'd ever noticed and no one saw him leave.

Except for a little white mouse that dashed out from under the bed skirt, squeezed itself under the door, and ran into the nothingness with a flick of its tail.

V burst through her bedroom mirror with enough force to make her sit up straight.

"What?" she said, feeling stupid, half awake. "What's happened?"

"It's burning. Joseph Crow's place—it's burning!" V pointed as if it were happening just over his shoulder. Consuela threw back her blankets and stood up, thankfully dressed.

"Can you show me?" she asked. He nodded dumbly and took her hand without asking permission. Moving like a fire engine slicing through traffic, he stepped through the mirror and she forgot to close her eyes.

The Mirror Realm was a split-second slice across her retinas, tricking her with painful splinters of fragmented silver light. She blinked against the pain-tears. Her eyes stung and kept on stinging as they crossed onto the open plain.

Smoke billowed and filled the sky; the singed specks of ash in the air were horribly hot and real. Consuela coughed, squinting against the light and heat as V crushed her hand in his. He felt cold.

The tepee was a huge pillar of white-orange fire capped in black smoke, its triangular insides outlined in ash. Some of the fire had spread to the grass, but they were feeble flames.

V stared. Consuela could see the fire reflected in his eyes, yellow-red-gold obliterating the brown. She didn't have to ask if Joseph Crow had been inside, she already knew. But the expression on V's face—glazed, mouth slightly open—she didn't need a different skin to sense what he felt. *Rapturous. Yearning. Guilty. Afraid.* It was a wordless radiance that bubbled off his skin.

She shared the fear, at least.

"How can this be happening?" she asked. "Things don't . . . do this sort of thing in the Flow. They don't change."

"Nothing affects the Flow but us," V whispered woodenly. "Joseph Crow had a fire because there was a fire in the pit when he crossed over, but it always stays in its circle."

"Like my bathroom stays misty," she said. "How could it spread?"

V took a long time to answer, his eyes never blinking.

"Everything reverts back to its original form unless one of us changes it."

Silence shielded them against the roar and crackle of the fire as it burned. Someone had changed it. Someone from the Flow.

"Will it change back?"

The violin-voice ignored the rush of fiery death song.

// No. //

"Tender . . . ?" Consuela said, trying to make the word fit the crime. "Could Tender do this?"

V's eyes sank to the ground, although their look still smoldered. "No," he said. "No, he can't. Only I can do that."

// I can taste it again // I can smell it everywhere // Change // hot and burning. //

Consuela dropped his hand, forgetting, until that moment, that she'd been holding it.

"What do you mean?" she said.

The noise of the crackling, popping, impossible flames chattered in her ears. Bits of singed surreality kissed her skin and seethed. V said nothing. It made her nervous. Angry.

"You wanted to show me," she pressed. "You wanted to show me this." A flash of insight: "You *wanted* me to ask!"

V wouldn't look at her. He struggled with something that wasn't there, something that belonged in his hands, which opened and closed with need.

"I . . . used to set fires," V admitted.

"Fires?" Her brain slipped on his words. They made no sense.

He nodded. "Little ones, mostly," he said. "Sometimes big ones."

// Beautiful. Wild. Free. They whispered . . . //

Consuela remembered the curtained room singed at the edges.

He glanced at the burning wreckage and the ecstasy-shame evaporated. His rapture gone, a hollow emptiness remained.

"This," he said, taking out a cigarette lighter and turning it over. "This is the one thing I have that can cross over." It sparkled, reflecting malevolent light. "It's the only thing I know of that could do something like this."

Consuela thought about her skin of flame, the box of matches from her scented candles. Her candles regressed to being unlit. There were always fourteen matches in the matchbox, no matter how many she watched burn. *Nothing changes in the Flow, unless we change it. Could I do this with my fire-skin, if I wanted to? Does it work that way?*

"Did you?" she finally asked. "Did you do this?"

"No!" V shouted, but the electric chorus doubted.

// Tender! // It has to be Tender! // Me? // It couldn't be me . . . //

Consuela faltered. How could he not know?

The central pole finally gave way, collapsing the tent in a cough of sparks.

Consuela placed a hand on his arm. V flinched. She spoke softly. "Then let's find out who did." Her hand sought his and he took it. A tentative touch, permission to be let in. "Bring me back," she said, and V's face pinched with worry. "Just for a minute," she assured him. "I can find out. Evidence, remember?"

He knelt and picked up a small beaded pouch. Circles of polished mirror were stitched carefully into the leather with bright red, black, and yellow thread. V lifted it up by its thong and cupped the tiny reflection to his eye, staring hard.

"Hang on," he muttered, and squeezed her hand. She didn't have time to squeeze back as they flipped over, spiraled under, and stepped out onto her carpet.

She didn't bother with explanations or with shyness or rebuke. Unzipping her skin, she marched toward her closet, shedding it along with her clothes as if it were nothing more than an undershirt, an afterthought. Consuela grabbed her fire-skin and welcomed it on.

It rushed over her gladly as she tipped back her head to revel in the wash of heat. Crackling from her toes, up her spine, and into her eyes, the fire plumed out the top of her head in a forelock of flame. She glanced at herself in the mirror with a satisfied smile, all but ignoring the awed look on V's face.

She was a terrible, beautiful, burning

// Angel. //

V stood, transfixed. In his eyes, she saw it: she was his own private heaven, his own private hell. He could not look away. His eyes burned inside her.

// Beautiful // Wild // Burning // Free //

// Angel. // Angel Bones. //

Consuela smiled, hearing herself through him. She took his hand, which did not burn. Her voice, roaring and airy, said, "Let's go."

He followed like a worshipper.

They sheared through the silvered glass. Returning, Consuela swooped in a hurricane dive, swiveling into the heart of the pyre. Racing along its insides, she felt the organic dwindle and burn—hides, pelts, wood, sinew—only the bits of metal and stone sang with heat, impervious to unmaking. Would that Joseph Crow had been the same. Perhaps he'd managed his bird form and taken wing? But no. She smelled the acid flux of burned feathers and sensed that the only living things crept deep beneath her, safely tucked under the earth.

She returned to the matter of the fire, scenting its beginnings; the foreign perfume of treachery, ferreting out its secrets better than any pyrotechnician could. She found the answer, but it brought her no joy.

Satisfied, Consuela leaped from the inferno, surprised by the gentle pang as she divorced herself from the parent flame. In this small way, perhaps, she understood V. The fire was her lover, her parent, her friend—all-encompassing and welcoming as no other human being had ever been except her father and her mother, far away in the realm of flesh. Fire had no prejudice, judgment, or reserve.

Fire was free. And damning.

V held the totem pouch like a talisman, looking half inclined to flee. *From me? From Tender? From the scene of the crime?* Consuela flung her arms in dismissive wings that roared, burning through the air. She was done with superstitious guessing; she wanted facts.

"Give me the lighter," she said in a soft roar. V did.

Holding it in her palm, she turned the thing over, tasting its cheap, metal surface, kitten tongues of flame divining the microscopic truth. She even sniffed it to confirm the obvious—a sharp tickle of plastic and fuel—thankful that when she was in her preternatural skins she was more inured to human emotion, less easily affected by mortal things like suicide and murder. Her heart and tears were elsewhere. She handed back the lighter.

"This set the flame," Consuela said darkly. "I could taste it in fire."

V paled.

"No," he said weakly. "That's impossible."

"It is possible and it happened," she said under the flames. V shook his head as if he hadn't heard her at all. "Only your fingers have touched it. I can taste the oil."

V kept staring, his head barely shaking no.

"Why did you bring me here?" she asked. "Was it to confess?"

He curled like she'd physically punched him.

"No!" V snapped, and balled his fists. "I didn't do it! I'd know!" But he didn't sound so sure. He fell heavily to his knees, pitching forward in a sort of weird supplication. "I'd know! Wouldn't I? I'd *know*!"

But doubt sang under his words, a black undercurrent dragging him down. He pressed his head to the dirt, rapping his forehead against pebbles and grass, arms crossed over his stomach. Unfurling like great wings off of his back, the sound of metallic strings reverberated into pleas.

// I couldn't do this! // Joseph Crow // You told me // My only wish // Tender! // Only a dream // Another pain-nightmare // Pain // Fire // Burning . . . I didn't do this! // Please // No // No! // I DIDN'T DO THIS! I COULDN'T DO THIS AGAIN! //

The force of his denial pushed her backs, the unspoken words beat at the surface of her skin. Consuela stumbled, astonished.

Again?

V lifted his face, one hand in the dirt, and reached for her.

She surged. The flames waxed ominously. "Get away from me."

"No, please, listen . . ."

"*Get away!*"

She jerked her arm back, launching into a rainbow arc of flame and punching an acetylene trail through the Flow's deadened sky.

CONSUELA seared through her open window, landing in a puff of ash. She grabbed Sissy's discarded bath towel and threw it angrily over the mirror, diving into her bedroom to do the same with her sheets. She smothered every shiny surface. As she went, her tears evaporated, throwing steam off her eyes.

A rushing-wind vacuum sound ended abruptly in a *thump*. Consuela swirled, staring hotly at her closet, where the freestanding mirror stood draped like a ghost.

"Bones?" V called through the flat plane. "Bones, are you there?"

He sounded a little panicked, a little hopeful, desperate.

Consuela's skin roared in response.

"Bones." He sounded thankful, exasperated. "Remove the sheet, please."

Consuela said nothing. She seethed. Burned.

"You're not mourning, are you?" V sounded more ashamed than annoyed. "I can't come into a house of mourning." Another swooshing impact, and not a ripple against the sheet. "Dammit, Bones. We can't afford to do this now!"

She wandered nearer to the bedsheet, inspecting it at a distance, hardly believing that such a little thing could keep him at bay.

"Bones," V called out again. "It's not safe. You're in danger . . ."

"From you?" She hadn't meant to snap back. Hadn't meant to speak at all.

"Dio mío cielo . . ." V muttered. "Can you *please* let me in?"

"Did you do it?" she shot back.

"No!" V said.

"But you're not sure," Consuela said. There was a short pause. "What happened, V?" Consuela asked. "Tell me what happened."

"I don't know! I don't remember anything!" V insisted. "Can I come in?"

She shook her head needlessly. "Not until you explain."

"I never remember . . ." V started and sighed. ". . . when I go back." The last line was an admission of something close to repulsion. Guilt.

"I don't understand," she said, sitting in front of her shrouded mirror. "You mean when you try to save people?"

"No," his voice rasped. Without a face, he wasn't a gorgeous god, or an angel, he was just V.

"When the pain comes," V stammered. "Whenever anyone tries to bring me back, I'm pulled into the pain. You can't imagine . . . I can't stand it." Another soft thump on the inside of the mirror and she could all but picture him leaning against its flip side, speaking over his shoulder back at her. "I don't remember what happens in those in-between times, but I usually end up somewhere else in the Flow." His voice dropped off. "Like sleepwalking," he said.

// Lost without memory. Stinking of pain. //

Consuela hesitated, the flames of her fingers plucking the edge of the bedsheet as he talked.

"The Yad said I was subconsciously running to escape it, and that's why I ended up here in the first place." V sighed with a trembling ripple in his breath. "He kept saying that eventually, I'd have to stop running."

With a soft tug, she brought the sheet cascading down. She looked into her own reflection, knowing V sat on the other side.

"Then what?" Consuela asked the mirror.

V leaned through the silver pool, looking her right in the eye.

"Then I'd either live or die," V said.

She shook her head, sending up crackles and curls. "So you're in pain . . . ?" she said, awkwardly.

"All the time," he said. They both stood as he stepped in beside her. "It's low-key, dealable, but—" He unbuttoned his shirt slowly, a mass of black bruises spread across his chest, but Consuela saw they weren't bruises; they were patches of darkness, like the shadows of the Flow etched on his flesh. "—I come out of it looking like this."

Consuela clenched her fingers to keep from touching him, but his eyes made it hard.

So she said, "Why?"

"I don't know. When I become aware of my body, I'm aware of more pain. If I can stay deep enough in the Flow, I can escape it for a while. But when my family tries to revive me, or the doctors get particularly creative . . ." V stopped, sensing something in Consuela's sudden stillness. His monologue slid into regret. He looked sorrier than ever.

"You didn't know that our bodies are still out there, did you?" he whispered. "That we're just souls stuck here waiting to die."

And although she wanted to deny it, it made perfect sense. Her soul, her self, was here—the rest had to be somewhere else. Back in the real world.

"And you're . . . where?" she asked.

"In an intensive burn ward," V said casually. "Suffering full-body burns." He glanced at his hands, his arms, then hers, aflame.

Consuela shuddered under the licking flames. "That's what you meant by 'again,'" she said. "You burned yourself."

The muscles around V's mouth trembled and he bit his lip to still it. His fist beat against his thigh and he dropped his head, nodding into his chest.

"It was an accident," he said. // *Getting trapped there. The fire . . . The fire just got away . . .* // "I lost control of it." V cracked his neck. "They keep me under—way under— but in the Flow, I'm whole. I'm me. I have all my fingers and my hair and my face and my nose. But when they try to pull me back . . ." He shrugged. "I don't let them. I bow out."

// *Coward.* // *No!* // *I can't take the pain.* //

Consuela saw the husk of Joseph Crow's place in her mind. *Did this mean Joseph Crow died in the real world? Or did Joseph Crow die here, first? Did he die there and, somehow, his death crossed over? Which world is the reflection and which one's real?*

"Where am I?" she whispered to no one.

"In a hospital," V said. "Most of us are."

// *I found you.* //

She stared at him. "Where? How?"

V sighed. "Sissy has her computer," he said. "If it's out there, she can find it. Medical records, news reports— she can find anyone with enough information. And there aren't a lot of Consuela Louisa Aguilar Chavezes around." He rubbed his palms against his jeans as if trying to get warm despite being in the company of a living, burning thing. "So I found you. // *The shell of you.* // I hoped that bringing you to your body might help get you home."

"Would it?"

"Maybe. It always pulls me," V said. "That's why I avoid going as long as I can. But once you know where your body is, you can never not-know again. It haunts you like your own personal ghost. You're never wholly *here* again."

Consuela considered that and him. "Can I ask you something?"

"Anything."

She burned, hesitant and looming. "Who are your assignments?" she asked quietly. "What's the pattern?"

He knew why she was asking; a ripple passed over his mottled chest. He steeled himself before answering.

"I save those who are victims of their own choices."

Stunned, Consuela struggled to make that fit.

V waited a tense moment in silence. "Can I ask you a question?"

Consuela looked up.

"Are you ready to leave?" he asked.

Consuela swallowed, tasting her resolve with her tongue.

"No," she said, her voice warm. "I haven't saved you yet."

Something unspoken passed between them.

Consuela stepped cautiously forward. V flinched. She wanted to say that she was being careful not to touch him—that although he would not burn, her fire might be a painful reminder—but the sentence only continued in her head: *A reminder of pain. His pain. V's pain. Her* thoughts fell neat as dominoes: *Tender eats pain. Controls it. Tender needs pain. He can't help it, he's hungry. V is always in pain. Tender helps him. Tender needs to feed. V wants to escape the pain, but Tender wants . . . what?*

Violins sobbed in unison, snapping her aware.

// Do it! Say it! // Damn me, Angel! // You can't save me! // No one can! //

She could. And she couldn't. It wasn't him.

Don't give up, V. Don't give up.

Consuela curled against him, a nimbus embracing him. He shuddered in her halo.

She whispered into his sleeve: "Know thyself."

He looked up, startled, eyes wet and confused.

"It wasn't you," she said. "I know it wasn't you." And she was surprised to find that she meant it. There was some connection between V and pain, and pain and the Flow, and Tender and V, and somehow, she would find the answer. It was a compulsion as strong as any she'd known. But there was something more that she could give.

"I forgive you now."

He fell against her.

Consuela hugged V tighter and let his tears dissolve into mist.

chapter twelve

"It is more than an opening out: we rend ourselves open. Everything—music, love, friendship—ends in tumult and violence."

—OCTAVIO PAZ

tHe den was filled with a hot, lazy smell, fuggy and somnolent, thick with pheromones and the milky weight of sleep. Under the coarse animal scent tinged with urine and rotting leaves, there was barely a whisper of the warm breath that Tender needed in order to locate her face.

Specifically, he needed to watch for her nose, and that would help target her eyes. Tender didn't bother to concern himself with her arms, claws, and teeth—if she got a chance to use them, he'd be nothing but dead. And that was "dead" in a painfully crunchy, definitive sense.

Tender wanted to die on his own terms, which did not include being mauled by an archaic she-bear.

Madeline Ingstaad was a mountain of flesh and fur. She'd assumed her ursine form in the late stages of hibernation. Everyone in the Flow knew it was coming when Maddy kept yawning or nodded off more than twice during a conversation. Tender had watched her lumber off, scratching herself high on one hip, making her way back here with the sort of instinctual tread of feet knowing their own way back to bed. Maddy otherwise avoided this place of her awakening. She'd been up and about in a sort of sleepwalker trance, patrolling on instinct, but had finally settled back into the cadence of a coma.

Even when she was sleeping, Tender had a healthy respect for Maddy. She was not like Joseph Crow, who flaunted his beast beneath a haughty veneer of ritual. She was what she was, and she lived it with a calm acceptance that Tender thought honest and admirable when she was inhuman. Her mind tapped into an ancient place of northern auroras, scrimshaw, and ice. She had a ponderous certainty and a lazy eye under one almond-shaped lid. He'd once mistakenly thought she had Down syndrome, not knowing that she was one-fourth Ainu.

Now the mushroomy odors surrounded Tender as he waited for the air to adjust, slowly including his scent. He could picture the tiny particulate matter, the bits of bear and fart and earth clinging to his clothes and skin. He closed his own eyes to steady his breathing, reciting one hundred digits of pi. At each series of eighty-eight, he took another step toward the monster on the floor.

Black nostrils flared once, testing the air with the one part of her brain that lay awake, nearly smothered under the cortex of slumber. Tender watched those snot-flecked holes like tiny mouths that might roar alarms at any minute. Pushing his hand through jellied tar, he felt for the hilt and drew out his sword, adding its sour stink to the mix. The acrid tang mixed with the damp bear sleep-scent that clung wetly to the underside of her belly and the mattress of leaves. To Tender, the stench was familiar and welcome—that of him, winning. A delicious shiver raced along his arms and the insides of his legs.

He leveled the oozing, black sword above one delicate, sleeping eye. He knew he'd have to shove it home, right into her brain. If he were to have any chance at all, he'd have to kill her instantly. He hoped that the blade was thin enough to make it through the eye-hole and deep into her skull. Maybe it'd get stuck in her bone, halfway? Maybe she'd wake up any second and stare right at him? He thought briefly of Bones, her empty eye sockets, and how much bigger a bear's must be. Anyone could be made vulnerable with their guard down and alone.

Tender had planned everything on the menses of Maddy's sleep, on the erasure of Nikki's empathy, on following the intricate, inevitable probability charts Abacus had traced upon his dodecahedron walls. It was all there, citing everything clearly.

His plan would work. Maddy wouldn't wake up. Ever again.

None of them would.

And then he could stop, too.

π

aRe you saying Tender did it?" Sissy pushed past Consuela and V, throwing open her file cabinet and rifling through its drawer. She sounded official as she yanked out a stuffed manila folder.

"No," Consuela said, before realizing that she really meant yes. She glanced at V, who looked away. He'd been uncomfortable seeing her in the skin of flame, so she'd changed back to herself before going to the Watcher. The air was itchy and uncomfortable; it crisped their voices, making hairs stand on end. Sissy slammed down the folder.

"Of course he did it," she said angrily. "He has to have

done it, but we don't have *proof*. There are rules in the Flow. We should find out 'why' and 'how' and only Tender knows the answers . . ." Sissy sounded exasperated, two steps away from hysteria. "But first we have to find him and stop him, and I have no idea who he is."

"What does that have to do with anything?" Consuela asked.

"Tender can walk through the Flow instead of along it," V said. "He's impossible to find if he doesn't want to be found." He beat his thigh with a nervous fist. "He comes to us, not vice versa."

"And if we can't stop him here in the Flow, we have to stop him back in the world. The real world. By any means necessary," Sissy said hotly. Implications sank their teeth into the quiet. She shuffled some of the papers in the file. "But we have to know where to look."

"There was a room," Consuela whispered. "A room with a chair and some things on a table. We thought it could be Tender's."

"Where?" Sissy asked.

"Left of the sunset meadow and close to the blue room," V said.

"The name on the cup says 'Talbot,'" Consuela added. "But you have to sit in the chair to see it."

"Be careful when you do," V said. "It's a sensory memory."

"Really?" Sissy said, and dropped her voice, all business. "Okay. I'll go check it out." She rubbed her hands fitfully. "It just . . . it makes no sense. Tender has to clean up all that mess. Do you know how much pain violence leaves behind?" She shivered and ran her fingers through her hair. "He hates it. He *hates* feeding. And he's been here how long? Why would he do that? Why now?" She didn't expect Consuela or V to have the answers, none of them did. The questions hung in the air.

"We need our own protection," she said finally. "We need a plan." She forced a little brightness into her voice. "So now it looks like I have a job that only you can do, Bones. We can't take any more chances; I want you to check on Maddy. Get visual confirmation that she's still there."

// No! // The violin-thought-voice outran V's own.

"Are you crazy?" he asked.

Consuela glanced at them, confused. "What?"

The Watcher swiveled in her chair like a CEO. "Without her skin, Bones has no scent," she explained to V. "She can go undetected by Maddy until she's close enough to see her without waking her up." Sissy nodded to herself and threaded her fingers in her lap. "I'd send an eye to look for myself, but we can't risk it now. It'll have to be you." The Watcher squeezed her hands together. "Take off your skin—you're a stranger to her and Maddy depends on her sense of smell," Sissy added half apologetically. "She tends to attack first and ask questions later."

"She doesn't know the way," V protested.

"I'll show her," Sissy said. "Maddy knows my scent and that I'm safe." The Watcher smiled. "I'll be happy to lend a hand."

V frowned, crossing his arms. "Then I'm going, too. As far as the lea."

"Fine," Sissy agreed. "It's better that you stay together."

"What about you?" Consuela asked.

Sissy took out a roll of fax paper tied with red string. "I'll be okay," she said. "I have to stay and do some digging, you two check on Madeline." She managed a small smile before the grief resurfaced. "Just make sure she's okay and then get the hell out. We'll wake her if we have to, but she'd likely go berserk."

"Okay," Consuela agreed. "Where are we going?"

V stood up as Sissy massaged her wrist.

"Where angels fear to tread," he said.

I am completely and utterly weirded out," Consuela said as she picked her way over the rocky ground.

"This coming from a skeleton?" V said, and gave her a

hand up. The irony was not lost on either of them as they watched their guide scuttle by. "You knew how Sissy's powers worked."

"Yes, but I was always with the majority piece," Consuela said. "I never saw the rest."

V smirked. "Welcome to the Flow."

"Gee," she grumbled. "Thanks."

Sissy's disembodied hand tapped impatiently against the rocks.

Consuela followed as Sissy's left hand crawled like a tan-colored scorpion up the rise. The wrist ended at a soft nub of fleshed-over stump. The manicured fingernails made little *tick-tacking* noises as it moved. Consuela felt them arpeggio down the length of her spine.

I may be weird, Consuela thought. *But that's just creepy!*

"I'll be able to go as far as the stone up there." V pointed up the incline to where a giant boulder sat like a fat toad sprouting moss. "After that, the winds would carry my scent straight into her den." The way he said it made it clear that he didn't want that to happen.

"Right," she said. "Rule number one: Do Not Wake the Sleeping Bear."

"She's not sleeping," V said. "She's hibernating. Hunting the Dream-time or whatever." He used a hand to steady himself and wiped his palm free of dirt. "Maddy's more than a bear, she's whatever the ancient form of what it was first like to be a bear—a Neolithic Bear, a Jurassic Bear—she's the Goddess of Bears," he said. "She's huge."

"Sounds lovely," Consuela muttered.

// *She is,* // the violins rang. Consuela stepped awkwardly over the next knot of tree roots and around an odd twinge of jealousy.

"Maddy is the resident warrior," V continued. "She saves people by demolishing whatever threatens them. The way she talks about it, she can either do it in the real world or in dreams."

Consuela swept bits of mulch off of her gleaming bones. "We can cross into dreams?"

V shook his head. "She's the only one that I know of," he confessed. "Although the Watcher spoke of a Kiwi girl who did it, too. But she wasn't here for very long."

Consuela swallowed without tongue or throat. "Did she die?"

"Who knows?" V said up the trail, not looking back. "That's what it's like most of the time—one day they're here and then all that's left of them is their spot in the Flow. The number of people can vary, but there's only a handful of us who are here at a time and only one who's been here for a lifetime."

Tender.

She thought back to the matchstick. A candle snuffed. Somewhere out there were the bodies of Nikki and the Yad, dead in the Flow and in the real world, too. *It could happen at any time, to any one of us, without warning.* The idea of being killed by one of their own seemed particularly cruel. Part of her didn't want to believe it—Tender was almost too intense, but she wouldn't call him a killer. She remembered his boyish smile.

Then she remembered the ants and stumbled.

Sissy's hand flattened itself at the base of the giant boulder. V stepped off the path and sat, his back pressed against the stone.

"This is it," he said quietly. "I'll wait here. But if there's any problem, I'll be right over."

Consuela stared at the disembodied hand and back at him. "If anything goes wrong, I'll be a stack of bone splinters."

Actually, she had no idea what might happen if a giant bear smashed her skeleton form. She knew that her iridescent structure was stronger than real human bone, but she didn't know what might happen against the Queen of the Bears.

"I'll be there," V promised, and held up the compact, flipping it open like a cop's badge and clicking it closed. "If I need to, I can get in, but it might make a bad situation worse," he said. "Be careful."

"I will," she said, and tapped the compact case. "Will that be enough?" It was awfully small.

"Full-length mirrors are easier, but tough to lug around." He clicked it open again for her to see and drew a thumb over the surface of the mirror to clean it. "I need to see my eye, and then I can see inside." V pointed to his own eye, which he widened for her benefit. "There's a door inside my pupil. If I can see it, I can walk through." He tilted the tiny reflection so that Consuela could see the pink-blue-pearl shimmer of her cheekbone and maxilla. V's smile lit up his face, transforming his dark handsomeness into oil-portrait beauty.

"From mirror to mirror, ad infinitum," he said reverently. "The world is full of mirrors, so it's easy to get lost. I think, once upon a time, it was easier because mirrors were rare."

"I thought only Sissy and Tender had powers that have existed before," Consuela said.

V shook his head. "I mark the corners of mirrors to know which ones I've used, and I've seen other markings. I know someone's done this before." He turned the silvered disk over in his hands. "There's too much out there—magic mirrors, covering mirrors, seven years' bad luck—someone knew something about this, once. I know I'm not the only one."

She had a twin feeling of being infinitesimal and déjà vu. If she hadn't been here in some incarnation before, had there ever been others like her? Like the *calaveras* dancing in flowers and flames?

"So what am I, then?" she wondered aloud.

V gestured with his chin. "Stalling," he said. Sissy's hand drummed its fingernails impatiently against the ground.

"Right," Consuela said. "I'll be back."

"I'll be waiting."

// *Bones. Angel Bones,* // he thrummed, achingly pure.

She stepped up and tapped the back of Sissy's hand, which sprang alert and, waving its fingers in a chipper good-bye to V, scuttled on its way. Consuela, obediently, followed.

As soon as she emerged onto level ground, Consuela could see the gaping cave in the hillside. It was framed by large rocks overgrown with wild grass and sheltered from the sun and weather with a flat duckbill outcropping like a baseball cap. Sissy's hand scurried toward the den on a well-worn track of trampled-down weeds.

"Coming," Consuela muttered as she hurried after the hand.

All she would have to do was catch a glimpse of Maddy the She-Bear, to know that she was okay. But the possibility nagged her: What if she wasn't okay? What if she was chopped into bits like the Yad or beheaded like Nikki? She'd never seen a dead body, let alone a murdered one. The thought twisted her stomach, even though she didn't have one. *No. She's fine. She's a warrior. She'll be fine.*

But Consuela agreed with Sissy—she'd feel better knowing for sure.

Nearing the entrance of the bear cave, Consuela had to mount the large rocks like stairs, cresting their peaks before clambering down. She hoped that her bones didn't make too much noise clacking against the rock. She sounded like wind chimes made of bamboo sticks.

The fetid, wild scents emerged with a whiff, washing over Consuela's body and prickling in her nasal cavities. She recognized the smells of wilderness and woods. It was as if her bones remembered a time when the world had been shared equally by man, animal, and earth. Here was a power old and slumbering.

The bearess was home.

Consuela hesitated, wondering if this was enough to confirm Maddy's well-being, even though she couldn't yet see a shape in the darkness. Did she really have to go on?

Sissy's hand, heedless of Consuela's pause, pulled itself along the grassy lip of the cave side and dropped like a stone. Consuela shook her head as if to clear it. Of course she'd have to go inside and look. She couldn't take someone else's word for it. She wouldn't repeat her mistake with Abacus by listening to Tender and not seeing for herself. She'd failed Sissy once. She had to trust her own eyes.

As soon as her foot touched the leafy floor, she knew that something was wrong. Winking like candles on the edge of her vision, Consuela stood still, trying to place what it was.

A flash of color made her turn. Flickering beside her, a brazen butterfly fought against the exhaling breeze. It was a bold creature of black and Florida orange. The monarch hovered over a patch of milkweed, battling to stay aloft in the draft. It settled on her arm.

The monarch poked her with its proboscis as if searching for what made her sweet. A powerful urge reached up inside her and answered with a honeyed wisdom.

Yes. I know you, she thought. And she did.

Raising her limbs to the sky, she called it down. A cloud of flittering life unwound, curling itself around her like a ribbon; Cinderella's magical ball gown descending in a rush of wings. The flock of tiny, tickle-me legs prodded and planted as their bodies became one; a thousand glittering compound eyes, a thousand antennae testing the wind, a thousand-times-four wings opening and clos-ing; drinking in the scents of millions. Her body all of butterflies.

The world snapped open.

The world snapped shut.

And Tender emerged from the cave with a sword.

She fluttered in mute amazement; the smells eking off of him were coppery and hot. Shadows lit him in grainy black and white. Dark fluids dripped off the blade.

He stopped. Saw her.

Consuela took off for the sky.

She was a swarm of disparate entities carried on the heady breath of spring. Forewings and hind wings climbed into the air. She smelled V below and saw him helplessly shouting something. But whatever he said dis-sipated like pollen in the wind.

She tried to go, but alarm buzzed her hive mind. She struggled and failed to reach that peaceful surrender of being called, to escape and return to the world beyond. She flailed for a kite string to pull her out, to tug her toward the soul that needed saving . . . but then Tender stepped out onto nothingness and scattered her thoughts like bees.

Tender vaulted invisible stairs, the Flow materializing instantly under his feet, charging at her with his black sword held high. Pieces of her body bumped and crashed in panic. She fought against the wind, a constant capricious buffeting. It was all she could do to gather herself together. She raised the tiny flocks of her arms in front of her face as Tender swung the sword.

The blade ran right through her.

Insects parted and re-formed like two handfuls of water. She was as surprised as Tender, who stood forty feet in the air, black eyebrows high over wide, wide eyes. She drifted, feeling the insistent pull of her assignment, the need to go somewhere across worlds, but Tender stabbed again—two-handed—and her instinct to evade overrode the pull to comply.

The sword cleaved. There was a fluttering, a rippling, but nothing more.

Tender growled. A splash of reddish black speckled his lip.

He was blocking her, keeping her here. By attempting to kill her, he made it impossible for her to leave. Each time she coalesced, he followed, vainly trying to damage her rabble of wings. He hacked at her wildly, chasing her through the air. Consuela tore and re-formed, but there was no escape. It took time to scatter, time to merge; it was time she didn't have. She grew desperate with the inexplicable need to *leave now*! She could feel the compulsion pulling tighter, thinner, fraying along her edges and burning nerves raw. Panic rippled like static, passing from thorax to abdomen to antennae to eye, frantic little lightning shocks building pressure in her head.

Desperate, she swelled and swarmed—rushing Tender, trying to push through him, past him, surrounding his face and neck and hair as he batted his arms and screamed. She felt his breath on her face, touched his tongue.

A thousand wings gave voice: *"Tender?"*

He gripped the hilt and swung baseball-bat-blindly again and again. He took a deep, enraged breath and screamed. Her butterflies spun, reeling, a cloud punched by the wind. Her alarm became one single, achingly high note in her ears, piercing like a migraine—

—something inside her broke and went slack.

She merged with a snap, shocked, confused, and in pain.

"It would have been easier if you'd gone!" Tender shouted from far away, inches before her. "I gave you a choice! And you've made your choice!"

She quailed, meek and afraid. Disoriented, she couldn't hold on.

"But it's not your time, is it?" he granted with a wry smirk. He gave an offhand salute. "Until then, Bones. At the end of the world." He sank slowly down, wiping his hand through the thick sludge of the blade, fingering its tip as he eclipsed into the Flow and disappeared.

Consuela hovered, feeling hollow. Empty. Except her hand, which burned cold.

She didn't recognize where she was. Tender was gone. V and Sissy's hand were gone. Maddy was dead, but that wasn't it.

She searched for what was missing. She couldn't feel it. She couldn't find it.

The butterflies on her left hand had shriveled black.

That's when it hit her: she had nowhere to go.

Somewhere in the world, her assignment had died.

SHE crashed into her room in an undignified heap, splattering monarch wings haphazardly on the bed. Consuela unzipped her butterfly skin and hurled it to the floor, where it fluttered weakly, a soft mound of black bodies and veined sunset leaves. She looked at her left hand: there was an ugly patch of shadow painting several bones black. She ran to her closet, rubbing her palm anxiously against her thigh; she felt pins and needles and a piercing ache. She might have chosen the fire-skin—craving its warmth and destruction and heat—but a deeper part of her needed to be herself.

She yanked on her own skin, pulling it hard, stretching it painfully. Consuela pulled on her clothes and a pair of good running shoes.

V was the closest to guessing the truth. He was the next likely target. Maybe Consuela could find Wish and make her baby-tooth dream come true—she tried to think how she might phrase a wish to stop Tender as she fought with the straps on her shoes.

She upended her makeup case into the sink. Fumbling for her darkest lipstick, she unscrewed a finger length of Red Hotts, writing IT WAS TENDER on the mirror over the sink, the full-length, the vanity, and the one in her closet. One way or another, V would be sure to see it. She threw the tube away and turned toward the door.

"Bones!"

She spun around, heart in her throat.

A hand stuck out of her closet mirror. Lipstick-stained fingers beckoned; V had reached right through the N.

She lunged and grabbed his hand in both of hers, pressing his knuckles to her cheek like a rosary. She bowed her head and closed her eyes as he pulled her through.

She bounced off his chest with the force of his pull. Squeezing his hand tighter, Consuela buried herself against him. She was dimly aware of him, hugging her tightly, the weirdly alien chorus of his steel-violin-voice singing, // *Thank God! Thank God!* //

He kissed her forehead. Hard.

"Are you all right?" V asked her hairline.

She didn't know. All she could say was, "It was Tender!"

"I saw," he said. "I couldn't reach you."

Consuela shook her head. "Maddy . . . ?" she started to ask.

V squeezed her tighter. "I couldn't see, but I saw Tender. // *And the sword.* // *And the blood.* // He gritted his teeth at the memory. "Then you were both gone, so I brought the Watcher's hand back and went searching for you. And Wish."

Consuela was suddenly aware of her surroundings. She searched for something familiar, as if trying to place herself on a mall map: You Are Here.

"Where are we?" she asked.

They were in a long, brick corridor lined with painted lockers and wooden doors. It was a high school, but it could have been any high school. They all looked the same, smelled the same—a mix of antiseptic cleaner, hormones, and sweat socks. V had pulled them through a small vanity mirror mounted inside an open locker door.

"It's a straightaway connecting Wish's hideout to the outside," V said quickly. "He's been through here recently. I thought if I could find him, I could find you."

He dropped his eyes suddenly. // *My wish/For you.* // V shut the locker door with a sharp, metal bang. "He's alive somewhere. Come on."

There was something that burned hot as cinnamon in her mouth, along with the creeping tickle she recognized as her own fear. The feeling of wrongness spread through her again, much as it had on the lip of Maddy's cave. Being in her skin made her feel vulnerable. But it was more than that. She rubbed the blackened spot on her palm and hid it behind her back. The place was eerie, too quiet; the school hall lights doused like a thousand candles, dark.

V started down the hall, his boots squeaking echoes on tile. She followed in soft sneakers. The lonely sound of their footsteps only heightened the feeling that they might not be alone.

Passing through the emergency fire doors, V pushed his way into the stairwell. The air was stale with antiseptic as if it'd recently been washed, a chemical-soap smell. The rapid-fire patter of their feet on the stairs echoed like phantom pursuers. V exited onto the first floor with a squeal of hinges. He held the door open with his shoulder and they headed straight for the exit. A sudden sound brought them up short.

Consuela felt every pore on her skin contract.

"What was that?" she whispered.

It came again. A quick, metal hiss-click.

Fear stabbed her spine. V froze. He'd heard it, too.

Only about thirty feet to the edge of Flow, but neither of them moved.

A soft *snick* echoed down the hall. Again. And again. More than one now—tiny snippets of overlapping sound, filling the abandoned emptiness with noise.

The front doors slammed closed and audibly locked. She and V spun around as a cloud of motion rounded the corner.

She had the flash impression of impossibly thin birds: wide, sightless eyes and sharp, pointy beaks. Dozens came in a flock, converging, dense almost to black in the center.

Without speaking, V and Consuela turned and ran.

The whispering cackles grew louder as the things gave chase.

She was no good at running. Her fingernails bit into her palms and her breath chugged heavy and thick in her chest. Her heart hammered under a cold wash of fear, feet pounding and breasts bouncing painfully as she tried to stay by V.

The hall stretched and lengthened. Pulled like taffy in a distorted mirror, the bricks became long streaks and the

darkness intensified. Consuela and V shot down the hallway with the cloud in fast pursuit—she could feel sharp
things snapping at her heels and at the tips of her hair.

"What are they?" Consuela shouted over the sound.
V didn't answer. He grabbed her hand and pulled her
forward, locking her steps to his. She glanced back. Dull
light pierced the gloom, shining off a hundred flashes of
silver and black. She recognized the shapes. *Scissors.*

Heavy old scissors made of forged steel flew through
the air, snipping sharply, hungrily. Their combined clatter
sounded like the chatter of birds, but there was nothing
alive in them.

It wasn't real. It wasn't possible.

Tender?

The cloud of scissors banked and flew down the hall.
V made a sudden, sharp turn and pounded through a
classroom door.

They skipped around the teacher's desk, upsetting a
pile of binders and toppling two of the front desk chairs
as they ran into an adjoining room.

Chem lab. Black tables with sinks. Walls of dusty
cabinets. V and Consuela ran through the back of the
classroom and up between the rows.

V ducked into the teacher's alcove behind the black-
board as a lone pair of scissors speared through the

room at head height. Consuela threw her arms over her face with a scream, but the scissors veered past, aiming straight for V. She saw him brandish a dissection tray and smack the scissors out of the air, pushing them violently flat against the floor. He toppled a tall shelving unit filled with beakers on top of it—crashing metal and smashed glass raining over the struggling, snapping thing. V didn't stop to gloat.

"Come on!" he shouted.

Back into the hall, V had brought them full circle behind the storm of scissors and dodged in a tight turn up the stairs. Slamming up the steps, Consuela was aware of how tired this body was compared to the tireless, timeless *her* underneath. She was sore and sweaty, her eyes stung with fright. She was fleshy, heavy, exposed, full of fear and mortal blood. Consuela gave an involuntary cry as the scissors smashed through the tiny glass window two floors below and funneled wildly up the stairwell.

// Danger! //

"Move!" V barked as he burst onto the second floor. Consuela ran breathlessly as the door swung closed.

V was looking for something, but not finding it as he ran. Worry sprayed off of him like sweat.

"I need a bathroom," he hissed. The snipping sounds grew closer. "I need a mirror!"

The doors opposite the end of their hallway burst open in a flurry of sharp edges, the cloud of scissors split into two, blocking their escape. V shouldered his way quickly into a random classroom. Consuela squeezed past him and V pushed the nearby file cabinet over, grabbing the teacher's wooden desk and heaving it sideways with a shriek of metal-capped feet to block the door. Consuela glanced around. *No mirrors.*

V read her mind. "Check the drawers," he shouted as he ran to the shelves. He frantically swept over piles of papers, notebooks, textbooks, looking for a compact or teacher-confiscated purse. Consuela could hear the chittering, shrieking echoes and mad scraping against the door.

"They're after you," she gasped as she yanked drawers off their treads and shook them out onto the floor. *Nothing!* She threw it aside. "Why are they after you?!"

"I don't know," V shouted as he ran along the room's perimeter like a caged animal. "I don't know of anything like this happening before . . ." He smashed an overhead projector against the tiles and clawed inside. "I need a mirror!"

"No!" Consuela dove on the mess of shards on the floor. "You need a reflection." The raking scrapes intensified, rabid hounds' teeth on the wood. "You said you needed to see your eyes," she said, picking up and discarding large pieces of glass. "You don't need a mirror, right? Just something where you can see yourself."

"I've always used a mirror," V said, but he sounded unsure as he, too, picked through the glass. "I don't know if anything else will work."

Consuela cut herself and dropped the useless piece of glass, a small sliver stuck in her thumb. She sucked at the salt and spat out the tiny shard. She ran her tongue over the blood and *hated hated hated* the flesh she was in, but there was no time to change into Bones. A stab of scissors punctured the metal around the doorknob; a chorus erupted, battering at hinges like gunfire. The scissors were breaking through.

V was desperate for escape, his eyes wide and frightened. She felt helpless, trapped. *There's nothing I can do!*

Inspiration hit.

She grabbed his face.

V stared up at her, startled, afraid. Consuela sounded more confident than she felt.

"Look into my eyes," she said. He did. As he stared into her dark brown irises, deep into the black, she knew that he could see himself there. His own reflection. She saw it, too.

"Run," she whispered.

V relaxed and his body melted, swirling into an

upside-down cyclone, curling to a pinprick in the center of her eye. She forced herself not to blink. The last of him siphoned into nothing as the door splintered. Consuela cringed as the crashing wave of black-handled scissors broke over her, puffing into shadow-feathers that dissipated in a rush of undone wings.

Huddled on the floor, Consuela slowly uncurled, wisps of silver darkness fading like smoke. She inspected her hands and arms, covered with nothing more than tiny hairs on alert. She exhaled a shuddering breath, staccato in the quiet. Looking at the ruined doorway, the shattered glass, and the few drops of her own blood on the floor, she bent down as close as she could and caught sight of her miniature reflection in red.

"I'm safe," she confided, her voice eerily amplified in the room. "Hope you are, too."

chapter thirteen

"Love is an attempt at penetrating another being, but it can only succeed if the surrender is mutual."

—OCTAVIO PAZ

CONSUELA wheeled into Sissy's doorway. It was locked. She pounded on the wood.

"Sissy!" she cried.

"I'm here!" the familiar voice shouted back. "I'm coming."

The *snick-click* of the lock gave way and Consuela pushed into the room, wrapping her friend in a hug.

"Thank God," Consuela breathed with a squeeze, and let go.

Consuela shook where Sissy's lone hand touched her arm. "It's Tender! I saw him!" she said. "Tender's got a sword!"

Sissy gaped. "A sword?"

"At Maddy's. He killed Maddy. Then he tried to kill me!" Consuela shouted.

The Watcher stood, stunned. "He attacked you?"

Consuela nodded. "Then he tried to kill V!"

"With a sword?"

"With scissors! With phantom Flow scissors!" Consuela squeezed her eyes, knowing that she was babbling.

"Where's V?" Sissy sounded scared.

"He got away."

"Good. Great. Okay." She grabbed a dry-erase marker and wrote a v on the mirror. Her right hand was missing, so she scribbled with her left. "He'll see this. And at least we have that," Sissy said, and pointed upward with the pen. Tacked above the door was the roll of fax paper on which were handwritten runes in flaking, brown paint. Not paint—blood. Old blood. *The Yad's?* Sissy gave a half nod, her one eye glossy. "Yehudah made it for me as a last-ditch defense. We weren't sure if the ward could work this way, but I thought I'd put it up, just in case."

Consuela stared at the banner. There were no licking, black flames. She doubted it worked. It drooped above them like a dead paper flag.

"Tender's killing everyone," she said, her panic growing no matter how she swallowed it back. "Why is he killing everyone?" She clawed at her memories. "He kept talking about making the most impact—he showed me something with ants . . ."

"Slow down, slow down—you're not making any sense." Sissy tried to sound soothing, which was odd; Consuela had been the one comforting Sissy as of late. "I've got pieces searching," she said. "And you guys were right. Look." Consuela allowed herself to be led to her usual chair and sat down, feeling the unfamiliar scrape of the armrests against her thighs. *Was this chair always so narrow?*

Sissy fell into her desk chair, fingers flying comfortably over the keyboard, seeking calm in what she did best. "They say that once there used to be attendants for this—assistants, couriers, that sort of thing . . ." she said absently as she typed. "Now I use UPS." She was at the Web site, punching tracking numbers into their pull-down menus. Her voice sounded almost flippant as she concentrated. "I play this little game with myself about what part of me will find stuff first," Sissy muttered as Consuela looked over her shoulder. The screen was all confirmed shipping orders and addresses around the country. She squinted, trying to make sense of it, and rubbed her arms violently.

"Here we go . . ." Sissy gave a wicked little smirk. "The eyes have it."

"What?" Consuela stammered.

"Well, one eye, anyway," Sissy said. "Because the damn thing was a PO box number, I had to wait until they'd picked it up before I could look around. Tender's real name is Jason Talbot and he's at Mercy House in Willoughby, Ohio." She awkwardly wrote something on a Post-it note and handed it to Consuela, who stared at the little square of yellow paper as if it were a dead mouse.

"Bones?" Sissy prompted.

"We have to stop him," Consuela said, detached, uncomprehending. "Here. Now."

Sissy grabbed Consuela's hand in hers, crushing the note between them. She noticed then.

"Your hand . . ." Sissy began. Consuela pulled back, ashamed and embarrassed. The shadow pulsed with pain.

"It happened . . ."

". . . when you lost one," Sissy finished for her, stroking the spot delicately. "It happens sometimes. It hurts, both inside and out. That's why we all *need* Tender. He doesn't just tend the Flow, he tends all of us, takes away the pain. He's supposed to, anyway. He's supposed to . . ." Her voice changed, shaking.

"Yehudah said he couldn't trust Tender. That no one was supposed to be here for so long, living off pain." Sissy squeezed their hands and shook her head. "We can't *do* anything to stop him here. In the Flow, he's too strong. And with weapons, who can stop him? Maddy's dead."

"Wish . . . ?" Consuela started.

"I've been looking. He's either hiding, or dead, too," Sissy said, her calm breaking at the edges in high-pitched quivers. "Who knows who'll be next?" But she knew. They both did.

Consuela shivered with renewed panic. Death had come so close, it had pierced right through her. She put a hand over her belly.

"You can come with me," she begged. "I barely got away . . ."

"I can't," Sissy said, and grabbed her arm, hard. "Listen, Consuela, I found him. I found Tender in the real world. We've got him. I can't go out there, not in one piece. I'll be safe here. I promise." She said it so she could believe it because Consuela couldn't. Sissy was placing all of their hopes in her.

"Now listen," Sissy added with a tinge of menace. "If anyone can appear in the world and put the fear of God into someone, it's you. Do you hear me?"

Consuela nodded, feeling numb.

Sissy shook her with a little emphasis, boring into Consuela with her one blue eye. "Do whatever you have to do," she said. "Once he sees you, he'll *have* to listen—he can't do anything to you there, he's only mortal. You're *you*. Go out there, find him, and get him to stop!" Her eyes hardened, her words damning: "He deserves to die!"

Sissy grabbed Consuela and gave her a quick kiss on both cheeks. "For luck," she said. "For Yehudah and Nikki and everyone else. We're counting on you. Without us, there's no Flow. No one to save them from Tender or Death."

Consuela struggled, uncertain and needing certainty. She wanted to ask Sissy so many questions. Why was this happening? Why Tender? How? How long had he been here? How long had she been gone? Where was her body in the real world, right now? Was she drugged up in some hospital on the brink of death? Did her parents know what happened? Was she missing, presumed dead? Or was she really dead and just didn't know it yet? She wanted to know more about life, about death, and most of all, about the Flow. She wanted to ask enough questions to hold back time. But Consuela knew none of the answers would make one bit of difference. She had to go. Right now. She had to live, or die now. Her choice. Right now.

Consuela disengaged gently. She walked under the banner of dried blood from a dead guy she'd met trying to protect a baby boy. It all seemed so impossible and unreal. Even her hatred for Tender, her newfound fear of scissors, seemed to belong to someone else—some other skin long undone. At the door, she stopped.

"Abacus . . ." Consuela said in soft confession. "I never saw him. Tender said he was out and I believed him. He's probably dead, too," she whispered. "Forgive me?"

The Watcher nodded. "I forgive you," she said quietly. "You know, we called him William Chang, but his real name was Weizhe. Remember that. The living are left to remember." Her voice dropped to a whisper as Consuela opened the door.

"I am Cecily Amelia Gardner," Consuela heard her say. "Remember me, too."

RUNNING. Again. The Flow could be navigated once you got the knack. Wish had the knack, but unfortunately, Tender did, too. Wish stumbled while looking over his shoulder as he ran.

He wasn't here, yet, but like a shark with blood in the water, Tender could smell betrayal in the Flow. Wish knew—Tender wasn't here, but would be soon. And, like a shark, Tender was made for killing.

Wish didn't know if he swam with the fishes or was closing in on shore.

It didn't matter anymore.

He'd done what he could. For now.

He ran.

CONSUELA debated appearing as a figure aflame, but the fire felt as slippery as oil as she struggled it on. It felt wrong. Everything felt wrong.

There's no time!

The thought made her angry and her skin flared in response. Consuela tore the fire from her body and let it whisper to the floor. It burned, but not hot enough for her.

She burned. Frightened, angry, and doubtful, she burned.

Consuela looked into the lipstick-lettered mirror, searching for truth in her own sockets—but, in truth, searching for V. Instead, she noticed herself, her glittering bones streaked with red. Stripped of her skin, it was as if she had peeled away what it meant to be human, leaving behind the hard, cold, beautiful, and terrible truth that Death eventually comes to us all.

This is me.

Bones. Angel Bones.

She didn't need a skin. She could go as herself. Life. Death.

Bones stood grim in the mirror.

She was coming for Tender.

If that didn't stop him, perhaps nothing would.

t**He** name and the address hummed in her brain as she settled to a stop. Sissy hadn't needed to tell her that this was the place; Consuela recognized the door.

She stepped through it while a nurse in purple scrubs passed by, carrying a tray of pills in plastic cups like tiny bowls of Halloween candy. There was a quiet bustle in the room punctuated by strange, wordless sounds, the scrape and rattle of chairs, the snap of checkers. Soothing, steady instructions from male nurses in loose orange clothing ran a lulling undertone, while beneath it all, a rich baritone voice read aloud.

Consuela hesitated in the spotlight reality of the ward, the invulnerable feeling of righteousness evaporating in the face of something so mortal. It was bright and vibrant and colorful. It smelled like a hospital under heat lamps. It smelled like Tender.

She turned around slowly as she walked, taking in the sparsely furnished room and its sparsely dressed patients and its vividly patient crew. She wandered to where she knew the chair would be, in front of a large window, the sunlight playing merrily with the muted colors dancing in her bones. Opal rainbows reflected on the walls in sprays of aurora light. She circled around to look directly at the tall boy in the chair.

He stared, sightless, out the window, his face hollow and slack. His eyes reflected the pale light outside, unencumbered by eyebrows that were clipped short to smears of five o'clock shadow. His head was similarly buzz-cut; the blond bristles made his ears stick out like trophy handles and his neck seem extra long. A light blue T-shirt hung straight from his shoulders. His hands were folded, politely useless in his lap. He was neat and clean and utterly still. Without his cocky, charismatic spark, he was pale and calm as milk.

This wasn't Tender. If not for the pug nose and the shape of his lips, Consuela would not have recognized him as Jason Talbot either.

Her attention flicked to the man sitting in the opposite chair. He was a large man, bald and ruddy, wearing a business suit and a pair of glasses that nestled against unsurprisingly thick, bushy, salt-and-pepper eyebrows. Consuela remembered seeing those glasses before. The table beside him still held the adjustable lamp and a fresh cup of coffee. The man read from the large book in his lap, its title written in stamped foil letters.

"' . . . To exclude the cold, one half of this door was fast closed, and the other was opened but a very little way. Such a scanty portion of light was admitted through these means, that it was difficult, on first coming in, to see anything . . . ' "

His rich narrator's voice told Consuela everything.

He had been reading to Jason for a very long time. Not just today, but perhaps every day. He'd read reams of pages from huge, old books; hundreds, thousands, because he thought that Jason would like the stories, or the cadence of words, or might even remember the sound of his father's voice. There might once have been a hope that the words would make Jason smile or cry or come back to life, though the words of his family thus far had not done so. There was something in his timbre that said that that's how it had started, anyway. Sometime long ago.

Now he read because he had promised himself—or Jason or someone else—that he would. That promise kept him coming back and reading from the great works of literature instead of the old, battered children's books that littered the plastic hospital bins. He read Jason the books a young man could appreciate, the ones he'd be expected to know in school; books filled with ideas a clever mind would find challenging and intriguing, a mind that might be still lurking somewhere just out of reach.

His father read because he'd promised to read, and he had a good voice for reading—but now the intonations were tired, the pauses skipped, and the vowels flat. Once in a while Mr. Talbot might show some interest in a line or a well-written phrase, but more often he read with the unconscious awareness of having an audience, of being overheard by someone, even if that someone was not his son.

Mr. Talbot paused in his reading of *A Tale of Two Cities* to take a sip of coffee and adjust his glasses on his own pug nose.

". . . 'You can bear a little more light?'" he continued, "'I must bear it, if you let it in . . .'"

Consuela backed away, bumping into the windowsill. She held her breath and watched Tender's face register nothing of this world. She waved a shimmering hand in front of him. Iridescent light caressed his sharp features, passing over his face like mist. *A grayful of nothing*, she thought. Like cream poured into coffee that billowed to fill the darkness, changing the nature of everything it touched, the image of Tender clouded and revealed itself to her.

The world snapped open.

The world snapped shut.

And, in that moment, Consuela understood.

Tender had lived years—nearly his whole life—in the Flow; a place meant for the few who were caught in the cracks for a time. They were the souls that kept others from crossing too soon, filling the porous, pitted holes where the living might slip unseen. They were a last defense, guarding those who still belonged to life as they, themselves, no longer did. But this was only supposed to be a temporary occupation. They died, like everyone died, before the Flow might overtake them. New angels arrived every day to save the living and take one last dance on the heads of pins.

They were young, but each of them had experienced some life, some history, to make sense of the unreal. They manifested their extraordinariness—their abilities reflecting who they really were. They took some small part of what was real with them so that they could adjust. But they knew that this wasn't real, wasn't permanent—Sissy, Wish, Joseph, and V—they knew the difference between the real world, their past lives, and the Flow.

But Tender never did.

She could imagine that tiny window where Jason might touch the real world and feed a mind hungry to understand and be understood; one that wanted, needed, to take control of a world that he could affect, to make up for the one in which he had no control.

Jason Talbot had been trapped in this body, trapped in the Flow, with no escape, no end, and no handle on the real. The Flow was only meant to be a layover, with a continuous changing of the guard—but Tender had lived there all of his life without ever living his own.

Never ending, never changing.

What would that do to a strong-willed mind, naked and brilliant, but unable to touch? How long had he been staring out an imaginary, one-way window? How long had he been trapped in the Flow? What would he do with his power over pain once he'd learned to control it?

Consuela looked deeply into Tender's dark-as-night eyes and saw, reflected, tiny bright skulls. She touched his face with her hand. He felt nothing. She felt that, too.

He couldn't see her. She couldn't tell him. She couldn't stop him here in the world. There wasn't anything anyone could do.

A wordless shriek made her start and Mr. Talbot stopped reading. A girl in a pink dress and violently copper hair gaped at Consuela, screaming and slapping the side of her head. Two nurses hurried to help. Consuela stood up, surprised and embarrassed, and spun away in a blur of glimmer and shine.

CONSUELA ran to her room and picked up her skin, taking comfort in the tactile memory of being human, once, even if only temporarily. She hugged herself to her chest. She'd been alive, she'd been real, she'd had a home and a family and friends and a life, strangely sad that Tender had had none of those things—or, worse, he had them, but didn't know it, or—worst of all—that he knew it, and mourned it every day.

She hoped that maybe he really didn't know how much his father missed him and loved him. Then she was mad at herself for feeling anything for Tender. Then guilty for being heartless. She had no eyes for crying, yet tears spiked the corners of her sockets. Consuela shivered and felt rippling-sick.

She draped her skin gently on her bedsheet and turned toward her mirror . . .

No.

All the mirrors had been splashed black. The paint, dried and crusty and caked in layers, had been smeared in thick liquid shrouds.

She picked at it, pulling off bits and soft chunks that stuck in globs to her finger bones. Consuela took the screwdriver off of the desk and tried chipping the seam between glass and frame, trying to loosen a sheet like ice on a windshield. She heard a squealing scrape, and stopped. She'd scratched the glass. What would that do if V needed to get through? She dropped the screwdriver on the carpet, speckled with dried black drops.

"V," she whispered, and touched the cold, lumpy surface. Someone had come into her room and painted his doors shut. As one of the Flow, they'd changed it—her place—and it wouldn't change back. Her room had been violated, vandalized like Joseph Crow's. She felt victimized, hunted, trapped.

Tender, the fear whispered. She spun in place, searching. Even when she was Bones, he could affect her this way.

She had to get out of here. She had to find V.

Running to her bathroom, she found all the mirrors obliterated in the same sloppy, tarlike massacre. Consuela ignored them and rummaged through the collection of upended lipsticks, eye pencils, mascaras, and base in her sink; she snapped open case after case of shadow and blush, looking for even the tiniest mirror.

She saw it near her curling iron: a silver compact case that she recognized, although it wasn't hers. Gratefully, she clicked it open, heedless of its oddly shimmering surface. She pressed her finger against it, willing V to be there.

And he was! She could feel it!

Consuela surrendered to the touch of his hand and the telltale pull, not realizing until it was too late that he hadn't drawn her forward, but was trying to push her back.

CONSUELA slid into the dark, pressed close against V. The entrance shrank behind her, squeezing over her foot, and disappeared. Even without light, she felt the enclosed space wrapped tightly around them.

"V . . ." she said.

// *Bones.* // The violin song rang through her shadow veins, sorrowful and thankful all at once.

"He made a mirror out of the Flow," V whispered back; his heartbeat thudded in her ears. "He placed it in your room and trapped me here. Now he's got you, too."

Thoughts ricocheted around inside her head. "Tender?" she gasped. She still saw him as limp and lifeless, staring with shaven brows at Mercy House.

"Who else?" V growled, smoothing his hands down her humerus bones. If he was shocked to feel only the silky-shell surface, he gave no indication.

She blinked against the darkness, her mind still reeling. "Why?"

Tender's voice rang down into the chamber of no walls, no floor, and no light. "Actually, I'm conducting an experiment," he said. "I'm curious to test your theory, seeing how far you'd go to save another, or how far you'd go to save yourself, or if it's all just words," Tender quipped. Bodiless, the sound was mockingly everywhere. Consuela thought that he might be speaking only to her. She felt the vibrations of his voice in her bones.

"It's down to the last few," Tender said casually. "Both of you have been instrumental and, thereby, worthy to see it through. So: whoever makes it out may live a little longer, but we all know there's only so much borrowed time."

"He's insane," V said flatly. She couldn't quite agree, but why trap them here? Why try to kill everyone? What good would it do to empty the Flow? Tender would still be stuck here. Alone. He still couldn't get back to the real world.

A little hint of something other than sadistic daring tinged his words. "I've been watching you two—it's a rare thing—but I've seen it before," he said. "Young love. Desperate times. Strange bedfellows and all that. So preciously predictable." He sighed. "So let's play this out: who will sacrifice themself for the other? One of you is likely to get out. The other is likely to stay in the Flow. I mean this fairly literally, since you are basically in a pocket of the stuff. It's seamless on the other side— there's no up or down . . . or out, for that matter, although I trust in your joint inventiveness. The prize is a chance to live a little while longer, riddled with guilt at leaving the other behind, and the opportunity to seek revenge. The loser, obviously, dies. Or, hey, don't choose and see what happens—that's a choice, too. I am generous because I'm leaving it entirely up to you; the Flow was never so kind. However, time is short." There was a slight pause, just enough to heighten Consuela's panic. V's hands held on to her bones. "Ever wonder if we actually have to *breathe* in the Flow . . . ?"

"Tender!" Consuela shouted. "Don't do this!"

"I didn't," Tender said. "*You* did."

She felt his anger like a gavel. His embarrassment was her epitaph.

A vacuum sealed. Consuela felt her lungs constrict. Spots appeared before her eyes. Was it her imagination, or had she stopped breathing? Did skeletons breathe? Did angels? Or ghosts? The darkness became a velvet blanket smothering her. The absence of light was like a force pushing against her sockets, burrowing into her brain. She ground her teeth.

"Look away," V said, which made no sense until he flicked on a light. The cigarette lighter sparked like a flashbulb in the dark. It took a while for the winks of red and white to resolve into his profile, blackness underlining his eyes, nose, and lower lip. He held the little finger of flame high. "You okay?"

She placed her palms flat against his chest, taking comfort in his solidity. "I've been better," she admitted. "Is he gone?"

V reached out to touch the walls. Consuela splayed her fingers, but pulled back when the blackness gave sickeningly under her hand. Only the space underfoot felt solid. They pressed against each other.

"He's gone crazy," V muttered.

Consuela only shook her head. Tender wasn't crazy, not here; he was sane—which had to be worse when he'd been trapped for this long. Trapped with no way out.

"He wants it to *end*," Consuela said. "He wants to be the one to do it and take everyone down with him." They were just ants, crawling, broken, and scrambling under his boot. She felt the awesome pressure of enclosure, the venom of claustrophobia seeping into her veins. It trembled on her nonexistent tongue. It was at that moment that she knew that Tender had written the poem.

"Never ending," she gagged. "It's his hell." *I can't breathe!*

"Don't panic," V said sternly, the flip side of calm. "We're going to get out of this. We will. Trust me. Listen to the sound of my voice, all right? Think about something else." His last words choked out of him as he fumbled in the darkness. "Talk to me," V said over his shoulder. "You make skins, right? Tell me how it works."

"I don't know," Consuela croaked, fingers clawing at her missing trachea. "If I think about it too much, it doesn't work." She kept talking past the yammering panic, swallowing reflexively. "I just . . . do it. It's the same when I undo it."

V kept her talking, feeling the spongy walls for any chink, waving the lighter like a lantern above their heads.

"Undo it?" he prompted. "How?"

She shuddered against the suffocating fear and began following V's methodic prodding, grateful for something to do as she spoke. "I can change the skin back into its parts. The water is just water, the air disappears. My feather skin became a big pile of black fluff."

V reached above his head as high as he could, fingers extended, touching nothing.

"What did you do with it?" he said as he strained.

Consuela shook her head. She couldn't find escape anywhere! Was this how Tender felt all the time? Was that what he was trying to teach them? Or would he really . . . ? *Yes, he would. I saw him with that bloody sword.*

"I threw it out the window," she said.

"Really?" V said. "Why?"

"I don't know," she admitted. Consuela wasn't sure why she'd done any of the things she'd been doing of late. Any time she stopped and thought about it, she ended up in tears. Better not to stop and think, just do it. Action. It had saved Rodriguez and the guy in the building, the drunken woman in a field, and a drowning boy. When she thought about herself and how helpless she felt, how much she missed home, she turned into a useless heap. It struck her that this was always when she'd hear V's violin-voice singing her name. The one that now called her "angel" in secret. *Angel Bones.* It sounded very ominous now. Macabre. Hopeless. But she couldn't give up. Consuela kept searching.

V knelt on the floor and ran his hands over their feet, where shoes and bones touched blackness, pushing his hand, then his fist, hard against the Flow.

"Anything?" she asked. He shook his head. She ran a hand over her skull. "Shine the light here." V moved the lighter obediently toward her in case she'd seen something new. Instead, she pointed to herself.

"Can you see yourself in this?" Consuela indicated the smooth plate of her skull, knowing that the abalone shimmer was dull, muted with color and light.

"No." said V. "It's too . . . *//Hypnotic/Beautiful/ Deep //* . . . milky."

They were both uncomfortably silent.

"I don't have eyes to look into," she said, almost chuckling, but afraid to let the laughter bubble out. "But there's blood," she said, suddenly serious.

"Blood? What blood?" V demanded.

"When you'd gone—I saw myself in a drop of blood," Consuela said, remembering the scissors, which might have torn her to ribbons, but instead had puffed into smoke. Tender had meant them for V. This trap was meant for the both of them. "I'm okay. It was when I'd cut my finger on the glass. There was a spot of blood on the floor and I could see my reflection. I thought you could see me."

"I didn't look," he admitted. "I didn't think about that. Liquid."

"While it's wet, it can reflect. But I can't bleed," Consuela said slowly. "You can."

"I can," he said. "But I can't take you with me. Moving through reflections isn't like moving through mirrors—it's a tight squeeze. I barely got through the last time and I was alone." V sighed. "I might be able to get out that way, but what about you?"

"I'll get out," she said bravely.

"How?" V pressed.

"I don't know," she said. "Somehow."

V shook his head. "Not good enough."

"V . . ."

"No." He said it one step shy of "please."

He took a step closer. "I'm supposed to protect you," he said. "That doesn't end now."

Consuela met his eyes, saying something she'd dared to wonder about.

"Was I supposed to die in that changing room?" V said nothing. "I don't think so," she added carefully. "I think that I'm supposed to be here."

"I don't know," he confessed.

"You were compelled to save me, and you did. I'm here. Now." Consuela said it and her thoughts tumbled into order. "And I can save you."

The world snapped open.

The world snapped shut.

I'm here to save you. Save us. Save the Flow. She felt it like it was one of her skins, sure and solid. *But how?*

"I can make it out through the reflection, all right?" he said. "But I'm not going unless I know that you can, too. Make a skin and get out first." She shook her head. Her denial of the possibility seemed to feed his conviction. "Use anything," V insisted. "Use the lighter. My shirt. The dark . . ."

"I can't. It has to be something . . . organic." She struggled to put it into words. "I don't think there's anything I can use, because it's not real. Really real."

Shadows wavered and flickered like laughter in the silence.

"The fire is real," V said quietly.

"I already have a skin of fire back in my room," Consuela said. "I don't think I can make another one; it feels already done." It was a feeling she trusted, but it left her helpless. "I don't know what else I could use."

One-handed, V began patting his pockets, checking his clothes for something—anything—while his other hand held up the feeble flicker of light. He stopped suddenly with his hand flat against his chest.

"Use me."

"What?" said Consuela.

"That's it," V whispered. "Use me. Make a skin of me."

// I can save you. //

"No." She hissed back, "That's not possible."

"You said something organic, something real."

"Not *a person!*" she said, when she meant to say, "Not *you!*" The idea made her sick.

V shook his head. "You're not listening to yourself," he said. "You can make a skin of anything organic, anything real. I'm both." He hushed her next protest with a chopping wave. "No! Listen, if it works, you can get out of here using me—my powers, right? My skin. You can get us through a reflection. You won't need a mirror."

Consuela kept shaking her head, unable to express her horror without her eyes.

"I won't do it," she muttered. "I can't."

V shook off her words. "You can and you will. We have to get out, tell the others, and stop him."

"What if there aren't any others?" she shot back.

"Then *you* will have to stop him."

Consuela tasted fresh panic. "I can't . . ."

"Stop it!" V spat. "You can. This will work."

309

He was right, it could. It should.

"What if I can't turn you back?" she said.

"This *will* work!" V insisted. "Like reflecting in your eyes, right?" He touched one hand to her jawbone, lifting her skull upward. He spoke directly into her faceless face. "You thought outside the lines before. You showed me it could work. Believe it. Believe me." V touched his eye. "Just a reflection," he said, and touched his chest. "Just organic. You understand? Consuela: This. Will. Work."

She didn't trust her voice. Her mind spun with the idea of a thousand feathers loose on her bed. What if a person just turned into . . . parts? V?

"I can save you," V said quietly. "Let me save you."

// This is what I'm here for/Consuela/Angel/Bones //

// I can save you. //

// Let me save you. //

She shook her head against the montage of grisly doubts in her mind.

"No. Not just you, not just me—it has to save us both," she said, projecting a certainty she didn't feel. She touched his arm, speaking quickly. "All right. Tell me how it works, what to look for in there"—*the Mirror Realm*—"and I'll get us out."

V was suddenly taken aback. Her hand on his flesh, he realized the ramifications of what he'd been asking, begging, her to do.

"Keep your . . . my eyes open," he said carefully. "See the black door and walk through it without moving your feet. Like through the Flow: with intention. When you're in, look for the Vs drawn in the top right-hand corners. Those are the mirrors I've used. The tall one with the condensation is yours. It'll most likely be on your left, but you never know. Don't wander through any strange mirrors. Always aim for the one you know."

She nodded. He did, too. A sort of understanding passed between them, leaving an awkward acceptance behind.

"Give me your hand." The way V said it, she had to obey, the way she had since first coming to the Flow. She saw his hand on hers and wildflowers and Christmas lights and a half-remembered kiss. Consuela offered her hand, forcing herself to watch his every movement, trying not to think too much about what was happening or what might come next.

He rolled up his sleeve and turned his arm over. Taking her slim finger bones in his grip, he pressed the talon ends to his skin and resolutely pressed down. Both gasped as her fingertips pierced the skin, blood welling up in little vampire pools, a tiny spray of red flung almost to his wrist. He let his arm fall and fisted his grip, pumping blood down his forearm, massaging out a thin pool drop by drop. Thankfully, it didn't soak into the Flow. V grunted against the pain and sweat speckled his face.

// I hate pain. //

They knelt over the growing red splash. The lighter in his hand shook slightly, setting the shadows dancing. When the patch of blood spread as wide as his palm, V placed the lighter to one side, snapping its lever down with a rubber band wound around its middle. V pressed his hand over the wounds and wound his sleeve around them, glancing at the lighter, then at her.

"I can see the outline of your body," he said. *// Naked in the firelight. //*

Consuela was glad the bones would not betray her blush or her fear. She hoped, though, that perhaps V might see her smile.

Her lips were ghosted shadow and half-reflected light.

The Flow snapped open.

The Flow snapped shut.

Together, they entered the impossible.

V gently picked up her hand and placed it lightly in his own. He spread his fingers and threaded them through hers—finger-flesh, finger-bone, finger-flesh, finger-bone—like piano keys and living things. V lifted their joined hands up to his eyes, trailing their forearms together. It looked as if he waltzed with death.

He held their hands up so that she could see.

"You can do this," he said. "I trust you."

Entranced, Consuela said nothing, but turned her hand within his—still touching—and walked around his body, keeping close and quiet. She tried to think of him like the air, like the water and the flame, like the feathers and butterflies, but his smell brought her back to how very alive he was.

He was human—he was V—how could she make him into a skin? *What would I be taking? Can I accept what he's offering? Will I be able to give it back when it's done?* The questions tumbled in her mind and fed a secret, shameful place that delighted in the awesome power she would have over him if it worked; and the terribly awesome power she'd have—sanctioned murder—if it didn't.

Consuela circled closer, trying to help them get used to each other: a breath away from touching, casually creasing clothes, the kiss of skin on bone. She hovered like a moth flying closer to the flame. But she was the fire coming to consume him, and V, the moth, was letting her happen.

Irresistible, she thought.

// *Please,* // he thrummed. // *Do it.* //

Stepping slowly behind him, she dragged her skull

against his shoulder, tracing her way to his back, following the curve of his ribs as a guide. His breathing was a forced-down gasping, trying to maintain control in a moment tense with permission, unconditional, unknown, and closer to worship than fear.

V closed his eyes, his head lolled forward. His hair hung down. His black lashes cast long shadows, just touching his cheek.

"I trust you," he said, perhaps more to himself than to her.

// Do it. // Now. //

"Relax," Consuela coaxed. "Let me in."

Consuela lifted her right hand under the weight of his palm, flexing her fingers to match each of his, spreading them wide like a puppeteer. She bent both of them at the wrist and pushed her hand upward into his.

He gasped, but she did not retreat.

She rested her head against his shoulder and felt the charged anticipation there. Curiosity, electricity, pain. She tasted it in the air.

"Relax," she said, and placed her left hand against his shoulder blade, a giant albino spider against his shirt. Consuela touched its surface in a clinical way, then pushed her fingers into his back, caressing the inside/underside of his arm, sliding into his left hand like a glove.

V's head whipped back and he groaned once into the

dark. He squeezed his eyes against the sensation and she bowed her head reverently as she entered his spine. She felt his body push and part like heavy curtains against her face, and she walked in—warm and welcome—stepping through his calf muscle into the boot of his foot. First one, and then the other, before she opened him fully as skin.

She was surprised to hear an echo of his consciousness as his head covered hers, alive, entombed, a human skin; it was his last gasp of letting go.

"Be in me." It rang inside her, *his* voice instead of his usual, unusual violin song. It touched her that in that last second, he trusted her to the end.

Consuela stepped into his body, letting it zip closed behind her.

She looked up and out.

Her eyes saw from behind his eyes, like his irises were soft contacts over her own; her nose could smell beneath his nose, and she swallowed, scratching her throat along his Adam's apple. V was still there, spread thinly all over her. He was still alive, but she was the one living him.

She placed his hand upon her chest and wondered whose heartbeat she felt there.

Consuela turned slowly in place. She could feel the larger, callused feet, the odd weight between her legs, the itch of stubble on her face . . . It was a wholly unfamiliar feeling, moving in the suit of him, but she couldn't wonder about it any longer. She/he/they had to go.

She lowered herself gently, not yet trusting her borrowed body. Consuela spread her wide hand over the surface of the blood. She could imagine her bones resting on his hand, now in his hand—together they would get through this. She felt their confidence in each other. These hands, entwined, enmeshed, would see it done.

She flexed her fingers and picked up the lighter, feeling the cool kiss of metal, and smelled the tiny tang of fuel. *So human . . .* V felt so alive, so virile and vulnerable, it humbled her to be inside him. Yet part of her loved it, lusted for it, craved the complete invasion of another's soul—*not soul,* she reminded herself, *just his body. His body. Not mine.* She fumbled for the lighter. Knocked it over. It went out. Plunged into darkness and an unfamiliar body, Consuela yelped and hoped that V couldn't hear her panicked thoughts in his head.

It took four tries before she sparked the lighter back to life. Fingers shaking, she held its single flame over the thin pool of blood. She felt the raw sting in his arm where the punctures still bled, but she pushed the pain aside and lowered his face to the floor. She waved the lighter back and forth, trying to catch both his eye and the blood in the weak, gold light. Finally, she saw it: the tiny curve of his iris—a bit of the corner, framed in dark lashes, and a hint of his cheek. She saw the opening in his pupil, felt a tug—it was enough.

Smirking a little, she pushed forward. Even with the vertigo of sight and sound, she was inhumanly proud. Tender could not have expected this.

TENDER stared down into the pit wondering, watching, what they would do. Which one would go while the other remained? Who would be his sacrifice? Who would try to confront him later when he'd all but won?

He couldn't hear them, but he liked to watch. He gloated at their vain searching. He reveled in their argument. He could almost taste their shadowy pain. He was surprised when V pierced his arm, feeling every bit the Peeping Tom at their intimacy thereafter. It excited him more than he wanted to admit, desire pressing warmly against the inside of his skin. Tender touched the edge of his own arm as she cut and caressed his own chest, imagining the kiss of pain as she entered V's back.

He was horrified, mesmerized, awestruck. It took him many minutes before he comprehended their perfect plan, and by then, it was too late to do anything but admire it.

His next thoughts fell like hammer blows, smashing his brain.

Bones had made a skin of V. V could walk through blood. Bones could not do these things, but had while wearing V. Bones could make a skin of anything. Anyone. Any power could be hers. V could be dead. Could be free. Could be damned. Bones could skin them all like seals and wear their fur like sacred coats. Bones could be . . . V could be . . . He could then be dead/lost/free . . .

Bones, the game changer, could do it all. Anything any one of them could do.

He wouldn't have to do anything, anymore.

Tender sat back, stunned, in a makeshift chair and never even felt the tears fall down his face.

chapter fourteen

"... [D]eath revenges us against life, strips it of all its vanities and pretensions and converts it into what it really is: a few neat bones and a dreadful grimace."

—OCTAVIO PAZ

SHE swirled into an open darkness. Shapes of light spiraled in all directions, spinning into the distance every which way.

Squares and rectangles and ovals of various sizes shone like bright, gray windows against the black— other shapes, muted, were nearly hidden unless she stared at them out of the corner of his eye. Consuela guessed that the television-bright spots were mirrors; the shadowy ones, merely reflections, like spoons. *Or pools of blood.* The one behind her slowly shimmered closed as it dried.

There was an eternity of space; mirrors mounted like glow-in-the-dark stars stuck along invisible subway-tunnel walls. They spun end over end—no up, no down—dizzying in every direction.

The Mirror Realm, she thought. Worlds within worlds within the world of the Flow. *Just how many realities are there in here?*

In the center of the mirror universe, she felt very small and very alone.

Except, of course, for the skin she wore. V was a living, breathing film spread over her body—stretching in places, bulky in others, but very much a foreign presence and eerily mute.

She took a tentative step with his foot, then another, and a third. Noticing that she did not always travel in a straight line, Consuela pinpointed an oval mirror, and although she walked toward it, the robin's-egg shape corkscrewed until it hung nearly above her head by the time she reached it. She didn't feel upside down. She didn't feel awake.

Consuela swallowed against the fresh panic in V's borrowed chest.

All she had to do was find a way out. She could slip through any of these shapes, but she didn't trust the unblinking stares of the faceless, mundane mirrors. She kept walking, noticing that what she'd taken for scratches on the glass were really symbols, tick marks, and even initials. One said clearly RGB, another hieroglyph looked suspiciously like a mouse, and another outline was a flat hand with an eye etched into its palm. Consuela wondered how many mirror-walkers had been here before. What tied them to this world or united them in the Flow? Was there something V had in common with them? And, if there were others like V and Sissy and Tender, what about her? Had there been any skin-shaping skeletons before her?

She touched a mirror as she wandered by, pulling his hand back as it slid through with a feeling of microfilament pressure and a Xerox line of light.

V's hand was wet with blood. *My blood. No, his blood.* And she'd left red fingerprints on the inside of the glass.

They moved on.

Consuela kept her eyes focused on the left, a wall that slowly rotated as she moved through the spirals of mirror space. There were hundreds—no, thousands—of mirrors in this world. She began to worry about whether she'd ever find one of V's marks, or if she were lost, would she ever find her way out? The vacuum of sound was like an overplayed song, pressing against V's eardrums with an echo of heavy heartbeats.

His arm stung. His eyes, too. For whatever reason,

she was scared to make a sound. Afraid, with some little-girl wild nightmare feeling, of waking something in the dark that would jump out and devour her. This seemed a place for monsters.

She debated whether she should get out of him now, unmake V, and have him lead them both out. She'd have company. She'd know if he was okay. But she didn't know if she could survive in here without V on, didn't feel certain she could undo him safely at all, let alone in the Mirror Realm, and a small, greedy part of her felt powerful and confident knowing that she lay safely tucked behind someone else's skin. The hurt was not her hurt. The heart was not her heart. V was an armor she could wear over herself, a sort of protection realized in the flesh—his flesh—over her bones.

She saw above her a mark drawn in ink; a black letter v just as he'd said.

Consuela dipped her face low to the surface, careful not to touch. She saw a simple bedroom with a matching bed set and neatly tucked linens; a lady's hairbrush, journal, and hair spray adorned the vanity desk. Four layers of decorative pillows artfully filled half the bed and a rolled-weave throw rug splayed over a dark hardwood floor. The lamp was frosted glass. The fixtures, too. Consuela wondered whose room it was, but no one came in or out and she moved on.

She wondered if these places were part of the Flow or of the world? Could V pass through anywhere, like Maddy had done in dreams? What were the limits of their powers? Could they somehow escape Tender here, if they had to hide?

A spasm knifed his gut.

She coughed with his lips and his throat voiced the gasp. His hands were huge and automatically pressed deep into his side. She tried to identify the feeling when a flulike rippling flared in his kidneys. She cried out, a deep growl.

What's happening? She stared at his hands, which shook. She felt his face prickle with sweat. Chattering teeth peppered her ears in a haunting, mariachi shiver that begged her knees to buckle, her feet to jog. She felt like he had to puke.

V's body was rejecting her.

Not here, she thought sharply, wincing. *Not now!* Consuela had to get them safely out.

She looked wildly with his eyes for that elusive painted v. She'd yank them outside any one of these, if she had to—she would not risk his life by hiding beneath his skin. She felt ashamed for having even thought of it, punished by God for being arrogant. But she was scared, terrified, of getting lost in this place. She had to find the mirror back to her room.

But there were so many mirrors.

She ran, crablike, hunched and doubled over. The pain stabbed again. Clutching his stomach, biting his cheek, she limped down the corridors of bright geometric space. A whine escaped his lips. Tears blurred his eyes.

Consuela blinked, unable to lift her arms to wipe the wetness away, afraid that if she let go, the gaseous bubble in their gut would pop and they would both burst, splattered over curved walls that no one would see.

Fear kept her sweating and stumbling, grimacing with his lips and grunting with his throat. She glanced around desperately for one of his marks. *A little farther. Just a little bit farther . . .*

And there, like a constellation in the agoraphobic black, she saw the doorway speckled in misty dewdrops sporting the all-important v. The droplets were trapped under a sheet of matte black like a million crystal beads held in stasis by the Flow.

Then Consuela remembered: the mirror had been painted over.

She whimpered, beginning to crumple in half, feeling the next wave of nausea, the next push to release. They had to get out or they would die here. Now.

There were no clear mirrors in her bathroom, but

there were reflective surfaces—the faucets, the drains, the towel racks—if she could find them. Consuela squinted against the tears in his eyes and the pain spiking in his side.

She searched around her painted-over gateway, nearly crawling from the pain, before she saw it: the sink faucet was a pale, shimmering, oblong glow. She recognized its shape. But it hung upside down, above her head, horrifyingly out of reach.

A sudden lurch and she swallowed back bile. *No choice. No time left.*

She ran for it, diving their body sideways and up, willing it to somersault without gravity or reason like an astronaut in outer space, and she was very much surprised when it worked, condensing into a dizzying funnel.

They sheared through on a knife of dull silver light.

SHE fell into her bathroom, borrowed strength bleeding out of her all at once.

Consuela, the skeleton, hit the tile floor with a clatter. V, a heavy, wet thump, landed beside her. She'd expelled him. Or he, her. Self-preservation. Alien meat. Separated, they were wholly apart and miraculously whole. They flopped around spastically like fish without breath.

For a moment, she felt the loss, a frantic need to pull him back onto her—her into him—like a security blanket. But then she realized that he was not part of her. Not really. She forcibly kept herself to herself.

They spent long moments coughing on the floor, using their own lungs, their own air. Thrashing and stumbling on their own hands and feet, learning to be separate and in control once more. Neither of them looked at the other.

"Can I take a shower?" V asked the tile floor.

Consuela waved her skeletal hand toward the closet. "Towels in there," she said as she lurched to standing. Racing to her bundle of self-skin on her bedspread, she pressed it protectively to her chest. Consuela closed the bathroom door and heard the shower's splash-applause.

She shouldered herself over her body, slipping on her raiment of hair, eyes, and skin. The water changed tempo as it drummed against something solid, and Consuela tried not to think too much about V naked in her shower. Dressing quickly, she hooked her birthstone cross around her throat as the water squeaked to silence.

She heard the glass door of the shower click open and closed, the heavy footfalls on tile and the flump of thick towels. She listened to his every step and move as he dressed. She could picture his feet slipping down pant legs. She could hear his fingers fumble with the buttons of his shirt. Consuela heard V approach the door, conscious of her consciousness of him, and how aware she was about where he was, even outside herself. When his hand touched the doorknob, she felt it on her skin.

He opened the door shyly. V stood, wet and dressed, whole and alive. His hair still dripping, the water turned his tousles to curls. He rubbed at his face and neck.

He tried to smile, but it was weak, unsure. "I told you that you could do it."

Consuela self-consciously combed her hair with her hands.

"You okay?" she asked.

"Well, I've never had anyone 'in' me before."

Consuela grinned. "I think that means you lost your virginity."

"Ha ha. You wish." V laughed. Or tried to laugh. She tried, too. They sounded like crumpled paper.

They were laughing off the nervousness, but the awkwardness remained.

Then they were laughing off the awkwardness, but the nervousness remained.

Ruffling his hair with one of her towels, V spoke first. "It was frightening and // *intimate* // nice."

Consuela smiled, wondering if he ever heard the thoughts he gave off. She toyed with the cross on her chain.

"We should go," she said.

"Wait—" He stepped forward. Her face hovered near his chest. Consuela's chin grazed the very edge of his shirt. She could see a button up close—black threads, four holes. She felt the warmth of his closeness. She smelled bar soap and lavender mist. V sighed and she felt his breath in her hair.

This felt very different with skin.

// Oh. //

V noticed her paint-splattered room and the lack of exits.

"Did you do this?" he asked.

"No." That was all she needed to say. They both frowned.

"The obvious route's the door," V said.

"I wouldn't."

He sensed her nervousness. "You don't trust it?"

She shook her head. "No. I think Tender did something to it. Booby-trapped it, like the mirror." Tender had wanted her to go through it. She didn't want to go there now.

"Okay," V said, throwing the damp towel over the back of her chair. "So here's the plan: you suit up in your skin of fire and we'll go check on Sissy. Use the window." He headed back to the bathroom, pointing. "I'll get my mirror."

Consuela trailed after him. They returned into the steamy warmth of the bathroom, perfumed with her own herbal shampoo. Now V smelled like her, she thought. Or she smelled like V. Would there be something residual, like the scent of lavender soap, after she'd worn his skin? Would she be able to walk through mirrors? Could he create skins?

V picked up the compact by the sink.

"Tender took this and left it for you," V said. "He probably painted all the other ones over so you'd have no choice but to use this." He gripped the case in his fist. "Open it," he said, handing the compact to her.

Consuela clicked the top back and saw a small circle of oily film floating like a flattened bead.

"It's not a mirror . . ."

"It's the Flow," V said. "Tender laced it with the Flow. Or something like it," he said. It was shiny, black, and gummy.

"I think that's what he eats," Consuela said, looking at her own palm. "What he digests."

"Lovely." V grimaced and, grabbing a hand towel, wiped the surface with one hundred percent Egyptian cotton. Ghosting his breath upon it, he polished it neat, scrubbing it clean. On the towel, the darkness clung like gum. "Remind me to get a new one if we make it out of this."

Consuela's smile faltered. "Don't talk like that."

"I'm sorry," he said. "I'm here. You're here. We made it. We're going to get out of this and we're going to get you home." V projected the confidence he'd always had with that promise, but now it lingered, tinged with regret.

// Away from here/the Flow/me/Everything/I have to/I'll have to let you go. //

"V . . ."

"We should really go now," V said quickly. "I'll head out and you get going. Be sure to bring this with you so Tender won't get his hands on it." He tried to look reassuring. "I'll see you soon."

V lifted the case to his eye. Nothing happened. His gaze jumped erratically, searching; still nothing. V frowned, closed his eyes, opened them, and glared. Consuela eyed the clean bit of mirror.

// No . . . //

V shifted from foot to foot, agitated.

"What is it?" she asked.

"I don't know." He shoved the mirror at her like an accusation. "You try it."

"Me?" Consuela asked. "I can't."

"Maybe not," he said. "Try it anyway."

She took the compact and tried to ignore his eyes on her as she looked deep into her own brown windows of her soul. Consuela blinked and handed the compact back quickly.

"Nothing," she said. "Maybe it's the mirror . . . ?"

"No," V snapped. "I can't see it. The doorway."

// This can't be happening/Not possible!/Not now! //

He glanced around helplessly, his fingers in fists.

Consuela searched for something to say. What she saw was a tiny white spider on the ceiling.

"Wish," she whispered.

"Where?"

"No. One of his wishes," she said, titling her head to follow the tiny arachnid's tread. "What was he doing here?" Consuela asked aloud. It seemed like everyone had been in her room.

V shook his head, wiping the condensation off his face. "Probably looking for you," he said. "Making sure you're okay."

"I don't know," she said. "He's Tender's 'best friend.'"

Consuela felt their time growing shorter, their options shrinking, pushing to one, lone conclusion: confrontation on Tender's terms. *See you at the end of the world.* And where was Wish? Was he still alive? How much did he know? Whose side was he on?

"Do you trust Wish?" Consuela asked.

V dropped his eyes. "I don't know . . ."

"Do you *trust* him?"

// Wish/Joseph/Yad/Abacus, // I don't even trust my-self. // Who set that fire? //

"I. DON'T. KNOW!" V shouted. It rang off the tile.

Consuela hopped her butt up on the counter, slipping a foot in the sink.

"Well, I don't," she said, and slapped her hand flat against the spider.

V slammed against the floor.

chapter fifteen

"Each of us dies the death he is looking for, the death he has made for himself."

—OCTAVIO PAZ

"V!"

Consuela jumped down, but her outstretched hands passed through his body as if he wore a skin of smoke. Her left palm burned. V rolled over, watching his chest move through her hands, pushing himself to sit up—looking more astounded than pained.

"It doesn't hurt," he said, more to himself than her. He sounded surprised.

Consuela met his eyes. "V?" she whispered.

"It's happening again," he said vaguely. "But it doesn't hurt." His eyes met hers. He looked afraid to be happy, afraid to believe it. "I'm going back."

"Back?" Consuela said, her throat constricting around the word. "Back where?"

V stood up, glancing through his ephemeral body.

"Back," he said wondrously. "Back up. Back home, I guess. Back." His face was full of relief and an odd sort of joy. The masterpiece portrait revealed.

The next moment, it crumpled with the sound of violin tears.

// No! // Not now! // I can save you! //

"V . . ." Consuela shook her head. He was dying. Living. Going back to life. "No, V . . ."

"Consuela." He said her name slowly. It hurt to hear it said that way. Like good-bye, despite anything they wanted. He raised his hands but they were insubstantial as ghosts. "I can feel it . . ."

She wanted to be generous and let him go, but she was crying and afraid.

"V, please, fight it. Stay!"

He raised a misty hand to her face. He couldn't touch her. She couldn't feel him. The shampoo smell hung wet in the room.

"Help me fight it," he said, trying to find purchase in her hair. "Help me stay."

"How? V!" She tried grabbing his hand and holding his knuckles to her face. If she closed her eyes hard enough, she could feel them there.

"Stay with me!" she begged, selfish and scared. "I can't do this!" *Not against Tender! Not alone!*

V was growing more tenuous by the moment, particles of him blowing away as if under a steady breath.

"I feel it coming," he said. "I'm sorry." He meant it. She was crying. His gentle eyes sparked dark once more. "They're calling me . . . and I'm ready to try." V spoke from far away, a distance that was growing deeper.

"You can do this," he said. "You can do anything. Remember: you don't need me—you don't need anyone."

// *But I needed you.* // *Brave Angel.* // *I'm not afraid anymore.* //

"Thank you for believing me." He smiled again, that portrait smile.

"Don't give up," Consuela pleaded through tears. "I have to save you."

"You did save me, Bones," he said softly. "And I was supposed to save *you.*"

She looked at his eyes and every panic softened. He was here. He was with her. He'd saved her from death. He'd given her this. And time. And a chance. And him.

Consuela whispered, "You did."

Giovanni smiled like the sun.

"If there's any way, I will find you again," he said. "I promise."

He gathered himself with effort, tried one last time. His hand passed through her face as he reached.

"Consuela."

. . .

Gone.

She groped at the space that twinkled with shorn stars, the dwindling, last moments of V.

Now she was alone. The shock of it washed over her. She'd wake up soon.

An echo of electric hums thrummed through the room.

// I will find you again. //

BONES walked into the basement room. She was unsurprised to find the door unlocked, she was unsurprised to find the fax hanging useless above the door, and equally unsurprised to find the room exactly as she had left it, save for a few returned cardboard boxes and Sissy slumped in her father's chair.

Sissy's honey-brown hair shrouded her face, her creamy skin still beautiful, her fingernails immaculately filed—one hand had been attached sickeningly backward and bent into a crude gesture, the middle finger raised. Her body caved around the gaping hole in her torso, which had hammered her into the leather chair back. The seat and the floor were soaked in her blood; her pretty shoes dangled in the puddle and the weight of the chair sank its wheels into wet carpet. Consuela knew that it would never change back.

The Watcher had been pinned like a butterfly and, just as casually, discarded and left as a message. For her.

Consuela turned away. Sissy was gone. There was no one here to tell anything anymore.

She touched the shelves briefly, the chair, the books, the hidden Scotch. Sissy'd never gotten the shower she'd asked for, not really, just a cold, hard slap to sober her up.

That one, lonely thing made Consuela sadder still.

The rest of her burned as black as her palm.

She snatched the roll of paper off its tacks, tearing the pulp and dried blood to shreds, sprinkling them like snow on the sleepover floor. Consuela pushed behind the ruined thing in the chair and pecked the keyboard keys with her finger bones so that they'd stay.

Cecily Amelia Gardner, she typed. **I will remember you.**

teNDeR snarled in frustration. *How hard could this be?* He could always find Wish anywhere, anytime, without even trying, and now, so near the end of things, the little bugger eluded him. *Annoying little flea speck.*

He swept the sky from black into a hallucinatory gray complete with streams of gold and purple like watercolor paintbrushes washed in warm milk. He testily poked at Maddy's remains at the base of the den. Nested in leaves, her bare body was a bloated rag doll on the ground. Naked and plump, she was unmarred except for her gouged-out eye; her face was turned discreetly to the earth and tiny brown insects peppered her belly.

He jiggled her breast with the toe of his boot. It sloshed loosely.

Girls are gross.

Tender squinted into the sunlight, casting his eyes like a fly-fisher's line; he caught the flurry of black ants, a red squirrel, a chipmunk, and one or two monarchs clapping lazily on the trees. No white animals. Wish hadn't been here.

Tender vowed that he'd make things exponentially more painful for every minute he'd have to spend hunting Wish down.

He had laid the trap. Now he just needed the bait.

CONSUELA let her feet carry her into the folds of the Flow, following the instinct that led her to the real world and beyond, to Sissy's door, to Maddy's den, to V's portal of glass. It was true, if she let herself, she could feel them all inside her—outside her—following the trail like Sissy's cell-phone signal. Once she'd made the connection, she couldn't lose it. But it was tough to concentrate on such raw nerves.

But a skeleton didn't have nerves. She was a solid, silvery apparition of vengeance and bone.

Bones.

She hardened with every step that took her closer to Wish.

SHe exploded into the fenced-in forest line. Her quarry crouched behind the crab-apple tree.

"Wish!" she shouted.

"Shh!" he hissed back. That surprised her. Not that he was fearful—but that he wasn't scared of her. He was clearly scared of something else. Consuela was incidental.

"I found a spider in my room," she said.

Wish ignored her. "Where's V?"

"He's gone," she said.

Wish nodded, his cheek pressed close to the bark.

"Good," he said.

"Good?!" Consuela couldn't believe what she was hearing.

"You can't trust him," Wish explained. "T's got him by the balls."

"What?"

Wish tapped his fingers on the tree. "Don't know

how he does it, but I've seen it happen more than once. Like a puppeteer with an invisible hand up V's hole. Doesn't look easy, and V moves like a tank, but T would do just about anything to get you now . . ." He hadn't needed to include himself on that short list. "So I stopped him."

"Who? Tender?"

"Shh! No," Wish said. "V."

She rubbed a hand over her face. Her fingers scraped against her sockets.

"Wish, you're not making any sense," she said, coming closer.

"He could use V to get to you." Wish spelled it out as if to a child. "So I blocked all the mirrors and left him a wish of 'fare well' in your room." He snorted a little as he said it. "Should keep V out, for a while, anyway. Sorry about the paint job. It's the only thing I got that can cross. Or block."

Consuela gaped, impressed, disbelieving.

"V was *helping* me!" she insisted. "He was trying to help you, too! We were all trying to stop Tender . . ."

"*Shut the fuck up, for Pete's sake!*" Wish spat in panic. "Don't say his name! He can hear the shape of it in the Flow." He shook his greasy brown cowlicks. "V could only help if he stayed in control, but the minute that changed, you'd be dead." He scanned the open soccer field. "Burned to a crisp."

"Like Joseph Crow?" she said. Wish nodded, tight.

"I couldn't stop him," he said softly. "Either one of 'em. Never could. Just got the hell out of the way," he said with a sorry smile and tapped a button that read, SCREW THE WOMEN AND CHILDREN—ME FIRST!

She wanted to believe him. Needed desperately not to be the only one left.

"So what are you doing?" she asked.

"Hiding."

"Hiding?" Consuela said in disbelief. "How?"

"Very, very well." Wish smiled as he said it. "T can't see me."

She was certain that Wish had lost his mind. The tree trunk was hardly any cover at all.

"Listen, Wish . . ."

He grew angry. "No, Bones, I mean it!"

The air rippled and tore, forced open with the blackened, pitted point of a sword. One, two boots later, and Tender sauntered through.

Wish cowered, silent and scared. Consuela turned to see the real face of Tender—animate, alive, and malevolent.

He smiled.

"Bones," Tender said lovingly. "You're out."

"Tender," she murmured. "Jason . . ."

"Don't!" Tender slashed the air as if his hand were the sword. The Flow curdled and burned as his gesture passed. "Don't make it worse for yourself than it already is," he said, cocking his head to one side. "Where's V?" he asked. "Hung in your closet like a cloak?" His eyes glittered, grin widening. "Maybe a robe that you can sleep with, curled up against your skin?"

Consuela tried to ignore him. Fear prickled her spine and ground in her molars. She was all too aware of the smear of shadow in her hand.

Tender swung the sword casually. "Where's Wish?" he asked.

She'd checked to see that he was safe, jerking her head back, too late—horribly, far too late. Tender raised his sword, hot and hiss-popping.

"He's here?" Tender laughed, following the tilt of her face. He marched into the thin copse where Wish squatted, undetected. The skinny boy squeezed his eyes and mouth shut as Tender passed.

"Well done! I didn't think you had it in you, Abe," Tender called out as he walked. "I mean I knew you were a coward, but I didn't think you were so good at it." He tapped the sword out like a blind cane, touching this tree and that.

Consuela didn't meet Wish's eyes; she didn't want to give him away again. Tender really couldn't see him there. She had to distract him, somehow.

She took a deep breath. "Sissy . . ."

"Oh, please." Tender sneered. He spared her a glance that was one word: disappointed. "'Avenge me' is just a pretty way of committing murder and asking someone else to take the fall. Are you really that stupid?" He stalked the trees. "Maybe you are. You should have taken me up on my offer and gotten out, Bones, and left the Flow to me. You would've never missed it. It would have been just a bad dream."

Silenced, she willed that there was one wish left for her—that Wish would break off his tooth and she'd come up with something to save them all. That miracles could occur. That Tender would not find his friend. That they would somehow all escape. That they would win in the end and that she wouldn't be alone. And maybe V would come back in the nick of time . . .

But this wasn't the time for wishful thinking.

Exasperated, Tender stopped by the fence, straightened, and sighed.

"Okay, have it your way," he said with a shrug. "I know in your rabbit heart there beats the fantasy of a knight." Tender taunted the air, but his eyes were trained on Consuela. "Let's see if you can stand by and watch as I smash Bones to bits."

Consuela started backing away as Tender strode purposefully toward her. He gave a couple of strong swipes with the blade that split the air with a wood-chipper moan. He kept coming, gaining speed.

"'S not like Sissy's," he warned under his breath. "I knew you were there, Wish; somewhere outside the door. Did you hear her scream? Did you hear her die? I know you couldn't bear to see it, so close your eyes, buddy, because this one's full screen!"

It was chilling the way Tender came at her while talking to somebody else. She hadn't a skin, hadn't a power, and raising her arm bones in defense only excited him more. His chest expanded, his round nostrils flared wide. He was coming too fast! *Too fast!* He had to slow down, give her time . . .

Tender gripped the hilt in both hands like a baseball bat. He spoke over his shoulder.

"Funny thing is, I have no idea what'll happen when this hits." He said it so simply, like a boy with a pipe bomb at school—curious to see what would happen because whatever the consequences, it would be *interesting*.

His shoulders shifted. She shrank back.

Tender sensed Wish coming as the thinner boy whirled

into view, branch in hand. It looked as if Wish had planned to club him from behind. But Tender turned and casually smashed the sword pommel into Wish's face.

Blood exploded, sending Wish backward, spitting out swearwords and teeth. Hands clapped against his nose, Wish bubbled and gagged.

"There you are," Tender said gently. "I had a choice, you know, whether to knock out your teeth or cut off your thumbs. Either way, no more wishes for you."

"No' mah wish," Wish spat thickly.

Tender mocked him by cupping a hand to his ear. "What's that?"

"No' *MAH* wish!" Wish's eyes sparked tears and daggers. He shouted, *"Yourz!"*

It registered in Tender's face, a flip book of thoughts/emotions/memories shuffled in his eyes; the final page settled dark and foreboding under his low, black brows.

"See, now you've made me mad."

Tender spun the sword in his hand and advanced on Wish, who scrambled, stumbling, prone.

"Tender! No!" Consuela wrapped herself around Tender's back in a crow's cage of limbs. Her jawbone clamped into the pit of his shoulder, her fingers dug into his pale throat. He stumbled under her unexpected weight, but it wasn't enough to trap his arms.

345

Tender laughed. Wish grimaced, missing both front teeth, his pink tongue splashed with runny blood. Consuela squeezed Tender harder, yanking her radii under his chin. Gagging, Tender grabbed the top of her skull, holding his sword out like a game of keep-away.

"Want me to snap your neck?" he hissed. "That's not what I want, but I'll do it, I swear."

She didn't care. At that moment she knew it wasn't Wish's turn to die.

Let me save you, the past whispered.

But those words were meant for her.

Tender let go of his weapon, smacking both hands against her parietal lobe, braced to pop her skull from her spine over the crux of his shoulder. She knew it was coming as she clawed his neck, using his jaw as a hinge, digging her sharp fingertips in. Consuela didn't have the strength. She couldn't stop him.

Wish rushed forward, a frontal assault, which Tender welcomed with surprising largesse, snatching the buried hilt backhanded and cleaving the sword through the air.

The blade caught Wish in his side, momentum digging it deep.

Wish squealed. Consuela fell. Tender coughed.

There was a moment where everything stopped, frozen and silent, as the Flow wobbled like gelatin back into place.

Time bubbled, popped, and started anew.

Stumbling erect, dragging the blade, Tender held his throat and croaked, "Done." Parting a phantom curtain, he plunged into the Flowing darkness. Gone.

Consuela scrabbled through the dirt to where Wish lay bleeding, the edges of rib poking out with some pinkish, wet ballooning pooling over his jeans. He clawed at his mouth with spastic fingers. She knew what he was trying to do. Consuela felt for his hand, but he slapped it away. His one act of defiance might have brought her to tears, but she felt nothing but numb denial.

"Give me my wish," she whispered hotly, propping his head on her hand. "I can wish you safe! I can wish that none of this happened!"

He tried to laugh, his eyes rolling, his tongue wagging blind. "Heh. Doez'n' work like tha'." Wish's head lolled dangerously. He tapped his eyetooth with one quivering digit. "Break it. Blease."

Consuela didn't hesitate. She cinched the tiny fang in her pincher grip. Snapped it. Wish groaned nasally and cupped his quivering hand. She placed the tooth in his palm.

"He wished . . . no' t' be so *aware* of everything all th' time." Wish's eyes crinkled as he dry-laughed and winced. "So I made m'self one o' th' everything, righ'? Can't see you, then. Invizzible. To him." He poked his wobbling finger at her, like he had rheumatoid arthritis. Not like he was really dying in her arms. "Only t' him."

347

Wish tried to sit up, but failed, eyes bright.

"Tender's wish . . ." he said. "I give i' to you."

She stared as he struggled to lift his head. Pursing his lips, he blew a stuttering breath flecked with spittle and blood. The tiny tooth in his palm dissolved into dust, taking off as a tiny, white cricket flitting erratically with the sound of cellophane. She watched as it disappeared into the tall grass.

When she looked down, Wish was dead.

chapter sixteen

"Man collaborates actively in defending universal order, which is always being threatened by chaos. And when it collapses he must create a new one, this time his own."

—OCTAVIO PAZ

He wasn't running. There was no need to run. There were only the two of them left, after all.

Tender stood in the vast, unwoven Flow, muted flashes and slipstream rainbows moving sluggishly through the fog. He stirred a patch with the tip of his boot as if trying halfheartedly to unearth a coin stuck in the dirt. His sword was gone, sheathed somewhere.

Consuela crept forward, her bones sinking into the Flow, unheard and unseen and miraculously unfelt. Wish's cloak of invisibility wafted over her as firm and whole as any skin. She wore it like armor, but was oth-

349

erwise unarmed. She planned to rend Tender apart with her bare hands, if necessary.

Where was his sword?

She'd tracked him here and it needed to end. Here. Now.

She stood right in front of him—invisible, ineffable—glaring hatefully at him.

This was it. She shook imperceptibly, her fingertips buzzing. Tender stared at his boot while she willed herself to do something terrible.

But she couldn't. Not like this.

He'd have to know, and know it was her—that she'd been the one who had stopped him once and for all.

Consuela circled him slowly until she stood next to him, able to follow the gaze of his eyes, the twist of his lip as he was lost deep in thought. His neck still bore the red rash of her attack, the raked lines on pale flesh like Gothic jewelry. His heavy eyebrows were drawn down, the smooth bump of his pug nose made his profile almost cherubic. Yad's Angel of Death.

She was losing her resolve to kill in cold blood.

She tried to think of Wish and feel hate. Of V and hate. Of Sissy and hate. But the hate wouldn't come, just the cold knowing that if she were to have any chance against him, she'd have to keep him from getting the sword. Better yet, she should take it, claim it first. But she was afraid—deathly afraid—of what would happen if she tried and failed.

Consuela leaned nearer to him, daring herself to get as close as she could to his mad, feral smell of hot copper and antiseptic. She peered over his shoulder, but was unable to see what he played at with his boot. She watched him as she'd watched Rodriguez that forever-sometime ago. That was when she had met her calling—preventing a suicide. Preventing a man, a boy, and a drunk woman from dying, from giving up hope. Remembering her own helpless fury at losing some stranger while she protected herself. She still wore the painful shadow of failure on her bones.

She had watched V leave, found Sissy's body, held Wish as he died, but still, she hadn't given up hope.

There was a way out of this. There was a way she could win. She could stop Tender. Save herself. Save the Flow and everyone it touched.

The world snapped open.

The world snapped shut.

I save those about to give up hope.

It struck her like a gong.

Vulnerable and invisible, Consuela opened herself to Tender. Feeling what he felt, being as she'd always been, unfurling like a marigold, opening wider and wider as layers peeled away, exposing the heart of it. Consuela evoked her power, attuned to him, and listened/saw.

Pain. The only word there was "pain." Whether off in the distance or in the back of his brain, a sickening taste in his mouth or a sharp scent in his nose, a hot pressure on his eardrums or a grumbling, roiling blackness in the pit of his bowels, it was all there—in every sense—an abiding, ever-present, familiar love-hatred with pain.

Again, she couldn't pity him. Knowing what he'd done, she couldn't.

Wish, Joseph, Yehudah, Sissy . . . and all the others she never met, would never meet, crowded for space in her brain.

Sissy's voice rang sharply in her mind. *He deserves to die!*

As dispassionately as she dared, Consuela inserted her left hand through Tender's spine and, at his gasp of surprise, fished around for the hilt. She found it, hard and slick, pressed against the inside of his belly button. It smoldered against the shadow stain on her palm, hot and angry.

Tender's head snapped back. His breath came in popping coughs. Consuela leaned her face close to his pink, perfect ear.

"Surprise," she said.

His cough transformed into wobbly, cracking laughter.

"Hello, Bones." Tender swallowed, the pain black and red against his eyelids when he closed them. "Come to do me in?"

She pulled the hilt a little and heard him wince. "Like you did to Wish and Sissy and Joseph Crow . . . ?"

"Uh-uh," he corrected with a lilt in his voice, his arms, paralyzed in shock, splayed wide. "Of course I killed Joseph Crow, but I never touched him."

"Meaning?" she said.

Tender licked his lips and stared up into the void. "Well, after our last tête-à-tête, I wasn't able to get anywhere near him or his wigwam, so I had someone else do it. Someone you know and love—"

"V," she interrupted. "I know. How?"

If Tender was disappointed by her failure to be surprised, he was too distracted by her hand through his body to show it. "My job is to clean up the darkness," he choked out. "And there's plenty of darkness to go around; we each have a little darkness of our very own . . ." He glared at his clawed hand, squeezing an invisible ball with mighty effort, and Consuela felt tendrils of fire race up her left hand, through the core of her arm, and convulse in her rib cage. The pain pulled her down.

She staggered, but the feeling receded like a wave of

nausea. She gave a ripping twist to the sword handle. Tender twitched, crying out, then pouted. He dropped his hand with a minuscule shrug.

"It takes some time to get used to the flavor, the vibe," he said slowly. "You're new. But I've been here a lot longer than V. I know how to pull his strings. And to me, he's putty in my hand." Tender grinned with malicious glee. "But, then again, he was poly-cotton in yours."

Consuela grimaced and adjusted her grip. "So are you."

"Yes," he said with a strange ecstasy. "So am I."

It nauseated her that this somehow excited him—her proximity and invasion of his body more like rape than her fragile intimacy with V. It wrenched something inside her, filling her mouth with the memory of bile.

"You're sick," she spat, blaming him.

"Maybe," he coughed. "But I'm not dead. Or hooked up to machines in some hospital ward bleeding deductibles dry." He felt her tremble. "Eh? That had bite," he said. "Sissy never told you where your body's at or what you've put your parents through . . ."

Consuela's fist was a nest of bones. One of them locked in him. "Shut up!"

Tender mocked her childishly. "Make me!"

She pushed herself into him, up to the shoulder, elbowing aside the blackness that oozed like liquid acid instead of ribs, kidneys, or anything human. It stung and stank and stuck. It hurt her to do this—to be in him this way. She shook her head, wishing this wasn't how it had to be.

But it was. He was. This was.

She had to do this.

"You have to be stopped," Consuela whispered, trying to convince herself.

"Of course I have to be stopped!" Tender yelled suddenly. "Stop me!"

He deserves to die!

With a sickened sob, Consuela parted him like stained curtains, spreading her hands wide into his arms, crucified against the uncaring Flow. She felt the miasma of Tender splashing against her bones, smeary and sticky, oily and inked. She was about to bow her head under the black tidal wave of him when she heard his voice, like V's last thoughts in her head under a long litany of broken numbers.

"Take my burden."

Consuela stopped.

Halfway through him, she realized the truth: Tender *wanted* to give up. He didn't want to do this anymore. It was a burden, a hateful thing, to be half living in pain, feeding off it and everything else in the Flow. V said it, too. But V's pain was only temporary when he could find respite here. Tender had no respite—he'd been all but born here, living out his function as the janitor of the Flow. He lived pain, ate it, for years and years and years. The Yad knew. No one was meant to be here that long. No one was ever meant to bear that burden more than temporarily. The Flow flows—from one thing to another. No one was meant to stay.

"Take my burden."

If she made a skin of Tender, would she have to clean the Flow? If she failed to wear him, would the Flow collapse under the weight of pain and shadow? If she hung him up forever, would another ever come to take his place? Could the Flow exist without him? Without any of them?

That was what he'd wanted all along.

Consuela remembered, with horror, the idea of their souls returning to this world to serve their selfless function time and time again, forever. If Tender believed that he was destined to eat pain in this formless void for all eternity, how awful would that be?

She stood on the edge between mother-of-pearl and shadow, muted light and sopping darkness, Consuela and Tender—her arms through his arms, her foot half into his calf. His body teetered in the raptured shock of it—the entrance, the ending, to all that he craved.

He tricked me, she thought. *I don't want this.*

She removed her foot, squelching free. Tender's eyes snapped open, and he shrieked a wordless, soundless *"NO!"*

It was no more than a sigh, a hoarse wisp without wind. Tears ran down his upturned face.

Consuela saw it, felt it, with her body still in his.

"He deserves to die," Sissy'd said.

And it was true, but not the way she'd meant.

Consuela stepped back, arms out, holding Tender's skin aloft. She saw him in his chair in a room with the sounds of Dickens and rattling meds and scraping chairs and Jason deaf to everything but the hunger pangs of pain. He deserved to die, but as a kindness, not as a vengeance.

She could save him. It was in her power to undo him as water or as V.

She stopped, bowed, and prayed. *May God grant me mercy . . .*

God, Jesus, Mary, and Joseph,
Let this be undone.

His body dissolved into a wet splash of unmade blood and flesh and gore.

tENDeR soaked into the Flow like a memory or dream banished at dawn. Consuela watched his undoing with a kind of odd peace; the shifting, opalescent gray swallowing everything, leaving behind only her.

She wondered if the creeping fear she felt was agora-phobia or claustrophobia—it was tough to tell without there being any real substance to the world. That was how she felt: insubstantial. Unreal. She thought of V disappearing like blinks of light spun on Abacus's walls.

She wanted to go to her room. Pull on her skin. Take a bath. Start over.

Consuela saw what had caught Tender's attention.

Under the puffs of lavender-blue-gray Flow, a shape solidified as if carved in ice. Consuela knelt down and blew gently, like Wish breathing baby teeth to life. She stood back, trying to make out the zigzag shape.

If she turned her head and squinted, it looked like something she ought to have recognized—a pictogram of a river, or a mountain range on a map. When she saw the tiny, forked Y at the end, it clicked into place.

"Snake," she whispered, and placed her hand upon it. The trapdoor whorled open and Consuela peeked through.

The meadow was an open invitation of blue skies, white clouds, pale green scrub brush, and raw, red earth. The tent was still a sad, ruined pile—a blackened thing of char and ash—but it was no longer the only spot of black in the world.

High above, she could see a bird wheeling.

Consuela smiled, grateful. She was not alone.

SHE'D showered, dressed, and cleaned her room, most of the work having been done by the slow, steady reversion of the Flow—her supernatural maid service. Only Wish's industrial paint job remained. That, and the aching bruise of shadow on her hand.

Consuela was carefully digging long flakes of paint with the blunt end of a ballpoint pen. Chiseling pieces like dried Play-Doh, she made a pile of thick curls on her pillowcase. She turned one over in her hand, pressed a few parallel lines with the cap clip, and dropped it on top of her dresser. A single black feather: a reminder like the rest.

She'd found the present Wish had left her: the small baby tooth, like a child's forgotten prize, nestled against her flannel sheets, hidden as per fairy prerequisite underneath her pillow.

In retrospect, she thought she'd figured out the perfect wish: *I wish that this was all just a dream.* But the tooth was here and Wish was gone. She placed the tiny bit of bone in her jewelry box, a reminder that the most precious things, like chances, pass quickly—here one second, gone forever the next. Like Sissy. Like Wish.

Like V?

An insistent pecking rapped against her windowpane. Consuela hurried to let the black bird inside.

"Joseph Crow!" she said happily as he settled on her bedpost.

"You found Coyote's door," he said with approval. "And you survived."

"You did, too," she said. "I'm glad."

"It was no sure thing," Joseph Crow acknowledged with a huff of his feathered breast. "While the tent burned, I lit the sage bundles and was able to change."

She sat on her bed and leaned into the mattress. "You flew away?"

The crow shook its head, beak swinging like a compass needle. "I couldn't. The flames were too high. I dug underground. Root totem, mole." Joseph Crow snorted through his tiny nostrils. "Everyone thinks the power is in the big, showy animals like eagle or bear, but the mole is a good animal."

Consuela shrugged, smiling. She was deliriously happy to be having a conversation—any conversation—with another human being, even if he was in a bird's body, and was eager to keep it going.

"Well, you're not a mole now," she said.

"No. But a mole can gather sage and stoke it in the fire that's still burning under the wreckage. I changed into

Crow in order to move quickly, to warn the Watcher . . ." Joseph Crow's voice slithered off into an uncomfortable quiet. "But I was too late."

Consuela nodded. "I understand." It was a useless, though true, thing to say.

"I knew, then, what the Vulture intended. He wanted to eliminate everyone and, therefore, eliminate the Flow. End it all, and himself with it. I could not stop him in this form and I could not pick more sage, so I folded the Flow closed behind Coyote's trapdoor and marked it only for you." The bird's beady eye winked with a wrinkled, blue-black lid. "Played possum. He thought I was dead."

"So did I," she admitted.

Crow feathers ruffled. "As if," he said. "If any of us survived, he could not empty the Flow. He would have failed. I was hoping that you would find it sooner; I had only the one door."

She smiled, but the room settled into an awkward silence. She picked at the pilling, wondering if she'd be picking the same piece of fluff forever.

"Are there any others?" Joseph Crow asked.

Consuela shook her head, plucking a pilly bit free. "No."

Joseph Crow flexed his wings, flapping them a little as he repositioned his feet on the post. "There will be, soon enough. So I'd appreciate your help."

Consuela nodded. "What can I do?"

"I need you to gather the white sage and clear away a bit of the fire for me. Once I transform back into human, I can begin rebuilding." Joseph Crow flexed a claw. "As I said, beaks and claws are no good at pulling sage. They are tough, woody plants."

"Sure," Consuela said. "Although it might be easier with a pair of scissors." But the mention of scissors brought a nightmare chill—running and fear and Tender. And V. She glanced at her door with trepidation.

The crow cocked its head. "What's the matter?"

"That door," Consuela said, pointing at it accusingly. "I can get out through the windows in skins, or through the mirrors with V, I can even get back, through the Flow and in dreams, but I can't go through that door like this . . ." She touched her face, her soft skin, feeling her every vulnerability. "I think Tender did something to it."

Joseph Crow flew over, landing on the carpet. He hopped two-footed around the base of the door, peering under and pecking it. He fluttered back to face her.

"Have you tried it?" he asked.

Consuela shrugged. "I've been afraid to," she admitted.

"How many doors remain closed to us because we've been afraid?" he mocked. Tipping his head back as if swallowing a worm, Joseph Crow flew to her desk chair to be at eye level as he spoke.

"What do you want?" he asked.

What do I want? It was no small question. *I want to be safe. To be real. To be alive. To go home.*

"You know." Joseph Crow said. "As well as you know yourself." The crow winked a beady black eye.

Know thyself.

"V was your angel," he said. "He spoke your truth. Did you hear him?"

Consuela nodded. "I did." *I always heard him.*

"You don't need me—you don't need anyone. You can do this. You can do anything."

She blinked, a hairbreadth from understanding, a guess on the tips of her lips.

Satisfied, Joseph Crow turned and readied himself for flight. She remembered the feeling: bunching her legs, tucking her wings.

"Do not forget to come by and pick the sage," he said, lifting a claw. "I'll be stuck like this until you do." He waved a wing and cast one quick look out the window. "We'll be waiting for you, Consuela Chavez, here in the Flow."

He flapped out of her room, the movement filling her mind with the empathic memory of feathered flight. She watched him disappear into the unzipped sky.

Consuela stood by the window and placed a hand against her chest, her fingers brushing the topaz cross. *Whose heart beats here?* She remembered once wondering and glanced at the door, knowing the answer all along: *Mine.*

She left the window open. Walked tentatively to her door. Remembering Grandma Celina, she grasped the handle. Stared at her hand—*her* hand, fingernails, cuticles, crinkles, and all. Skin and blood and bone, all her.

My skin is mine.

My skin is me.

This is my self—and I know myself.

That is my one thing.

Me. My skin. Myself.

The last piece slid into place:

I can cross over.

Consuela turned the handle, afraid to look, but then she saw it: hardwood floors, cream-colored walls, the worn, Indonesian runner, and the framed family portrait at the end of the hall.

She took one look back into her phantom bedroom, growing dim, and stepped out into her life in a brilliant burst of light.

chapter seventeen

"I believe that myths, like every living thing, are born, degenerate and die. I also believe that myths come back to life."

—OCTAVIO PAZ

It was the first time she'd been out on her own since the coma. Consuela's parents had been overprotective and jumpy since the brain tumor had been detected, but it was benign, so their panic was slowly easing off with time. Save for some slight nerve damage in her left hand, Consuela was fine, but her falling unconscious in the bathtub had done nothing for their willingness to leave her alone.

After some shameless begging and a talk with Consuela's physical therapist, her parents had agreed to give back some of her lost independence as well as her credit card. This solo shopping trip was a precious gift of trust.

Baby steps, the outpatient counselor assured her. *Baby steps.* Consuela still had to take the bus to school and the mall, her driver's license suspended until the doctors could prove that she wouldn't black out at the wheel.

Consuela knew that wouldn't happen, but couldn't share why. Unless she removed her skin, she'd remain part of this world. In the meantime, she'd have to suck up the bus rides and the every-twenty-minute parental check-in texts. As annoying as it was, it felt good to be home and loved.

That's why she could never tell her parents that when the tug of need was strong, she'd curl up in her closet and remove her skin so that she could go rescue some faraway stranger and slip back into her room, hoping that her lifeless body would go unnoticed until she returned. It was risky, but it was the best she could do. Consuela belonged to both worlds now, and she had responsibilities in each.

A skin of autumn leaves, another of ash, and a third, glittering one of spider silk hung in her closet. She'd kept the original skin of fire that crackled in its garment bag, and she'd undone the skin of butterflies so that they'd soared out of her window in a calliope of wings. It amazed her that no one in the real world saw these things. She, herself, couldn't see them unless she returned to her self as Bones.

Consuela. Bones. Angel Bones.

She smiled down as she made her way down the clothing aisles, riffling her fingers through the long rows of jeans. She felt the ones she was wearing rode too low on her hips; that fashion was so over. *One cannot live on impossible skins alone!*

Draping two pairs over her left arm, Consuela headed for the dressing rooms. She'd eventually find something that fit. They were just clothes. This was just skin. Today was just one day of her life, which was so much bigger than now. Consuela liked knowing exactly why she was here, what she was here for, and that no one else knew her secret double life. She could be a Guardian Angel with the benefit of coming home for dinner.

Consuela shut herself into the narrow stall and began unbuttoning, but stopped and stared at the mirror. Her pulse fluttered. Thought she saw something there . . .

She placed her hand on the cool glass, twisting it at the wrist to cover the image of her own eyes.

"No peeking," she whispered.

His reflection smiled back.

Acknowledgments

There is not enough chocolate in the world to thank everyone who helped make this book possible. Thanks to my editor, Julie Strauss-Gabel, who made the stars align, and to my agent, Michael Bourret, for heaps of sanity and sage advice. I am fortunate to have an incredible crew at Dutton, including Lisa Yoskowitz, Liza Kaplan, Emily Romero, Anna Jarzab, and Christina McTighe. Special thanks goes to Jeanine Henderson and Alberto Seveso for my beautiful cover and Rosanne Lauer and the copyedit team for making the words inside beautiful, too.

Before it ever got to Dutton, this story went through amazing critique partners, Susan VanHecke, Gayle Jacobsen-Huset, Robin Prehn, Kaelyn Porter, and Debbie Smart, as well as Angela Frazier, Maurissa Guibord, and Amy Henry, (with extra appreciation to Debi Faulkner,

Jody Mugele, and Rusty for the scary early Tender,
and to Jennifer Carson, Adrian Croft, and Deirdre
Mundy for the scarier later version of same).
Huge thanks to friends with red pens: Jenny &
Matt Bannock, Jeremy Bernstein, and Michel
Owen Miller who were there when it was barely
skin and bones. And I would have never made it
without my online writer communities including
the Debs, the Tenners, the Elevensies, #kidlitchat,
#YAlitchat, The Enchanted Inkpot, SCBWI, and
the Blueboarders—especially those who appeared
in real life: Sarah Jae-Jones and the Gothic Girls.
You are all worth my weight in Lindt.

For lifelong encouragement, thanks to Mom,
Dad, Corrie and Adam, Marilyn, Harold,
David, Shari, and my "dojo family": there is no
way I could have ever had the guts to pursue my
dream without you. To long-time friends Jennifer
Bagdade, Steve Deasy, and Ranjan Srivastava,
there aren't enough words (which is really
saying something)! For inspirational teachers:
Mr. Haberland, Mr. Larsen, and Mr. Philyaw;
Grandma, Grandpa, Bubbe, and Papa who
always believed in what I was meant to do—you
were right. As always.

Finally, a heart full of thanks to my Better-Than-Boyfriend, Jonathan, without whom my dream would have stayed nicely tucked into a drawer, and to my darling children who forgave Mommy's "one-more-minutes" and gave me hugs and kisses anyway. To you, the reader, who is holding this book, and to G-d for granting me this gift and this day:

Thank you.